Praise for Ellen Feldman and GOD BLESS THE CHILD

"Ellen Feldman is a remarkable writer...
Her ear for contemporary women's fiction
is virtually perfect."
—Anne Rivers Siddons

"*God Bless the Child* unfolds flawlessly...
dizzyingly splendid...plenty of suspense and
genuine excitement."
—*New York Times Book Review*

"...captivating...refreshing..."
—*Booklist*

"What headlines, big movies, and talk shows are
made of—you can't miss this book."
—Ilene Beckerman

"...rendered with an insistent eye for social detail in
prose rife with suspense and surprise."
—Elizabeth Richards

ELLEN FELDMAN

GOD BLESS THE CHILD

MIRA®

ISBN 1-55166-540-9

GOD BLESS THE CHILD

Visit us at www.mirabooks.com

Printed in U.S.A.

For
Michael, Mark, and Stephen,
Josh and Noah,
Philip and Alex,
and
Stephen,
good sons and fathers

Many people helped with information and
encouragement. I am especially grateful to Judith,
the counselor who gave me the facts about adoption
and showed me its human face; my editor,
Laurie Bernstein, who opened my eyes again
and again and again; and, as always, my agent,
Amanda Urban, who keeps it all in motion.

I cannot think of any need in childhood as
strong as the need for a father's protection.
                                    —Sigmund Freud

Motherhood is the strangest thing, it can
be like one's own Trojan horse.
                                    —Rebecca West

Mama may have, papa may have,
But God bless the child that's got his own.
                                    —Billie Holiday

One

Bailey Bender—named after Mildred Bailey, whose swingy rendition of "Thanks for the Memories" on the car radio had driven Bailey's mother past the A & P, past the post office, and halfway across the country before she realized she was pregnant and had to return, only temporarily, she swore, to Bailey's father—didn't think of herself as a failure. More like a case of arrested success. There'd been a time, years ago, when she'd been sure she was going to set the world on fire. There'd been a time after that when she'd figured she could hang in there. Now she was concentrating on the life after—after the career-track job, after marriage, after a lot of things she didn't want to think about anymore.

Of course, there was another way to look at it.

Some people would say she was stopping to smell the roses. But Bailey wasn't one of them.

Mostly she was trying to survive. She'd taken the money she'd made during the brief period when she was on the way up as a writer-slash-director-slash-producer of television news—at least what was left of it after the years trying to hang on freelancing in all those capacities—and bought a small house, which turned out to need more work than the engineer's report had indicated, on a wooded acre of land that wasn't exactly isolated, but in the summer when the trees were full there was no one else in sight. In the winter when they were bare, lighted windows hung in the darkness framing her neighbors eating dinner and watching television and arguing. She told herself it was better than listening to them through the thin walls of a Manhattan apartment, except when it was worse. At least the people she lived among now were known quantities rather than anonymous potential muggers and murderers and other familiar figures of the urban landscape. And she did take a certain pride in the fact that now when something went wrong, instead of calling the super, she got out her toolbox and hammered and wrenched and screwed her way into the body and soul of her house.

She'd also got a job at Livres of Grass, the local bookstore. The name was forgivable, or at least understandable, in view of the fact that the store sat on the tree-shaded main street of a town at the eastern end of Long Island that survived on the largesse of summer residents and weekend trippers. And in all fairness to Maude Thwait, who'd bought the store with a legacy from her late husband and against the advice of her two sons, the name had come with the business.

Technically Bailey worked in the store, but for two months every winter when Maude went to Arizona and for a good part of the rest of the year when Maude had other things on her mind, Bailey ran the store. It wasn't a bad arrangement. Maude trusted Bailey. Bailey liked Maude and the chance to read during slow afternoons, though there were fewer of those than she'd expected, what with the placing of special orders, and the unpacking of shipments, and the packing of unsold books to return to the publisher for credit; but Maude passed on the galleys she got for early reading and never minded when Bailey took a book home to finish. They were both expatriates from other worlds and felt faintly alien in this one, and some nights after they'd locked the door and turned off the lights in the front of the store, Maude took a bottle of Johnny Walker Red from the bottom drawer of her desk, and Bailey got the ice tray from the small refrigerator in the office at the back of the store, and they put their feet up on cartons of books and talked about everything under the sun, except their past lives, which they kept stowed away like old clothes that might come back in style some day but probably wouldn't. Though once as Maude was refilling their glasses, she did mention that her late husband had disapproved of women drinking straight whiskey. He'd thought mixed cocktails were more ladylike.

They were even making a living. During the summer Maude took on several part-timers and did a healthy business in pricey collections of the area's architectural gems and gardens, local histories of the good old days when the town was a village in more than name only and old salts plied the waters, and beach fiction. During the winter Bailey kept the store open for the few intrepid weekenders who braved the cold and desolation and the rare year-rounder who had a little discretionary income and was willing to spend it on something other than videos or kitchen gadgets or enough beer and whiskey to dull the pain or dispel the boredom or camouflage the loneliness.

But now it was early May, and summer rentals were up, and everyone was saying that the town in general and Livres of Grass in particular were in for a good season. Maude was pleased, but then, these days Maude was usually pleased. She'd had a successful career as And-His-Lovely-Wife that had spanned the years from cream cheese and pimiento loaves to crème fraîche, and seen two sons through childhood diseases, adolescent anxieties, and Ivy League educations. Now her late husband lay beneath a dignified granite headstone several towns away, and her sons had gone out into the world, and she was free to do exactly as she liked. What she liked was to read in bed long into the night, discuss with friends and customers what she was reading and what they ought to be reading during the day, and garden, wearing as little as possible, at odd hours of both. Sometimes when the summer foliage enfolded her property, she mucked about in nothing but sneakers and a pair of her late husband's boxer shorts. It was a relief, she'd confessed to Bailey once, after all those years of hoarding her charms, to be suddenly profligate with them, especially since they were no longer of value to anyone but her. Bailey, who hadn't quite shed her city apprehensions, warned of ticks, but Maude was fearless.

She was also impatient. Like most people who come to contentment late in life, Maude had a powerful sense of time running out.

Bailey saw her look at her watch again. There was no clock in the store. One of the cardinal rules of retailing was to suspend the customer in a timeless world of perpetual purchasing possibility. You didn't want people who were finally zeroing in on buys suddenly noticing they were twenty minutes late for something else.

"You can leave," Bailey said. She knew Maude had a long drive ahead of her that night, though her sons insisted she shouldn't drive at all and one of them had offered to come get her. "If things pick up, it won't be until people start coming out from town or back from the beach, and Nell will be here by then."

"She should be here now," Maude answered in the

'tone that had got her sons to a place in the world where they could offer advice she didn't take.

"She's never late," Bailey said.

"She never used to be late," Maude corrected her, and Bailey knew she was right.

Nell Harris was what used to be called, and probably still was, though Bailey couldn't be sure because she didn't have a daughter of her own to worry about, a late bloomer. At fourteen she'd looked ten and acted, alternately, like an unruly child and an opinionated old woman. She'd been angular and awkward and in constant collision with things and people and ideas. She'd also had big ambitions. At various times she'd planned on a career as a veterinarian (the preadolescent love affair with horses), astronaut (the space shuttle was in the news a lot), television journalist (that had something to do with Bailey), and, for a few weeks, actress (some things never change). The last Bailey had heard, Nell had decided the best way to save humankind and see something of the world was to study medicine—human, not animal—and sign on with an international relief organization. In the meantime, she was settling for whatever vicarious adventure she could pick up working part-time in the bookstore.

The day Nell had turned fourteen she'd gone to the school office to get her working papers, then come straight to the store and begged Maude for a job. Maude had asked if it was all right with Nell's parents, and Nell had told her it was. "My mom wasn't sure because of some of the, like, books she doesn't want me to read, but my dad thinks it's cool. He's like, 'As long as she's hanging out here all the time, she might as well get paid for it.' "

So Maude had called the labor hotline, checked the rules for employing minors, and taken Nell on part-time from May through September. And Nell had loved it. She'd loved the books, including several she knew her mother wouldn't want her to read but Maude and Bailey said were classics, and the people who came into the store, and Maude and Bailey. The arrangement had worked out so well that Nell had come back the following summer and again two weeks ago. But this year something had changed. Nell had blossomed, and suddenly her confidence had shrunk and her worries grown. She worried if her sweaters were as baggy and her shorts as short as the other girls' sweaters and shorts, if her body was as thin and her face as pretty as the bodies and faces in the ads in the magazines she now pored over, and if boys liked her. Her worries worried Bailey. She watched Nell, and saw her disappearing into a long, dark tunnel from which she wouldn't emerge until she was a seventy-year-old widow, and was shocked at the surge of protectiveness she felt. Or maybe it was only envy.

"She probably got tied up at school," Bailey said.

"She probably got tied up with Kevin Lonergan," Maude corrected her again, and again Bailey knew she was right, though she didn't know why it bothered her so much. Kevin wasn't a bad kid. He wasn't particularly smart, and he didn't have much of a sense of humor, though he laughed all the time. He had a big, brutal body with a lot of those well-defined muscles kids talked about as if they were name brands, and a hormonal level that kept an arm or leg in motion at all times, but his face was open and occasionally kind, even if there was usually a cigarette dangling from his soft, faintly girlish lips. He swore it didn't affect his wind and anyway, he'd give it up before he was thirty-five or forty, when it got really dangerous. At least he didn't have a tattoo or a ring in his nose or even a stud in his ear, though that probably had less to do with Kevin than his father, who, according to rumor, needed less incentive than self-mutilation to beat the hell out of Kevin, or at least he had until recently, when Kevin had achieved his current size. Bailey did know one thing for sure. Kevin Lonergan was never again going to be as happy as he was at this point-scoring, popularity-contest-winning, gland-throbbing moment in his life, but surely that was a reason to pity rather than dislike him. She supposed what bothered her wasn't Kevin, but his effect on Nell. That, and the fact that his term of endearment for her was Squirt.

Bailey walked to the front of the store and looked through the display window up and down Main Street. There was no sign of Nell, but Mack Reese was getting out of a pickup parked in front of the store. She watched him cross the sidewalk toward her. He wasn't wearing sunglasses and his face was so dark it made his eyes look the same washed-out color as his workshirt. He must have spent the weekend out on his boat fishing. He pulled the door open, and she noticed the way the shirt strained against his body. He was putting on weight again, so maybe he hadn't been fishing after all. Maybe he'd spent the weekend sitting out on the water drinking himself into amnesia.

As he came into the store, she saw that his face was leathery but not ravaged, and there was no hint of the unhealthy pallor that sometimes lurked just beneath his tan. She decided he hadn't been drinking, just oversublimating with Cream of the Hamptons and Ben & Jerry's. That was a shame because for the couple of weeks a year Mack decided to turn over a new leaf, he had a nice body—not designer-underwear-ad level, but a nice, compact machine with an athlete's ease of movement. The rest of the time he just seemed to be lumbering around in someone else's bulk.

"Afternoon, ladies."

"The term, MacKinley, is women," Maude said, but her voice was creamy with pleasure. She'd married an exemplary husband and raised two admirable sons. Mack was her first experience with a troublesome man.

Bailey glanced out the window again. "Nice pickup, Mack. Who'd you buy it from, Ma Joad?"

"You know what I'd do if I were you?" he called

across the store to Maude. "I'd fire the help you have now and hire someone who knows how to treat customers."

"Bailey didn't mean it," Maude called back.

"Maude's right," Bailey said. "I didn't. It's a terrific truck. As soon as you get the part-black-Lab mutt for the back, I'll let you take me for a ride."

"Watch yourself, Bailey; you're supposed to be one of us now."

She was supposed to be, though she knew she wasn't. She'd abandoned her old life but hadn't found a new one, or even a niche. Her former income tied her to the visitors, her current salary to the locals. She wasn't a writer or an artist out here for inspiration, but some shadowy recollection of ambition lingered, though she couldn't say what she was ambitious for. Even the accoutrements of her life marked her as a woman without a place. Her house couldn't hold a candle to the fiercely modern beach bungalows and painstakingly restored cottages of the weekenders, but neither did it resemble the overly gussied up properties of her house-proud neighbors or the Tobacco Road ambiance Mack and some of his friends cultivated. She didn't drive a Mercedes or even a Jeep, but her old Toyota was foreign made and plastered with bumper stickers to stop the ferry and the new A & P and other so-called improvements that would blight the neighborhood and ruin the views, even if they did bring in jobs to pay the mortgage and feed the kids. She was an anomaly, but then, she'd felt like that for a good part of her life.

She thought again of the last physical she'd had, when she was still working for one of the networks and cossetted with health benefits. The doctor had detected a faint abnormality in her heart—not a murmur, exactly, more like a whisper—and prescribed an echocardiogram.

The test had been a simple procedure, noninvasive, painless, surprisingly boring. For the better part of an hour she'd lain half naked on a table in a darkened room as a strange young man had told her to lie this way and turn that way and hold her breath, while he'd moved a chilly instrument over her flesh with one hand and manipulated the dials of a machine with the other. When it was over, he'd asked if she wanted to take a look. She'd said sure. Who wouldn't want a glimpse of her own heart?

"It's like a sonogram," he'd explained. "You know, where you can see the baby."

He'd moved the monitor a little so she could get a better look. There on the dark screen a white blob thumped and bumped and writhed in a mad dance of life. It looked like a hyperactive amoeba, or a special effect for a horror movie. She'd remembered her father's comment during the moon landings, that for all anyone knew they could be staging the whole show in some television studio in New Jersey. The picture on the screen had the same unreality. Bailey hadn't believed it was a heart. She certainly hadn't believed it was her heart. She'd felt no connection to it.

A few days later the doctor had called with the results of the test. It was just as she'd expected, she'd told Bailey, a patent foramen ovale with small flow from left to right. Bailey had asked for a translation. The doctor had told her she had a small hole in her heart. Talk about cheap symbolism. "Nothing to worry about," the doctor had assured her.

Mack moved to the table piled with current fiction, picked up a book, and stood reading the flap copy. He wasn't exactly a lip reader, but he made a noise, something between a hum and a mutter, while he read, and standing there listening to him, Bailey knew it was the kind of sound that was inoffensive, even endearing in a stranger, and an incitement to violence in anyone closer.

"This any good?" he asked through the muttering hum.

Bailey glanced at the book he was holding. "Does the school board know the kind of trash you read?"

"The school board doesn't even know if I can read. All they care about is whether I pass the little buggers on to the next grade so they can graduate and become irresponsible members of society." He was still holding up the book so she could see it. "It doesn't have to be good, it only has to put me to sleep."

"You won't like it."

"Not enough sex?"

"Too much violence."

He slid the book back onto the pile gently, as if he were afraid it might detonate, and moved to another table.

Bailey made her way to the back of the store to start unpacking a shipment, and Maude sat behind the sales desk studying a catalog, while Mack went on browsing. The only sound was the muttering hum he made as he read and the whisper of traffic outside the store. There were no horns or sirens, no screeching brakes or crashing metal, and they'd fulfilled the requirements of conversation for the moment. The situation was companionable, even peaceful, or it would have been if Bailey hadn't been worrying about Nell—not about what might have happened to her to make her late but about what was going to happen to her.

The bell above the door rang again, and Bailey turned in time to see Tina Coopersmith come barreling in and feel the atmosphere change perceptibly. Tina carried woe the way a front carries weather.

Everyone said Tina was selfless. She drove the infirm to chemo treatments and dialysis appointments, kept watch beside sick beds, and carried casseroles and cakes to the scenes of death, disaster, and divorce. But Bailey had the feeling Tina was merely infatuated with other people's afflictions.

She made her way down the store now in a swirl of Indian-print fabric and jangling jewelry, asking Maude if she'd heard the latest rumors about the bookstore chain that was going to open a branch in the new shopping center fifteen minutes away, and Bailey if she'd had that old oak over her deck removed because the hurricane season was just around the corner, and Mack about his son. Maude said the new bookstore in the shopping center was only a rumor, and Bailey said the tree was fine, and Mack didn't say anything at all. Bailey watched him turn away and wanted to tell Tina to get a life, only the strange thing was, she had one. She certainly had more of a life than Bailey. She had a husband and two daughters, and contributed articles on health, or as she called it, wellness, to a handful of newspapers and magazines. So there was no excuse.

Tina said she was looking for a book for Jeannie Harper, who was going into the hospital for a hip replacement, but before Maude or Bailey could suggest one, she asked if they'd heard about the accident, and Bailey knew from the trill in Tina's voice that something awful had happened to someone.

"It's heartbreaking." Tina shook her head, but she couldn't suppress the undercurrent of pleasure.

"What happened?" Maude asked, and there was a whisper of titillation in her voice too. Maude wasn't vicious, but she'd spent too many years with a good Christian man who'd had a horror of gossip to be able to resist a lurid story.

"The girl was dead when they found her."

Bailey felt a prickling sensation on the back of her neck. She put down the books she was holding and walked down the aisle between the display tables to where Tina was standing. "What girl was dead?"

"I can't believe you didn't hear," Tina said. She turned to Mack. "You must have heard. The kids can't stop talking about it."

Mack picked up another book without looking at her. "I heard."

"Rebecca came home from school with the story. She was really shaken."

"Who was it?" Bailey asked again.

"The police haven't released her name," Tina said.

"But who're people saying it was?"

"It isn't anyone local," Mack said.

Tina whirled around to face him. "Does that make it less terrible?"

He finally looked up from the book he'd been pretending to read. "Yeah, Tina, it does."

"She was still a human being. Somebody's child."

Mack slammed the book he was holding closed. It made a solid thud. "Thanks for the browse, Maude. I'll get working on that black-Lab mutt, Bailey." The bell jingled noisily as he left.

Tina looked after him. "What can you expect from a man who abandoned his own son?"

Maude shook her head. White hair floated over her sharp cheekbones like wispy clouds over a mountain climber's dream of a rock face. "MacKinley didn't abandon the boy. His wife divorced him and got custody."

"He never does anything with him," Tina insisted. "From what I hear, the only time he sees him is when they pass on the street. There ought to be a law. You have to have a license to drive a car or sell real estate or even install a toilet, but any idiot or incompetent can bring a human life into the world. It's a crime."

"Amen," Maude said.

Tina stood staring at her. She thought Maude was agreeing with her, but she might have been laughing at her. Then she remembered the accident and forgot her own worries.

"Alma Tyler found her. She has a key to the house. The Prinze house. You know, overlooking the pond. That's where they found her. Alma went in to clean. Mr. and Mrs. Prinze were supposed to be coming out today, but the boy was already there. Only he wasn't when Alma went in this morning. She rang the bell a couple of times, and when nobody answered, she used her key. At first she didn't think there was anything wrong. The place wasn't even that messed up. She said it was almost neat, considering the son was supposed to be there. You know how kids are, especially those kids. Spoiled rotten. So Alma was thinking she'd finish earlier than she'd thought. She'd already got a load of laundry in the machine before she saw her. The body, I mean. She was walking through the living room on her way upstairs, when she looked out to the patio and saw it lying there. Alma almost had a heart attack. I mean, she walks into the house expecting nothing but the usual kid's mess, and what does she find but this poor girl lying in a pool of blood. I get weak in the knees just thinking about it. Alma figures she fell or jumped or was pushed"—Tina pantomimed a shiver—"from the upstairs deck. Alma's brother-in-law, the one who's a contractor, put it up for them a few years ago. They used him for the deck but not the patio. They said they wanted to, made a big point about liking to use local people whenever they could and all that, but they were importing special Mediterranean stone so they needed a special stonemason. Alma says it doesn't look so special to her. Anyway, there she was, walking through the house, picking up stuff, and thinking there wasn't as much to pick up as she'd expected, and then she glances out the window and sees this body. I would have fainted. She just ran. Wouldn't even stay in the house long enough to call the police. She went next door for that." Tina shook her head. "It scares me just to think about it. I mean, one of the reasons we moved out here was for the quality of life. But I'm beginning to think no place is safe anymore."

Bailey went back to the cartons she'd begun unpacking. She was still listening, because Tina's voice was inescapable as a droning mosquito, but she wasn't paying attention. She didn't actually know Eliot and Caroline Prinze, though she knew enough about them. All summer long pictures of them at parties and benefits and sporting events appeared in the local weekly. Bailey even knew something about their reading tastes. Caroline Prinze bought novels and nonfiction on psychology and adolescents and women's issues. Eliot Prinze's interests were even more eclectic. In his line of work they had to be.

Eliot Prinze had started his career as a journalist, moved on to a column that was syndicated across the nation and around the world, and branched out to television commentary. For a while he was called a pundit. These days he was simply a personality. His maturely graying temples—in her earlier life Bailey had gone once or twice to his colorist, who made sure only the temples grayed, or so it was rumored; the colorist had been sworn to secrecy—and square, you-can-lean-on-me jaw inspired trust. His pet causes—the downtrodden, the disenfranchised, women, children, and victims—were those only a cad or conservative could hate. His speeches and public appearances commanded hefty five-figure fees. His TVQ rating was practically off the scale. If he'd been willing to do commercials, which he wasn't, he could have named his price.

Bailey knew Eliot Prinze wasn't as good as he looked. She'd lived around the fringes of his world. She'd worked with a woman who'd once worked—intimately, it turned out—with him. He wasn't as good as his public image made him seem, but he wasn't half as bad as he might have been or as a lot of men in his place would have been, given the aphrodisiacal effect that celebrity has on most women and public altruism has on the rest. To put it in a larger moral context, Eliot Prinze wasn't averse to the odd extramarital romp, but when it came to really important matters like establishing a living wage in emergent nations, or ending spousal abuse, or getting violence out of children's television, he was incorruptible.

Listening to Tina picking over the few known details of the accident like a vulture gnawing the remains of a meager kill, Bailey realized she knew more about the Prinzes than she did about some of her own neighbors, but she still didn't know enough to feel involved. And she had no idea who the girl was or what she'd been doing in the house. Tina was right. The incident was tragic. But Mack had been right, too. It had nothing to do with her.

As she carried a stack of books to the front of the store to shelve, she noticed a group of teenagers horsing around across the street and spotted Nell in the crowd of identical oversized shirts and droopy jeans and heavy black men's shoes, though the girl had her back to the store. Bailey recognized the long-legged, high-waisted body that always reminded her of a delicate seabird, and the shiny brown hair that swayed like a curtain, and Kevin Lonergan, who had an arm around Nell's neck in a hammerlock. He was pretending to wrestle, and when he pulled her around, Bailey got a glimpse of Nell's face. She was being strangled by love.

Two

Every morning Bailey got out of the king-sized bed that was a relic of her marriage, put on a T-shirt and rubber flip-flops in summer, a bathrobe, parka, and boots in winter, and walked down the long gravel drive through the oaks and birches and pepperidge trees that made a canopy overhead. When she reached the road, she picked up the blue plastic bags with *The New York Times* and *Newsday* inside and carried them back to the house. She used to do the same thing in her earlier life, wearing less and walking only a few steps to the front door of her apartment. Some habits died hard, though these days she got only two papers instead of four and no longer took them back to the bedroom to read to the accompaniment of the morning news shows.

On the day after Tina Coopersmith had come into the store with news of the accident, she stood reading the headlines while she waited for the coffee to drip through, then carried a mug and the papers out to the deck and settled at the table. The morning was cool, but the sun pouring through the trees made a pool of warmth for her to sit in.

She no longer worked her way through the papers as thoroughly as she used to when what was happening in Washington and the Middle East and cyberspace mattered to her professionally, but she still went through them systematically. There was a story about the accident a few pages into *Newsday* and a shorter one buried in the second section of the *Times* Though the incident was newsworthy to Tina and to a town that was changing quickly, but not so quickly that the recent theft of a handicapped parking sticker wasn't still reported in the local weekly, Bailey knew it wouldn't have made either of the larger papers if it hadn't been for the Prinze name. The girl, identified as Juliet Mercer, nineteen, a student at Vassar, had been a friend of the Prinzes' son, Charles. "A close and cherished friend of the entire family," a spokesperson for Eliot Prinze said. None of the Prinzes was in the house at the time of the accident. Mrs. Prinze and her son were in Manhattan; Mr. Prinze was in California. The police had released no details about the girl's death, though an unidentified source speculated about a possible suicide.

Bailey sat listening to the wren who'd taken up residence in the birdhouse making an unholy racket in an attempt to attract a mate and thought about the things that might make a nineteen-year-old girl commit suicide. Though she could imagine what they might be, she could no longer conceive of them as reasons for suicide. Nor could she imagine jumping off a second-floor deck to a stone patio as a means. The likelihood of instant death was too small, the chance of debilitating and grotesque injury too great. The unfamiliar house didn't make sense either. Bailey had known a grown man who'd opened his veins in the bathtub of his elderly mother's apartment and a woman who'd taken an overdose in her ex-husband's bed, and you didn't have to have a degree in psychiatry to know both incidents defined the phrase passive-aggressive, but why on earth would a young woman hurl herself off the deck of casual friends? Bailey decided she wouldn't, and hadn't, and ruled out suicide.

She stood, carried her mug and plate inside, and went upstairs to shower and dress. Maude was taking the day off, and she didn't want to be late.

Twenty minutes later she came back out on the deck to find Edward, the cat, sitting proudly beside the mangled body of a mouse he'd left for her on the welcome mat. When she'd first moved to the country, she'd tried to keep Edward indoors. He was a city-born-and-bred Abyssinian who knew more about hailing a cab to go to the vet than hunting and killing. But her determination had been no

match for the loamy breezes wafting through the
screens, the siren songs of birds, and genetic memory. Edward, formerly Mr. Murrow, had reverted to
the wild.

She disposed of the mouse, closed the sliding glass
door to the kitchen without bothering to lock it, and
walked across the grass, which she noticed needed
cutting, to the gray Toyota parked in a small clearing. And all the time she was doing it, she was watching herself. A woman getting on with her life. Alone,
but not necessarily lonely. Certainly no more lonely
than she'd been when she'd had a husband and a
Rolodex full of friends and colleagues and contacts.
She straightened her shoulders, as if someone were
watching. Relatively happy, even hopeful, though
the woman had warned Bailey against that. The
agency couldn't promise anything, she'd said.

Bailey had driven into town for the appointment
more than a week ago. Her eagerness had made her
early. For more than twenty minutes she'd had to sit
in the reception area looking at the pictures of smiling men and women bouncing blissful babies, and
holding laughing toddlers, and playing with happy
children. Early euphoria was the decorative scheme.

Finally the woman had come out to the reception
area, introduced herself, and led Bailey back to an office. She'd indicated a chair. Bailey had taken it.
She'd asked if Bailey wanted coffee. Bailey hadn't.
The woman had sat behind a desk and started to talk

in a soft, singsong voice that had an undertone of steel, the voice of the helping professional.

"We respect the triad," she'd warned.

"The triad?" Bailey had repeated.

"Birth parents, adoptive parents, child."

"Of course."

"We do not invade privacy. We do not use illegal methods. We do not find parents or children who do not want to be found."

"Of course," Bailey had repeated and tried to infuse the words with horror at the idea of such shenanigans.

"We're merely a clearinghouse bringing together those who do."

Bailey had assured the woman she understood.

That was when the woman had said she couldn't promise anything, especially after all these years, and warned Bailey against getting her hopes up.

Bailey had promised not to.

Only then, after the woman had heard the lie she'd been waiting for, had she taken a form from her drawer and a pen from the holder on her desk and asked Bailey to tell her whatever she knew. Bailey had. Finally.

She got into the car now, backed it around, and started down the sun-dappled driveway. A branch snapped against the windshield. It was only May. If she didn't get someone to cut back the trees soon, by the end of the summer she wouldn't have a driveway. The sparse gravel crunched beneath the tires. If she didn't get a new shipment, she'd be slipping and skidding next winter. The secrets real estate brokers never told.

She drove quickly and, she knew, a little recklessly along the winding back roads. Like Edward, she was city born and bred, and though she wasn't a bad driver, she wasn't an instinctive one. Unless she concentrated on the process, it tended to get away from her. She slowed as she came out onto the highway and cut her speed even more at the blinking lights in front of the school. A handful of students, the cutups and truants and troublemakers, were still straggling in. A thin boy with stooped shoulders slouched along, bringing up the rear of the group, the last of the local adolescent losers. Though his head, under the requisite peaked cap turned backward, was down, and she couldn't see his face, she recognized the slight frame hunched into a pathetic question mark of existence. It was Mack's son. She thought again of her trip to the agency. Her mother, the only person she'd told she was going, had pleaded with her not to. "Let sleeping dogs lie," Gilda had warned.

Bailey glanced at Mack's son again. But that had to do with Mack, and his former wife, and the boy himself. Besides, she'd rather know, even the worst.

She turned left into the lot behind the shop, parked the car, and walked around to the front of the store. A stack of local weeklies bound with plastic cord sat on the sidewalk. As she unlocked the door, she noticed the headline that ran across half the front page.

The Prinze name took up two columns. Beneath it an extremely pretty young woman with huge almond eyes smiled out at the world. Bailey opened the door and lugged the papers inside.

There were several customers that morning, and they all wanted help or conversation or gift wrapping. She didn't have a quiet moment until after one. Then she went to the small refrigerator in the office at the back of the store, took out the sandwich she'd brought, and carried it to the desk with the cash register and computer and impulse-buy joke books about cats and lawyers and men. She settled down with the local paper and turned, as she always did first, to the crime column. An unidentified man had walked out of a local pizza parlor without paying, but a police officer had caught up with him a block away and collected the two dollars. Phil Smith had parked his truck behind the post office and someone had thrown paint at it. Linda Gilbert reported that a passing motorist had fired a water pistol at her as she was coming out of the hardware store and hit her in the eye. These were the stories Bailey loved, the ones that reminded her, at the risk of sounding like Tina Coopersmith, why she'd moved here in the first place, or at least one of the reasons.

When she reached the end of the column, she turned back to the first page. There was a picture of the Prinze boy as well as the dead girl, and inside, where the article continued, of the house and of Eliot and Caroline Prinze. By the time Bailey had finished the article, she was beginning to think that the suicide theory wasn't so far-fetched after all. At least she had some inkling of what might make a nineteen-year-old girl commit suicide in a peculiar way in a strange house. It had to do with drink and sex and a fight after the sex. It also had to do with the fact that the boy had the kind of looks that could land him a six-figure contract modeling designer sportswear, if it weren't for the smile—they weren't allowed to smile in those ads—which could merely get him elected to national office. None of it was cause for suicide, but looking at the photograph of the boy, Bailey knew that a nineteen-year-old girl might not know that.

God knows it had taken her long enough to learn. There'd been a time when Bailey, like a lot of women of her generation, who'd come of age after the Pill and before AIDS, had thought she could handle stripped-down sex. No obligations, no expectations, just pleasure. But it was easier to slip out of clothing than feelings, and after a while she'd got tired of going through life in wrinkled, messed-up emotions. The realization had led her to marriage. It had also driven her to divorce.

She was still thinking about the possibility of suicide and feeling sorry for the dead girl in the newspaper—though, as Mack had said, not as sorry as she would have if the girl had been someone else, someone closer—when Mack came into the store.

"Hey, Bailey," he called, "get any new smut since yesterday?"

She looked up from the picture of Juliet Mercer. "Try to remember your fiduciary responsibility to all those nubile young things in your classes."

"That's the point. Sex is like teaching. Those who can, do. Those who can't, teach. Or in this case, read. Where's Maude?"

"Not coming in today."

"Not at all?"

"Not for a nanosecond."

"Is she home?"

"She's at her granddaughter's graduation. She left for Connecticut late yesterday afternoon and won't be back till tomorrow."

"Damn."

He walked to the front of the store and stood with his back to her looking out the window. That was when she realized he was dressed up, for Mack. His khakis were freshly pressed, and there were laundry creases in his white shirt. Mack was going somewhere, and it crossed her mind that he planned to hit Maude up for a loan to get there. Maude insisted she'd lent Mack money only once, and he'd paid her back with interest, but Bailey didn't believe her.

"Can I help?" She was sure he wouldn't ask her for money.

Instead of answering, he sat on the wrought iron bench that was supposed to encourage browsing and hunched forward with his elbows on his knees and his eyes on the floor. He was a grown man with a teenage son, two ex-wives, and more history than she wanted to think about, and he sat there like a spoiled kid who hadn't got his way. She swore she wasn't going to ask him what was wrong.

"What's wrong?"

"You were right about Ma Joad. The pickup broke down."

She tried not to smile. "I'm sorry."

"I'm supposed to take my kid out tonight. It's his birthday."

She thought of the pathetic figure she'd seen lurking on the school lawn that morning. Now she really was sorry.

He stood and shrugged. "He didn't want to go anyway."

"Why not?"

"The way he sees it, it's bad enough he has to run into me around town. He doesn't want to have to do things with me too. Only, his mother told him he has to. Which only confuses the kid more, and God knows he's screwed up enough. He can't figure why, if I'm such a loser and a louse and a fuckup—and those are the nice things she says about me—he has to spend time with me. I figured I'd make it easy on him, not to mention on me. Put some buffers between us. So I suggested he bring along some of his buddies. That really spooked him. At first I thought maybe he didn't have any. As far as I can figure, all he does is sit in front of the goddamn television all day anyway. Then I realized, it's not the friends, it's just me again. He doesn't want to see me, and he especially doesn't want his friends to see him with me. Hell, I wouldn't put it past the little fucker to have cut a class and sneaked over to the parking lot to screw up the engine himself."

"Then he's more enterprising than you give him credit for."

"Now you sound like his mother." He walked to the front of the store and stood staring at the street again, as if he expected the out-of-commission truck to appear by magic.

"Want to borrow my car?" she asked. She could get a ride home from someone in the real estate office next door.

"No."

"When you make up your mind, let me know."

He turned back and walked to the center of the store again. "Thanks, but no thanks."

"Why not? You were willing to borrow Maude's."

"That's different."

"Why?" she asked, though she knew. It had to do with a night almost a year ago after the Boys Harbor fireworks that neither of them had ever mentioned. She'd thought about the night, but she hadn't regretted it. She was past the point of looking for pieces of herself in other people's beds.

"Because Maude's gracious. She accepts my bluefish. She rejoices in my bluefish."

"Catch a tuna, and I'll rejoice."

"You're the first Jewish princess I've ever known."

"I bet you tell that to all the summer groupers over at Danceteria."

He walked to the front of the store again, looked out the window, and walked back. "I'll cut your grass for you."

"I can cut my own grass."

"That's not the way it looked last time I drove by."

"Just make sure you get the car back tonight. I have to go into town in the morning."

"*This* is town. That's the big city. What're you going in for?"

"None of your damn business."

"I was only being friendly."

She took her shoulder bag from the drawer beneath the desk, found the keys, and handed them to him. She thought of warning him to stay off the sauce, because it was her car, but she knew the one thing that would make someone with a drinking problem go on a binge was someone else telling him not to.

"Where're you taking him?" she asked as he started toward the front of the store again.

He turned back to her. "Where does any red-blooded American boy want to go? The mall. The one in Riverhead. That way he won't run into any-one he knows. Want to come? It's going to be a hell of an evening. First, dinner, a multicultural experience at the food court. Then shopping for still another pair of hundred-and-fifty-buck state-of-the-art Nikes so he can feel like Michael Jordan while he's lying around watching MTV. And finally one of those movies where not only do they blow away at least ten people before the credits, but they blow them away with such high-tech virtual-reality bullshit that you keep wanting to wipe the blood off your clothes."

"You must love that."

"I spend a lot of time buying popcorn and going to the men's room."

"If you disapprove of it so much, why are you doing it?"

He shook his head. "It's easy to see you've never been a father." He turned and started for the door again. "And according to my kid, my ex-wife, and a lot of other people, that makes two of us."

A few minutes later Nell came into the store. Bailey was sorry Maude wasn't there, because Nell was a quarter of an hour early for her shift.

"Alberta Schweitzer was taking Rebecca to the dentist so she gave me a ride," she explained.

"One of these days you're going to slip and call her that in front of Rebecca, and my ass is going to be in a sling."

"How're they going to know you're the one who christened her?"

"They'll know."

"Okay, Mrs. Coopersmith gave me a ride. You cool with that?"

"I'm cool with that."

"Whatever you call her, she's totally weird. I mean, my mom can be a pain, but she's beyond that. All she could talk about was the accident. Only she's sure it wasn't an accident. She's like, 'Drugs, blah, blah, blah, sex, blah, blah, blah, that's what happens when parents abdicate responsibility, blah, blah, blah.' Like Rebecca hasn't been smoking pot since she was twelve. Then after this whole, you know, morality trip, all I do is mention that I know Charlie Prinze, and all of a sudden she's a total groupie. 'What's he like?' she goes. 'What'd he say?' It was totally pathetic."

"You know Charlie Prinze!"

"See, you, too."

"It just seems an unlikely connection."

"Well, maybe not *know* but I talked to him once. In the Talkhouse."

Bailey didn't know why she was surprised. The Talkhouse was a bar and restaurant and music club where the locals went to eat and carouse, and the summer kids went to meet and carouse, and, according to rumor, a famous Hollywood star had gone the previous summer to get drunk and climb up on a table and carouse. Bailey should have known it was only a matter of time before Nell, fake ID in hand, went there, too. She thought of Nell's mother. Poor Loraine was always talking about how hard it was to raise children with decent values when television and rock lyrics and the Internet brought sex and violence right into your home, and Bailey had to admit Loraine had a point, but somehow all those electronic menaces paled beside the image of Nell rubbing elbows in a small noisy room with Hollywood stars and Charlie Prinze. Bailey wasn't suggesting the boy was responsible for the girl's death, but the mere innocence of it didn't make him fit company for a developing child. Not that Bailey had anything to say about it. She wasn't Nell's mother, though she had a feeling if she were, she'd have even less to say about it.

"He was with a bunch of kids like him, and all of a sudden he leaves them and comes up to me, and goes, 'Hi, I'm Charlie, who're you?' Just like that." She was quiet for a moment. "He was a little drunk, but he wasn't wasted or anything."

"Would you have known if he were wasted?"

"Hello? Sure, I'd know."

Bailey couldn't decide whether she found the statement reassuring or discouraging.

"The thing is, he wasn't, I don't know, superior. Most of those guys, when they come on to you, you can tell they're really making fun of you. Because you're not rich, and don't live in New York and go to private school, and have a polo player on your shirt. But he wasn't like that."

"At the risk of sounding like Tina Coopersmith, what was he like?"

Nell thought about the question for a moment. "He was . . . nice."

The boy was obviously a dangerous customer.

There was no getting away from the incident. An ordinary accident would have sparked talk, but a lurid death in a luxurious summer house of a teenager under the influence and in the wake of sex inflamed gossip in the guise of concern. All the regulars who came into the store mentioned it. Grace Freed, a local psychologist, wanted to put a sign in the window advertising a community meeting to discuss its effect on the local teenagers. The woman at the checkout counter in the IGA, and the man in the dry cleaning store, and every parent Bailey ran across that day fretted about it. Even at home she couldn't escape it. She was opening a can of Friskies while Edward pawed impatiently at her calves when the phone rang. As soon as she picked it up she recognized Annie Fenton's voice, though they hadn't spoken in more than a year.

At one time she and Annie had been friends as well as colleagues, but their paths had gradually diverged. While Bailey had made a few wrong moves— she wasn't regretting, merely admitting—Annie had made all the right ones, including marriage to Ted Holman, a writer twenty years her senior whose highly personal account of a lurid murder on an army base in the South had secured him a reputation as a pioneer of the New Journalism, and won the sergeant, who'd stabbed his wife and infant son to death, parole from a federal prison. That had been around the time Norman Mailer had sprung Jack Abbott, the golden age of the literary lion as champion of the downtrodden criminal, but Ted Holman had been more fortunate than Mailer. The sergeant hadn't killed again—so far. Ted's beat, he liked to say, was the dark netherworld of the human heart. Whenever a stalker shot a celebrity, a psychopath threw acid in the face of a model, or a serial murderer terrorized a community, an article or book by Ted Holman wasn't far behind. During the marriage, Annie had collaborated with him on some of them. Since their divorce, she'd been trying to cover the same beat on her own for a cable news channel. Annie asked how things were going, and Bailey said they were going just fine and waited to find out what Annie was really calling about.

"I've been following this Voluntary Simplicity Movement, and I think they're onto something." Annie sounded sincere, but of course that was one of the secrets of her success. She was a true believer, consecutively if not consistently. "I mean, when I stop to think about it, what am I doing with my life? Working long hours to make more money to buy more things I don't need. Then I think about you and your stripped-down life, and I'm green with envy. It's just like Walden Pond or something."

"This is the East End of Long Island, Annie. Walden Pond is Jet Ski Bay. The roads are crowded with hundred-thousand-dollar sports cars and four-wheel drives that have never touched mud. The favorite pastime is swapping junk in the guise of antique shows and yard sales. Last week I called the women's shelter to donate some old clothes and was told unless they were museum-quality designer pieces they could resell, they were full up. Less is not exactly more out here."

"Speaking of the local scene," Annie said, and Bailey could tell by her voice that she was getting to what she'd really called about, "what do you know about this accident at Eliot Prinze's?"

"Less than you, probably. I'm not exactly in the loop."

"Do you know anything about the girl?"

"Only what I read in the papers."

"What about the boy?"

"Same thing."

"You must know the parents, from parties and stuff."

"We don't move in the same circles."

Bailey could tell from the moment of silence on the other end of the phone that she'd made Annie uncomfortable. Voluntary simplicity might have a certain cachet, but involuntary exclusion was just embarrassing.

"Have you heard the suicide rumors?"

Bailey said she'd heard them, but didn't put much credence in them.

"I don't know," Annie said. "It's a possibility. If it were suicide, it certainly puts a different spin on things. The subject's been noodling around the edges for a while now. A talk show here, a made-for-telly movie there. But it's never had enough sex appeal. This could be the story that changes all that."

"You mean Juliet Mercer could do for teenage suicide what Anita Hill did for sexual harassment?"

"Exactly! I might come out to nose around a little. If I do, I'll give you a call. We can have dinner or lunch or a drink."

Bailey told Annie she'd love to have dinner or lunch or a drink, and got off the phone before the ante sank any lower, but the conversation had unsettled her. As she moved around the kitchen making dinner, she tried to be honest with herself. Maybe she missed that world after all. Maybe she'd made a mistake.

Years ago, when she'd started out, she'd believed in the intrinsic value of what she was doing. The people had a right to know. An informed electorate was a bulwark of democracy. To put it in less exalted terms, there were worse ways to spend her life than blowing the whistle on political skulduggery and financial scams and industrial pollution. And occasionally she had. Usually the segments she'd worked on hadn't aimed quite so high. She'd racked up a lot of footage of dead bodies and drug busts and lurid trials, not to mention abused children and injured animals and politicians who were shocked, simply shocked, to discover there was wrongdoing in the world, and hell-bent on combatting it. If some of the coverage was exploitive, a little of it was still worthwhile. And if she had to put up with superiors who lied through their teeth, and colleagues who stabbed in the back, and personal financial disaster that seemed always to be lurking just around the corner—hell, that was the American way. What she couldn't take was what she'd thought she'd gone into the business for, what some of her colleagues called investigative reporting.

The case that had finally soured her was the story of a woman whose husband, a rabbi, had been found dead in his sanctuary. The conditions of his death had puzzled the police, but they hadn't implicated his wife. Bailey and her colleagues had done that, in libelproof language and innuendo as substantial as smoke. The more they sniffed around, the more they found that smelled rotten. The wife, it turned out, drank a little too much, and took diet pills that made her emotionally unstable, or at least cranky, and had a habit of saying unkind things about her husband's flock. Years earlier she'd had a brief affair with a member of the flock. Aha, a motive! Years before that she'd been sexually abused by an uncle, or so the history pieced together by one particularly resourceful magazine suggested. Aha, the perp as victim! By the time the case began to wind down, the woman's life was an open book, what Bailey's father used to call a racy read. Only, the story wasn't quite over. The university where the woman taught, without tenure, fired her. Nothing personal, they assured her, merely downsizing the department. The flock didn't exactly abandon her, despite the unkind comments she'd made about them. They merely turned to their new spiritual leader and his wife, and got on with their own lives. At least her children stood by her, though they were understandably miffed to learn of her faithlessness to their late father, and when the opportunities came for one of them to work in Europe and the other to enroll in a school on the West Coast, she encouraged them to go, and they did.

It wasn't the worst story Bailey had covered, not by a long shot. What was one woman's loss of job and family, friends and face, of everything that made up her life except her life itself, compared with famines in Africa and ethnic wars in Eastern Europe and an epidemic of violence against women all around the world? But the story had frightened Bailey more because, unlike those oppressed and beleaguered and war-weary women around the world, and like Bailey, this woman had seemed safe. One minute her life had been secure as a fortress. From the sound of it, she'd been bored. The next, it had been a pile of rubble. The fragility had terrified Bailey. Her own part in demonstrating it had sickened her.

Not that she'd left her old life in high moral dudgeon. She'd hung on for a year longer, but she'd only been going through the motions, and the people who made the decisions and handed out the assignments had known as much. Her work had dwindled. Her income had shriveled. Her life had begun to atrophy. She'd cut and run while she still could. So maybe it hadn't had anything to do with the woman whose life she'd helped ruin. Maybe she simply hadn't been good enough at what she did. Or, as her mother occasionally pointed out, maybe she just hadn't believed she was good enough.

It was a little after ten when she heard the car. At first she stiffened. There were still times when the physical isolation of life in the country unnerved her. Beside her on the sofa, Edward lifted his head, ears pricked, senses alert, ready to attack. Then he relaxed, and she realized it was her own car in the driveway with Mack at the wheel. She considered going out and offering to drive him home, but she was only a few pages from the end of the new Richard Russo. Besides, her shoes were upstairs. Besides, Mack could take care of himself. Or rather, he couldn't, but that wasn't her problem.

Three

When she got into the car the next morning she noticed that he'd filled the tank. She also noticed that he, or his son, had left a paper bag with a pair of golden arches on the outside and a cup of melted ice and a cardboard container of limp, greasy french fries inside. They were a pair, all right. She got out of the car and carried the bag to the trash cans behind the house. On the way back to the car she glanced at her watch. She had plenty of time to stop at her mother's and make her appointment in town.

She pulled the car into a guest spot in the parking lot of Town and Country Towers. Bailey still remembered her mother's reaction when her father had brought home the brochure: "A luxury residence for mature couples and individuals that combines the cultural advantages of urban living with the security of Long Island's scenic south shore. Located less than ten miles from a major medical center, the Towers offers a three-tier program, ranging from independent apartment dwelling, through regular supervisory visitation, to compassionate round-the-clock nursing care." The glossy four-color brochure had set her mother's teeth on edge, but her father had been determined, a rare mental state for him. He'd have athletic facilities, cultural programs, and a variety of congenial neighbors; her mother would have the security of knowing that the second- and third-tier nursing facilities were just a wheelchair ride away.

Bailey climbed out of the car and started up the path. A curtain of wisteria clung to the raw red-brick building, and beds of impatiens and pachysandra did their best to camouflage the fact that the builder had torn up every tree in sight. The landscaping, like the euphemisms that flew in the place, provided insufficient cover.

She passed through the automated sliding glass doors. The stench of institutional cooking and industrial-strength disinfectant made her stomach lurch and her eyes sting. She signed in at the desk. The guard didn't lift his eyes from the paramilitary catalog he was studying. She hefted her shoulder bag, which, it occurred to her if not the guard, could have harbored a concealed weapon, and started toward the elevators. The dining room was empty at this hour, but from the solarium and television room and gym she could hear the screech and howl of elderly voices pitched to hearing-aid volume.

She stepped into the elevator, then held the door while a woman with a walker and another in a wheelchair navigated their way on. As the elevator rose, they studied her with the unabashed curiosity of small children. The ambulatory woman moved her walker several inches closer and put her face in Bailey's. "I hope you use sunscreen," she said. Bailey assured her she did. The woman shook her head. "If I knew then what I know now."

The door opened and Bailey started out of the elevator.

"What makes you think all of a sudden you're a rocket scientist?" she heard the woman in the wheelchair ask as the door closed.

She made her way down a long corridor between closed doors. The door frames were wide enough to accommodate wheelchairs and stretchers, and several of the small metal knockers had pink or blue ribbons tied to them. It was a grotesque parody of a hospital nursery, only here the color signified level of care rather than gender. In fact, when her parents had moved in four years earlier, her father had been one of only a handful of males on the premises.

Halfway down the hall she lifted a knocker with

a blue ribbon, struck it against the door, and stood
waiting. Though she could imagine her mother's
slow, painful progress on the other side of the door,
she knew Gilda's appearance would catch her off
guard. She always thought she was prepared for it,
and she was always wrong.

The door opened slowly. She felt the shock all over
again. Surely this frail old lady vibrating like a tun-
ing fork couldn't be the vibrant, full-bodied woman
whose long strides Bailey had once had to run to keep
up with and whose strong, carmine-tipped hand had
tugged her along. She bent, put her arms around her
mother and her cheek against the parchment skin, and
held her for a moment, as if the embrace could stop
the trembling. Then she let go and stepped back. Her
mother tried to smile. She managed a stiff grimace.

When the doctor had first used the word Parkinson's
and Bailey had read everything she could get her hands
on about the disease, she'd thought the tremor would
be the worst. She'd been wrong. At least the tremor was
movement, a kind of desperate life. The mask was
death, a shroud that had fallen over her mother's lovely,
lively face. Bailey could still remember the meticu-
lously shaped eyebrows, as expressive as punctuation
marks, over the huge black eyes that glowed and
sparked and burned, and the ripe lipstick-red mouth
that looked as if it were about to eat up the world. In
the old days Gilda's face had given away her every
emotion as if it were a gift, while her body had burst

with demands that even the highest styles and most rigorous corseting had been unable to camouflage.

Her mother's physical presence had been the lush landscape of her childhood, simultaneously dazzling and dwarfing her. She could still recall the pride of going places with her mother, and the embarrassment. Even as a child, Bailey's narrow features had had a kind of dignified restraint that was belied only by the thin mouth with the short upper lip that gave her, still, an air of startled breathlessness. And her rusty brown hair, which Gilda had tried to glamorize by calling strawberry blond, had been fine and straight and no match for her mother's storm of jet-black waves. People would look from her mother to her, and smile, and ask whose little girl was she.

It was different when she went places with her father. Daddy's little girl was the operative phrase then, although the term didn't really apply. Bailey was probably one of the few women Harry Bender had never managed to charm. But if the allure wasn't there, the resemblance was. Even toward the end, when his head had been bald and a white mustache had covered the short upper lip, people had commented on the similarity. All the widows in the Towers had remarked on it when they'd come, supposedly to visit her mother but actually to bear gifts to her father. They'd come carrying brisket ("It's his favorite") and chopped liver ("He can't get enough of it") and apple pie ("He loves my crust"). Her mother always said that with a diet like that, plus two meals a day in the dining room, no wonder he'd keeled over ten months after they'd moved in, but Bailey didn't agree. Life in the Towers, brief as it was, had been good for her father. By then he'd given up his job as a shoe salesman at Saks, the last in a succession of low-level jobs and failed enterprises, but he'd continued to pursue his real vocation: women. He hadn't been a womanizer. He'd just liked being around women. He'd liked the way they listened to his pronouncements and laughed at his jokes and doted on his presence. And he'd liked the way they repaid him for all that by taking care of him. They'd even taken care of his wife for him. After all, she was such a burden on the poor man. Though her mother never mentioned it, Bailey suspected Gilda had fewer friends since her husband had died.

As her mother turned to go back to the living room, Bailey noticed the well-cut trousers and shirt and wondered how long it had taken her mother to get into them that morning. Gilda wasn't particularly vain, but she was proud. She had no intention, she'd told Bailey, of spending her declining years locked in an apartment with a disheveled, badly dressed woman.

Bailey took her mother's arm to help her back to her chair. The skin above the elbow felt soft and waxy, like a melting candle that would hold the impression.

Gilda pulled her arm away. "I can manage."

She trembled her way to the chair in front of the window, where she spent most of her days now, and maneuvered herself into it. Bailey took the sofa across from her. The latest issue of *Vogue* a book about women of the American West, and biographies of Coco Chanel and Karen Horney lay on the coffee table between them. So did the buzzer that would summon help in case Gilda fell or became ill or was assaulted by an intruder. She was supposed to wear it on her person at all times. She never did. It was not, she pointed out every time the issue came up, an attractive accessory.

She put her elbow on the arm of her chair and rested her chin in her hand as if that would stop the tremor while she examined her daughter. Her face was immobile, but her eyes still held some life, and for a moment she was the smart, calculating woman who'd worked her way up from a job as a part-time saleswoman to a position as a buyer whom half the houses on Seventh Avenue had courted and feared.

"Nice outfit," she said. "Even if it's not pure linen. About twenty percent rayon, right? That's good. Keeps it from wrinkling as much. Your generation thinks synthetic is a sin. I've seen it with my own eyes. Labels that say, 'Guaranteed to wrinkle.' But if you ever tried to work a ten-hour day in the middle of August without air-conditioning in a hundred percent linen, you'd know a couple of synthetic fibers aren't such a crime." She went on staring at Bailey. "Color's flattering too. Warms up your complexion. It's nice to know something rubbed off." She tried to smile again. "Where are you going? I know you didn't get dressed like that just to come see me."

"Into town. I have an interview."

Gilda's face was still rigid, but the dark eyes flashed with excitement. She was convinced that if she'd had her daughter's advantages and opportunities, she'd be running a network by now. And Bailey wasn't sure she wasn't right.

"I knew you'd come to your senses. Cable or what?"

"I'm sorry. Not interview. Appointment. At another search agency."

Gilda's tremor accelerated, as if she were encouraging her daughter, but Bailey knew the movement was involuntary and deceptive. Gilda wasn't expressing agreement, she was merely suffering from a symptom. "So you're really serious about this."

"I told you I was."

"I don't understand why you have to go looking for trouble."

"What makes you so sure it's going to be trouble?"

"What makes you so sure it isn't?"

Bailey didn't answer.

"Look, you have a nice life." She held up one trembling hand. "All right, I admit it's not the life I'd choose for you. Living out there in the boondocks. With a bunch of dropouts and has-beens and losers. Working as a sales clerk."

"I'd hate to hear how you'd describe it if you didn't approve."

"It's just that I know you're capable of more. With your intelligence. With your education. You could have had a real career."

"I could have been a contender."

"You could have. You still can."

"Too late. Haven't you heard? There's been a technological revolution in the communications industry. I'm not up to speed."

The tremble accelerated into a violent pantomime of encouragement. "You could get up to speed in a couple of months. A couple of weeks."

"Even if I wanted to, and I don't, I'm not exactly a hot property. I was fired from three networks."

"That's the business you were in. You knew that when you went into it. At least, you should have. People are up and down and up again. Besides, you just said it. There's been a technological revolution. The networks don't control things anymore. You're lucky you're not tied to one of them."

"Talk about snatching victory from the jaws of defeat."

"That's better than giving up." Gilda sat for a moment trying to control the trembling. "I'm sorry. I didn't mean to get off on that again. We were talking about this search business."

"There's nothing to talk about. I've made up my mind. I'm going to do it. I'm already doing it."

"You're sure?"

"Positive."

Gilda sat for a moment, and Bailey knew she was debating something. "In that case, I have a list."

"I don't believe this."

"If you're going to do it, you ought to do it properly. There are lots of places you can go. Not just the original agency. I got a list."

"How?"

"What do you mean, how? Just because I can't mambo my way around a nightclub floor anymore doesn't mean I don't know how to use the phone. I let my fingers do the walking. Do you want it?"

She didn't. For one thing, she already had a list. For another, she wanted to do this on her own. "Sure."

Gilda leaned forward and began fumbling through the papers on the table. "Just don't say I didn't warn you."

Bailey shook her head. "You're an impossible woman."

Gilda beamed. "I know."

Bailey was early again, despite stopping at her mother's, but the woman at this agency, which was actually a tiny, makeshift office carved from an apartment, didn't keep her waiting. And she didn't give her any assurances about respecting the triad or not finding people who didn't want to be found. She insisted there was no lead too slight to follow, no shred of evidence too thin to run to the ground. Her voice was angry rather than professional. "We have a right to know," she argued. "We've been ostracized and penalized and punished by society long enough."

Who's this *we* Bailey wanted to ask but didn't. She didn't like the woman. She wasn't sure she approved of her methods. But she forked over her money, and filled out the forms, and promised to think about joining the woman's support group, though she knew she wouldn't.

She came outside into an ocean of children. They spilled out of buildings and surged along the cross streets and flooded down Madison Avenue. She'd forgotten this was the sacred terrain of the privileged private schools.

She tried to navigate through the blue blazers and gray trousers and plaid kilts, pushing and chasing and shouting and shoving and giggling and shrieking. One boy punched another, and the second one crashed into Bailey. A girl swung her backpack over her shoulder and hit Bailey in the arm. A smaller child in a red-and-white-checked pinafore over a gray jumper chased another in the same outfit straight into Bailey. She was beginning to get annoyed. Couldn't they see her? Then she realized: They couldn't. She was invisible to them. She wasn't a mother or a teacher or a nanny. She had no authority over them, no effect on their lives. She was just an adult, irrelevant, dispensable, doomed, their growing bodies and raging glands told them, to be cast onto the slag heap of obsolescence as soon as possible.

She kept walking. A gaggle of teenage girls milled

around in front of The Gap. One of them reminded
her of Nell, which reminded her that Nell's birthday
was coming up. She still hadn't decided what to get
her. It had to be small—she didn't want to overdo
it—but it had to be special.

More girls tumbled out of The Gap. She didn't
want to get her clothing. That was too unimaginative.
She couldn't get her a book. Nell had access to the
whole store. Music was out of the question. Buying
rap or hip-hop or whatever Nell was into this week
would make Bailey feel like an enabler.

She stopped in front of the window of a stationery
store. It was filled with sample invitations and overpriced fountain pens and sleek leather appointment
books to carry around in your handbag so you
wouldn't miss a trick. No inspiration there. Maybe
she ought to go back to The Gap after all. Then she saw
it, tucked away in a corner of the window. The spine
was dark green leather, and the covers were paisley-
patterned Venetian paper, and there was a small leather
tie to close it. She liked the tie. It implied privacy without overdoing it. The diary she'd kept at Nell's age had
come with a small brass lock and key. Even then she'd
known that using a lock and key to protect her fifteen-
year-old secrets was like using an Uzi to swat a fly.

She went into the store and asked to see the col-
lection of diaries. There were half a dozen cover
patterns and several more colors. She debated while
the man behind the counter made impatient noises

with his tongue against his teeth, then finally settled on the one that had caught her attention in the first place.

Tina Coopersmith was in midstory when Bailey came into the fish market, but as soon as she saw Bailey she backed up and started again.

"I was just telling Mike," Tina said, and from behind the counter Mike admitted in his lovely, lilting Irish brogue that she had in fact just been telling him.

"It wasn't an accident, and it wasn't suicide. The police haven't confirmed it, but everyone's saying it was foul play."

Bailey knew from the hushed frisson in Tina's voice that she'd been waiting all her life to use those two words.

"The police have been swarming all over the place. Town, county, you name it. Police cars up to gazoo. They've blocked off the area. I couldn't even get down the street."

Bailey didn't bother to ask why Tina was trying to get down a street in the strictly summer-people-with-major-money section of town.

Tina shook her head in a quick little shudder of horror. "Last year there was that rape in the cottage out near the point. Now this. It makes you wonder. I mean, we moved out here for—"

"Don't tell me," Bailey said; "let me guess. The quality of life."

"You can joke," Tina said, "but I tell you, I'm going to start locking my doors."

Edward was sitting on the deck waiting for her when she got home. She slid open the door, and they went into the house. The early evening sun spilled between the trees, through the glass doors, and across the pale wood floors like honey. She turned on the radio. The local station played jazz in the morning and evening, and now John Coltrane filled the house with a few of his favorite things.

The first woman had warned her not to get her hopes up. Gilda had insisted she was looking for trouble. The woman this afternoon only wanted to settle a score. But Bailey didn't care. She was full of optimism.

It was after midnight by the time she turned off the radio and the lights and went upstairs to bed. For the first six months she'd lived in the house, she'd fallen asleep with the radio playing. For the first year she'd slept with several lights on downstairs and one upstairs. Still, the sounds of floorboards creaking and branches brushing against windows and wild, unrecognizable things in the night had wrenched her awake every few hours. Then she'd lie in bed staring through the darkness at the double triangles of Edward's alerted ears and waiting for disaster. Her fear had been especially ironic because when she'd lived in one of the most dangerous cities in the western world, she'd rarely been afraid. Though she'd known that crime was rampant and been sensible enough not to take the subway or go near the park after dark, the presence of dog walkers on the street and neighbors in their apartments and doormen in the lobby had imparted a false sense of security. But gradually she'd got used to the noises of the house and the silence of the country and the absence of people. Now she slept with the radio quiet and the lights off and, during the summer, the doors open to the cool salty air.

She was getting into bed when she remembered Tina's comment in the fish store. She knew it was foolish. You couldn't take a woman who used the expression "foul play" seriously. And even if it had been that, a single incident wasn't exactly a crime wave. Certainly an intruder who had the ingenuity to find his way out to the East End would know enough to break into a summer house with a couple of Jags and Mercedes in the garage and Impressionist paintings on the walls rather than a small glass-and-weathered-cedar box without even a swimming pool in the yard. On the other hand, they never had found the rapist. At least, they hadn't taken down the photograph of the peaked cap he'd lost in the struggle, which was posted on the bulletin board outside the town clerk's office. For a while after the incident, she'd begun locking her doors again, but as the summer had progressed and the heat mounted and the breezes softened, the memory had faded, and she'd returned to her open-door policy.

Now she got out of bed, went back downstairs, and walked through the house sliding the glass doors closed and turning the locks.

Four

When she came downstairs the next morning, she was surprised to find all the doors closed and locked. It took her a moment to remember what she'd been afraid of. She went through the house sliding open the doors. Then she walked down the drive to get the papers.

The impulse came to her on the way back to the house. When she'd lived in town and had less time, she'd exercised compulsively. The first few months she'd been out here, she'd jogged regularly. Now she ran sporadically. But this morning she was bursting with energy.

She went upstairs and got into shorts, a T-shirt, and her old running shoes, still black with Central

Park grime. As she tied them, she decided it was time for a new pair.

There were only a handful of cars on the road, and they gave her a wide berth. When she reached the point, she counted five pickup trucks, though Mack's wasn't among them. Two of the trucks were empty, but in each of the others she could make out the twin silhouettes of a human head and, beside it in the front seat, the canine curve of his best friend. As she described a semicircular turn and started back, one of the men in one of the trucks raised a cardboard coffee container toward her in salute. The sun in her eyes made it impossible to tell who he was, but she waved in return. A few years ago she wouldn't have, but then, a few years ago she'd been a suspicious—or street-smart; it depended on your point of view—refugee from the city.

On the way home she noticed an osprey sitting on a nest. Overhead its mate circled with breakfast. Back on the two-lane highway, a police car slowed slightly as it approached. She felt a familiar flash of guilty fear, as if she'd been speeding, or making an illegal turn, or doing something she shouldn't have. Then she remembered: All she was doing was running, though she never was sure whether she was supposed to run with the traffic or against it.

As she came back up the driveway, she saw Nell sitting on the steps to the deck. Her chin rested on one hand while the other massaged Edward's stomach. Even in this harsh light, Nell's skin had a translucent glow. She gave off a promising luminescence, like the pale mystery in a film negative that has yet to be developed. Bailey squinted against the glare of her own love and longing and thought again about this business of having and not having children.

A few years earlier she'd helped an old friend through the birth pangs of single motherhood. After months of mucking about unsuccessfully with the bodily emissions of total strangers, the friend had decided on adoption. The application form had taken them back to those strained essays they'd written to get into college. Bailey had even spotted the trick question: "Why do you want a child?" There was no logical or even sane answer. People had children to complete their lives, or fulfill their dreams, or secure their old age. She knew ambitious women who had children as part of the package, like the power-path job and the designer briefcase, and she'd read studies of adolescent girls who had them because they didn't have anything else. It was different for men. In the struggle for survival of their genes, the only motivation biology knew, all they had to do was run around like something on the Discovery Channel, spraying as far and frequently as possible.

"What's up?" she asked Nell now. It was a greeting rather than a question. She knew that whatever was up, and something probably was because Nell hadn't stopped by for some time, it would take a while for it to come out.

"How far did you run?" Nell asked.

"Three miles. Actually, three point two, but who's counting?" She crossed the deck, slid open the screen door for Nell, and followed her into the kitchen.

Nell wandered around picking up things and putting them down while Bailey took a carton of orange juice from the refrigerator and two glasses from a cabinet, filled them, and handed one to Nell.

"I passed your mom on my way out to the point," Bailey said.

Nell didn't answer.

"At least, I think it was your mom. The car was going too fast for me to be sure."

"She always drives fast when she's pissed."

Bailey was beginning to understand what was up. "What's she pissed at?"

Nell's thin shoulders went up and down. "It isn't like she's got a lot of options. My dad or Hughie or me."

Bailey leaned against the counter and took a swallow of juice. "From where I stand that's a lot of options."

"Yeah, well, not these days. My dad's still going to his meetings and taking one day at a time, so she can't yell at him even if she wants to. And last week some lady came up to her in the IGA and said she wanted to put Hughie in this commercial, so all of a sudden he's Macaulay Culkin or something. That leaves me."

Bailey didn't say anything. It was too easy. Like shooting fish in a barrel. And too dangerous. Like catching a man on the rebound. She took the canister of coffee from the freezer.

"I came in about ten minutes late last night. Ten minutes. Like big whoop."

"She was probably worried."

Nell had been pacing the length of the kitchen. Now she stopped in front of the refrigerator, took off one of the magnetized oven mitts, slipped it on her hand, and stood staring at it as if she'd never seen anything so fascinating. "Nobody else has a curfew."

Since Nell had begun to change, the world had shrunk to two kinds of people—nobody else and everybody else.

"Where were you, anyway, that you were late?"

"Just hanging out."

Two kinds of people, Bailey thought, but only one pastime. Hanging out. She wondered at what point in recent history the entire spectrum of adolescent activity from loitering in front of ice cream stores and driving around in aimless circles to doing drugs and holding up innocent bystanders had been reduced to that single phrase.

"You and Kevin?" Silly question.

"We were just driving around."

"That's probably why she was worried."

"Yeah, like she really thinks I'm going to end up in a car crash or something."

"Stranger things have happened."

"Come on, Bailey, you know my mom. That's not what she's worried about."

She had a feeling Nell was right, but she didn't say anything.

Nell tugged off the mitt and flung it on the counter. "Forget it. Listen, I have to go."

Bailey followed her out to the deck. "You want to start running with me again?"

Nell took the three steps down to the grass in a single bound. "Sure."

"Tomorrow?"

"Maybe next weekend." She was already halfway across the yard.

Bailey stood on the deck watching Nell make her way down the driveway, passing from sun to shade to sun again. She moved on those delicate seabird legs with a quick, sure grace, like the terns and piping plovers and other once-endangered species now thriving on the protected breeding grounds of the area's beaches.

The next edition of the local weekly demoted the accident to a mere two-column headline on the front page. The article beneath it, unlike Tina Coopersmith, did not mention foul play. The police were questioning Charlie Prinze only because he was the last person to have seen Juliet Mercer alive. He was not a suspect. There was no mention of a crime. There weren't even any new facts, merely a few more details. During a lull in business, Maude sat behind the desk reading the account to Bailey.

Charlie Prinze and Juliet Mercer had started the evening in a local bar with several of their friends. They were, according to Charlie, just hanging out.

"I hate that phrase," Maude said. Bailey told her she wasn't too fond of it herself.

At around eleven they'd left the bar, gone back to the Prinze house, had some more to drink, and got down to sex. After the sex, he said, they'd had a fight. The police declined to say what the fight was about. Nor did they mention physical abuse, though a reference to bruises on the girl's body enabled any follower of recent trends to read between the lines. The boy obviously hailed from a long line of popular heroes—sports figures and movie stars, CEOs, and even a lead dancer with the New York City Ballet—whose favorite pastime was beating the hell out of their wives and girlfriends.

"So much for locked doors," Bailey said to Tina, who'd come into the store while Maude was reading.

"Keep going," Tina said.

Maude went back to the article. According to the boy, he'd slammed out of his parents' house in the middle of the argument, got in the BMW convertible his parents had given him for his last birthday, and driven back to the co-op apartment in Manhattan they'd bought him when he'd graduated from college.

"I blame it on the parents," Tina said.

"Who else?" Maude asked.

Tina looked at her uncertainly. Bailey didn't say anything because she hated to admit that for once she thought Tina had a point—almost. She wouldn't go so far as to say Charlie Prinze's parents were at fault for Charlie's behavior, which even if it wasn't criminal still sounded pretty unsavory, but she couldn't help wondering how it would feel to have raised a child like that.

Mack, on the other hand, found inspiration in the story. "It makes me realize," he said when he came into the store later and they were still talking about it, "that my kid isn't so messed up after all. The only one he wants to beat the shit out of is me."

Though the police hadn't said there was a crime, let alone charged anyone with it, most people agreed, where there was smoke, there was bound to be fire. They were outraged, they were scandalized, they were tantalized. And the fact that it didn't appear to be random violence by a stranger, like the rape and assault a year earlier, but personally directed mayhem with a steamy psychological subtext made it less threatening and more intriguing. People shook their heads over the moral implications while they lapped up the details.

Nell, of course, picked up on the fact. She'd changed, but she hadn't become stupid.

"Grown-ups are totally weird," she said to Bailey as they were driving home from the store one evening.

"If you're looking for an argument, you're not going to get it from me."

"They're all like, 'How awful, how awful,' but you can tell they're loving it."

Bailey admitted she had a point.

"You know what I really hate?" Nell asked after a while.

"What?"

"The way everyone thinks it's about them. Him," she corrected herself. "Her."

"What do you mean?"

"Like my mom. Last night we were doing the dishes, and out of nowhere she goes, 'I hope this teaches you a lesson.' Like it's some weird religious parable directed right at me. Like one morning God got up and went, 'Hey, I think I'll answer Loraine Harris's prayers and send Nell a sign.'"

Bailey kept her eyes on the road. "A sign of what?"

"The wages of sin. Of sex. Have it and you're dead."

Bailey didn't even slow for caution. And she didn't care if she was overstepping her bounds or subverting Nell's mother's beliefs. "Only if it's unprotected."

Nell hunched down in the seat and propped her heavy black shoes against the dashboard. "Hello? Don't you think I know that?"

Bailey glanced across the front seat. She wasn't sure what Nell knew. Her fine-boned profile was as clean and innocent as a Renaissance Madonna's, but the models for those Madonnas always turned out to

be the artist's mistress or some accomplished cour-
tesan. Besides, there was knowing and there was
knowing. But she let it go. If she pushed too hard,
the door would slam in her face.

As they pulled up in front of the house, Bailey noticed a shadow watching from behind the screen
door. It might be Nell's father, but it was probably
her mother. Loraine Harris always thanked Bailey for
driving Nell home, but Bailey suspected that Nell's
mother didn't trust or even like her.

"Besides," Nell said, "everyone says she was a slut."

"What in hell is that supposed to mean?"

"Hey, don't get angry at me. I'm just repeating
what all the kids are saying. The guys talk about
what a stud he is, but everyone says she was a slut."

So this, Bailey thought, was the revolution she'd
manned the barricades for. "Doesn't that strike you
as a little twisted? Two people do the same thing;
one's a hero, the other's a—" She hesitated; there
were only a handful of four-letter words she hated,
but that was one of them."—slut."

"I suppose it makes people feel better," Nell said.
"That way they don't have to feel bad that she's dead.
They figure she just got what she deserved."

"Is that what you think?"

"No way." Nell shouldered her backpack and
opened the car door. Then she hesitated and turned
back to Bailey. "Except she was, I don't know..."

"Slutty?"

"Forget it." Nell got out of the car and started toward the house.

"Hey!" Bailey called after her.

Nell turned back, but Bailey could tell from the way she stood with her backpack over one shoulder and the other hand on her hip that she was impatient. She didn't want to talk anymore. She wanted to get away.

"I almost forgot." Bailey twisted around, reached into the backseat, and took something from her canvas satchel. She held up a package wrapped in striped paper. "Your birthday present."

Nell shuffled back to the car. "I'm sorry."

"For what?" Bailey asked, but she knew for what. Nell wanted to talk when she wanted to about what she wanted to and stop when she wanted to. Those were the prerogatives of adolescence.

Bailey handed her the package. "Happy birthday."

"What is it?"

"Open it and see."

Nell put her backpack on the ground and, careful not to tear the paper, slid her finger under the Scotch tape. There was a time, so recent that even Bailey remembered it, when Nell would have torn off the paper in a frenzy of impatience.

She stood looking down at the diary for a moment, just long enough for Bailey to wonder if she should have gone for a cotton sweater.

"It's a diary," Bailey said.

"I know what it is. It's cool."

"I hope you like it."

"I love it."

"You don't have to keep it—as a diary, I mean. You can use it for anything you want; I just thought—"

"It's great! Thanks." Nell ducked, stuck her head in the window, and put her cheek against Bailey's. Then she picked up her backpack and started toward the house.

"Happy birthday," Bailey called after her again.

Without turning, Nell raised the diary in one hand and pumped her other fist in the air triumphantly.

Bailey was sitting on the side deck when she heard the sound in the driveway. She stood and followed the deck around to the other end, though she already knew who it was. The noise was too loud for any normally functioning vehicle.

She watched as Mack climbed down from the pickup. He stopped to hitch up his jeans. They rode low on his hips. She wondered if that meant he was in one of his turning-over-a-new-leaf phases. He reached back into the truck, took out a brown paper bag, and started across the yard toward her.

"You need a new muffler."

"That is a new muffler."

As he came up the stairs to the deck, she noticed the safety pin that held together his dark glasses. He really was the walking wounded.

He held the bag out to her. "You wanted tuna. I caught you tuna."

She looked at the brown paper bag. "Caught it?"

"I had to wrap it in something."

"Sure."

"If you don't believe me, call Mike. He'll tell you there's no way I was in there tonight buying a piece of tuna."

She took the bag from him. "Thanks."

"There's enough for two."

"I figured there would be," she said, though she hadn't been sure. Since the night of the Boys Harbor fireworks, he'd stopped by occasionally, but never with dinner.

She went into the house and put the fish in the refrigerator. When she came back out, he was lying on the lounge where she'd been sitting, reading the paper she'd left open.

"You know what I think? I think the Prinze kid never left. I think the two of them got up to something kinky on that upstairs deck, and she fell." He shook his head in wonder. "He must be one hell of an acrobat."

"You're worse than Tina."

"I wasn't the one who left the paper open to that page. Besides, she thinks it was foul play. I think it was love."

She asked him if he wanted iced tea.

"I almost forgot," he said and went back out to

the truck. When he returned, he was carrying a six-pack of nonalcoholic beer. "A tomboyish little brew." He handed her the pack. "Chilling brings out its complexities."

She took the beer into the kitchen and put several bottles in the freezer. "Is it going to bother you if I have a glass of wine?" she called back to him.

He came to the screen. "Hell, have two. Maybe I'll get lucky."

"It would take more than a couple of glasses of cheap chardonnay for that."

He slid open the screen door and stepped into the kitchen. "I don't know. You could do worse."

She took the bottle of wine from the refrigerator and poured a glass. "I already have."

He leaned against the counter and crossed his arms over his chest. "If you're talking about that guy last summer who used to sit in his vintage Austin-Healey doing deals on his cell phone so that all of Main Street could hear while he waited for you to close up the store, you're right. You did."

She looked up from the lettuce she'd begun washing. "He was one of the good ones."

He went on watching her. "I can believe it."

"Why don't you go start the grill? And try to remember, you have to open the gas valve first."

"Hey, I may be a bum, but I'm not a mechanical illiterate."

"You're not a bum."

"Be careful," he called from the deck. "It was exactly that thought that got my ex-wife in trouble."

He offered to set the table while she finished making the salad. When she carried the bowl out to the deck, she noticed that he hadn't quite mastered the niceties of what went where. Or else he was putting her on. She rearranged the cutlery and napkins, lit several citronella candles, and poured a bottle of nonalcoholic beer into his glass and more wine into hers.

"You sure this doesn't bother you?" she asked.

He was standing at the grill, and he glanced back over his shoulder. "Hard stuff would bother me. Real beer would bother me. I could name about a dozen controlled substances that would have bothered me at one time. But that doesn't bother me."

She reached into the kitchen to get a sweater from the coatrack and pulled it on. "A dozen?"

He took the fish off the grill, hacked it in two, and slid one piece onto her plate. "Okay, I exaggerate. It's my version of a war story."

She was surprised. She knew he'd been in Vietnam, and he knew she knew, but it had never come up between them. She also knew that wasn't an accident. He didn't talk about it, and she didn't have the nerve to ask about it.

"Don't look so guilty," he said. "If I hadn't been over there, I probably would've been here marching with you."

"How do you know I was marching?"

He leaned back in his chair and looked at her. "You gotta be kidding."

She shrugged. "I missed most of it. Too young, thank you very much. I got in just in time for the final act."

"Still, I bet you had a good time. I bet you had a hell of a good time."

It was a statement, not an accusation, and it was correct. She'd had a wonderful time. She'd had the time of her life.

There'd never been another spring like it, not in her life, not, she was sure, in the history of the world. In April she marched on Washington for the first time; in May she almost managed to get arrested along with Dr. Spock and twelve thousand other protesters; in June she and the rest of America awakened one morning to the Pentagon Papers. And there was more on the horizon. In the fall she was going off to Radcliffe. Gilda said it was her chance to save herself. She knew it was her chance to save the world. In the meantime she went on demonstrating and marching; manning telephones and canvassing neighborhoods; standing on street corners urging people to sign petitions and sitting in smoky rooms arguing about right and wrong, vehemently. Politics was personal and passionate and all mixed up with sex, though it wasn't yet sexual politics, which would have to wait until they stopped the war.

She was seduced by ideals, but when it happened, it wasn't a seduction. That would have been dishonest, corrupt, hypocritical—the kind of thing people

over thirty did. It would have been everything they
were fighting against. So that night when they found
themselves alone in the church basement that smelled
of stale coffee and cigarettes and freshly mimeo-
graphed flyers, he'd asked, casually, with a sweet
toss of his ponytail, if she wanted to fuck, and she'd
answered, with matching nonchalance, that she did.
It wasn't until later that she realized he'd been as terrified as she, and almost as uninitiated. Though he
hadn't been unprepared. He'd produced the neat little foil packet.

Maybe it hadn't been politics. Maybe if they'd
lived in another time, it would have happened the
night before he shipped out for France or the Philip-
pines, or after the prom or the big game. These days
it would happen while they were hanging out. Certainly the repeat performances in his car and the living room of the apartment where she'd grown up
weren't intrinsically political, though there had been
a poster of Che Guevara over the bed in his dorm
room. She knew now it probably would have happened anyway, but somehow, even after all these
years, she associated the heady experience of her first
sex with the political thrills of her youth. That spring
and summer, politics and sex had raged through her
system like hormones, making her pulse race and
glands ache and juices flow. Everything had throbbed,
including hope. It was only later, after a president
had gone down in flames and the last helicopter had

taken off from the roof of the American embassy and still nothing had changed, that disillusion set in.

It probably hadn't taken Mack that long. Across the table from her now, he stood, went into the kitchen, and came back with another fake beer.

"Is that stuff any good?"

He held the bottle out to her. "Try it."

She took a swig, then made a face.

"Yeah, that's exactly what it tastes like. Hey, did I ever tell you my real war story?" He sat across the table from her again. "Well, not exactly a war story. More like a coming-home-from-war story. It happened the first night I was back. I was still in uniform. That's how dumb I was. Calley was about to go on trial, and I'm walking into bars in the greater metropolitan area in a goddamn army uniform. Some girl started needling me. Nothing personal, just the usual generic stuff like 'baby-killer' and 'hey, hey, hey, how many kids did you kill today.' Now, I was hip. I'd been reading *Time* and *Newsweek* over there. So I told her I'd rather make love than war. That shut her up. In fact, it drove her right the hell off the bar stool. I wasn't too happy because, after all, it was my first night home, and I wouldn't't've minded getting laid—I'd heard about you hippies— but I figured, what the hell, at least I got her off my back. Then all of a sudden I see her coming back from the ladies' room, and she's still carrying her drink. She walked right up to me and threw it in my face. Only it wasn't her drink. She'd peed in the goddamn thing."

Bailey gasped. "That bitch!"

"Now, now, Bailey, remember sisterhood."

"What did you do?"

"Decked her. It was my last act of violence." He took another swig of beer. "Still, I got a lot of mileage out of the experience."

"What do you mean?"

"For years after that, every time I told the story to someone like you, I did get laid."

She pushed her chair back from the table. "Your luck just ran out," she said and began carrying plates into the kitchen.

He didn't offer to help her, though he did take the wire brush hanging on the side of the grill and give the grate a quick once-over. By the time she came outside again, he'd moved back to the side deck. He was sitting with his chair tipped back on two legs and his feet propped on the railing. She sat beside him and put her feet up on the railing, too, though she didn't tip her chair back. His right boating moccasin was torn along the seam. So, she noticed for the first time, was her left espadrille. The realization bothered her more than it should have. Maybe she was becoming one of them after all.

She leaned her head against the back of the chair. All around them the trees were swaying black shadows in the night, but directly overhead a circle of sky stretched like violet velvet. When she'd first moved out here, she'd been surprised to find that on some nights the sky never grew dark. Through a tangle of branches the moon glowed so close it looked like a neighbor's window.

He tipped his chair back another precarious fraction of an inch and locked his hands behind his head. She noticed an aroma of wild vegetation she didn't recognize, then realized it was his deodorant. She bet it was called Outdoors or even Musk. She imagined him standing in Revco, studying the names of the various scents, then, in an atavistic lurch toward some macho memory, reaching for that one.

"I got a call from my ex-wife today."

"Which one?"

"You're a mean-spirited woman, Bailey."

"It's a logical question," she said, though it wasn't. The only wife he ever mentioned was the second one, the mother of his son.

"Donna. Bella Donna. She's got a new boyfriend."

Bailey was surprised, not that his former wife had a boyfriend, but that he seemed to mind. She tried to remember how she'd felt the first time she'd run into Gideon with a woman. It had bothered her, but even at the time she'd known it hadn't bothered her enough, and that had bothered her more. What kind of woman can run into her former husband with a new woman and not feel some pang of passion—if not love or hate, then at least jealousy or envy?

From the sound of Mack's voice in the darkness he didn't have the same trouble coming up with the requisite emotions. She was surprised and, finally, a little envious.

"I'm sorry."

"I'm not. She's always easier to deal with when she's got somebody."

"Then what?"

"My kid's coming to live with me for the summer. Actually, she can't even wait for summer vacation. She wants him to move in right away. This new boyfriend has to go somewhere on business, and he wants her to go with him. So she's decided the kid can come live with me. Not do I want him to, or he wants to, but she's decided he should. She says I can take him fishing and clamming, which is supposed to make a man of him. On the other hand, now I'll have to grow up and shoulder some responsibility instead of wasting my summer fishing and clamming. I'm still working on the logic of that."

The logic of that, Bailey thought but didn't say, was that his son was a thirteen-year-old boy and he was a forty-eight-year-old man. Still, the accusation didn't seem entirely fair. During the years Mack had been married, he'd always got another job during the summer months. One year he'd worked for a landscape gardener, and another he'd been a house painter. He said he'd even spent a summer as a social director at a local spa, but she had a feeling he was putting her on about that. Since he and Donna had split up, each summer he got the necessary licenses so he could sell the fish and lobsters and clams and mussels he spent his days catching and gathering.

"I take it you don't like the idea."

"It's not that," he said, and she knew it was. "I just don't have room for him. I don't even have a place for him to sleep."

"Where does he sleep when he stays over?"

"He doesn't stay over. He hasn't for a couple of years. He used to sleep on the couch that opens up in what is euphemistically known as the living room, but he was only a kid then."

She thought of the slight figure she saw loitering about town. "He isn't exactly a bruiser now."

Mack didn't say anything to that.

"What does he think of the idea?"

He tipped the chair back a little farther. "How would I know? His entire vocabulary consists of a single, all-purpose grunt."

They were quiet for a while.

"What're you going to do?" she asked finally.

"Do I have a choice?"

At first she thought the question was rhetorical, then she realized he meant it. He was asking her advice. More than that, he was asking her to get him off the hook.

"No, you don't."

He brought his chair forward so it hit the deck with a bang. "I hope you have a kid someday. It'll serve you right."

She thought about this business of having kids again, not the sociological overview, but her own personal conflict. She'd thought about having a child. She and Gideon had talked about it. But they'd never done anything about it.

"I'm a little long in the tooth for that."

He didn't look at her, but she could tell that beside her in the darkness he was grinning. "I don't know. If we start now, we could probably get in under the wire."

"Great; then you'd have two kids to bitch about."

He got up. She did too. They walked around the deck to the steps. He stood with his hands jammed in his pockets looking out across the yard. "Now you think I'm a real son of a bitch."

She looked at him. His faded shirt glowed in the darkness, but his face, still turned away from her, was in shadows. "Come on, Mack. I always thought you were a real son of a bitch. Now I just think you're a real son of a bitch with a problem."

He swung the pickup out of the driveway and onto the road. He never should have opened his mouth. It wasn't as if he didn't love the kid. Sometimes when he caught a glimpse when the kid didn't know he was being watched and didn't have that sour, pissed scowl on his face, love twisted his insides like a physical cramp. Sometimes when he came across him unexpectedly, skulking around alone or hovering on the fringe of a group, his skinny shoulders hunched forward as if he could shrink himself out of existence, that rat's tail of hair creeping down his scrawny neck, the surge of protectiveness that jumped out from the shadows of everyday life frightened him. But how do you explain that to a kid who doesn't believe a word you say? How do you show that to a kid who won't even look you in the eye? He loved Will. He really did. He'd give up his own life for him. He just didn't know how he was going to live with him.

After Mack left she went back to the side deck and sat for a while thinking about him and his son. She didn't know the boy, though she saw him around town enough. He wasn't an attractive sight. His slight body was always curled into a cave of despair, and his head hung forward as if he were exposing his neck to the ax he expected to fall at any moment. His eyes, if you could manage to catch them, were shifty. She thought again of her mother's warning to let sleeping dogs lie. Mack didn't have that luxury, if it was a luxury.

She felt sorry for him. She even felt sorry for his former wife, because the only thing harder than living with a child like that was admitting you didn't want to live with him. But most of all, she felt sorry for the boy. He wasn't a baby anymore, and you couldn't blame it all on his parents, but he wasn't an adult either. It couldn't be fun to be thirteen years old and know nobody wanted you around.

Five

Though Gilda couldn't see it, and Bailey, even now, tried to fight it, she was her mother's daughter. Gilda worshiped at the altar of style. Bailey, against her better judgment and despite evidence to the contrary during the years they'd waged war, was a secret acolyte. In her old, supposedly glamorous life, her closet had overflowed with expensive designer clothes and canny bargain buys. These days her needs were simpler, but she still had enough jeans and T-shirts and sweaters to see her safely through old age and into the grave, with a few items left over for Goodwill and the Salvation Army. Nonetheless, she couldn't go to the local shopping center for vacuum cleaner bags or an alarm clock without a pit stop at some of the clothing stores. That afternoon she was checking out the ribbed T-shirts that had gone on sale in Banana Republic when she noticed Nell and her mother in the dressy section. Nell was standing in front of a three-way mirror in a thin slip dress and her clunky black shoes. Her arms were splayed stiffly a few inches from her sides, and her long neck was craned to one side as she studied herself through narrowed eyes. Behind her, Loraine Harris's face, still young, still fine-boned, still pretty enough to show where Nell had got her looks, was twisted into one of those overwrought smiles that could implode into tears in a second. Bailey wondered whether the smile meant that Loraine was remembering her own once-hopeful past, or anticipating Nell's future, or had merely lost the ability to distinguish between the two. She stood watching Nell and her mother in the three-way mirror and saw a disturbing reflection of her own feelings. They thought they wanted to protect Nell, to have her benefit from their mistakes rather than make her own, but maybe they were merely throwing their experiential weight around, warming themselves on the memory of it, wringing every ounce of pleasure from the shame of it, keeping themselves alive on the viability of it. If that was true, they were playing a desperate trick, though she wasn't sure on whom.

In the mirror Nell's eyes moved from her own reflection to her mother's; Loraine returned the gaze, and halfway across the store Bailey felt the current of love that surged between them. It was the positive

charge of that negative force that had sent Loraine careening the roads at unsafe speeds and driven Nell to
Bailey's house a week earlier, and the fact that it was
as fleeting as that other outburst didn't make Bailey
any less envious of it. That was all right. She understood the envy, just as she understood her need for
Nell. It was the disappointment in Nell and her
mother's closeness that shamed her. She thought she
wanted Nell happy, but maybe she only wanted Nell.

Nell broke from her mother's gaze, noticed Bailey
in the mirror, and turned and waved. Bailey crossed
the store to them.

"What do you think?" Nell stood in front of Bailey with the same stiff, splayed-arm posture.

"It's nice," Bailey said, and then because the answer sounded tepid: "You look beautiful." But that
wasn't right either. Beauty demands a certain har-
mony, and Nell looked uneasy. She reminded Bailey
of a toy poodle she'd had as a child. Poor Coco always came back from the grooming parlor hanging
her head in shame at the exposure of all that tender,
pink skin beneath the brutally shorn hair.

"What's it for?" Bailey asked, though she had a
pretty good idea. Recently one of the papers had run
an article about high school proms. She'd been hor-
rified at the photographs of childish girls painted and
combed and curried into replicas of the middle-aged
mothers they disdained. The reports of uncon-
scionable sums of money shelled out for uneaten

food and loud music and block-long limousines with chauffeurs who looked as if they had felonious pasts hadn't given her a lot of hope for the future either.

"Kevin's prom." Nell confirmed her worst expectations.

"It's way too expensive," Loraine said, "but how can I say no? She looks better in it than the model." She pointed to a display photograph of another young woman, this one pouting meanly, in the same dress. "Don't you think?"

Bailey did think, but something was still bothering her, something more than Nell's air of shorn-poodle uneasiness. She stood watching the reflections of Nell and her mother multiplied in the three-way mirror and tried to figure out what was wrong with the picture. Nell didn't look like an imitation of a middle-aged woman. The dress was too simple and the body it revealed too lithe for that. Loraine moved in and smoothed the silky fabric over the small globe of her daughter's behind. "It's her first grown-up dress," Loraine purred, and Bailey knew what was wrong. You couldn't send a half-naked nubile girl off with a boy whose hormones were in an uproar for a night of inflated expectations and expect any good to come of it. Even if you did go to church and have a direct line to the Almighty. Especially if you went to church and had a direct line to the Almighty. Someone was sending out what the experts in the field called a mixed message.

* * *

Bailey rested the shopping cart against the bumper of her car and opened the hatchback. Since the Pathmark in the shopping center had a wider selection than her local IGA, she tried to stock up whenever she was there, but she always found the gargantuan "family pacs" of chicken parts and cereals and toilet paper a little daunting. Today she'd asked a man who was hosing down the greens where she could find loose onions because all she saw were ten-pound bags, and he'd looked at her as if she were speaking a foreign tongue. The experience hadn't depressed her exactly, but it had made her feel somehow deviant.

She was putting the last plastic bag in the car when she heard someone calling her name and turned to see Tina Coopersmith pushing a shopping cart full of paper bags toward her. Bailey slammed the door of the hatchback, but it was no good. The plastic bags were still visible through the rear window. She braced herself for an ecological moment. Tina didn't even glance into the car. Bailey knew something big was up.

"Did you hear?"

"Hear what?" She hated encouraging Tina, but she was as curious as the next person.

"The boy did it! First they had sex, and then they got into a fight about something. He pushed her off the deck in the heat of passion." Tina's voice caressed the words *heat of passion* almost as lovingly as it had *foul play* "These kids." She shook her head. "I mean, you expect that kind of thing in New York. But not out here. That's why we moved here—"

"I know. For the quality of life."

Tina frowned. "I just wish they'd all go back where they belong."

"Bite your tongue. Main Street would close up, Maude would go bankrupt, and I'd be unemployed."

"You know what I mean. Leaving kids unsupervised in a house like that."

"Kids? According to the papers, he's in his twenties. And I don't see what the house has to do with it."

"You know what I mean. All that indulgence."

"They're young. They don't need Porthault linens or a king-sized bed to get randy." Bailey knew she was being contrary. She agreed that most of the summer kids were spoiled: overindulged, overvalued, and overwhelmed by the world that was theirs for the taking. She knew that sophisticated and dangerous things went on among kids, and adults, and kids and adults behind the iron gates and privet hedges of the big houses, and some of the smaller ones, for that matter. She knew the town wasn't as safe or sanitized as its broad beaches and litter-free main street and leafy winding roads made it seem. But that was the effect Tina had on her. She started around the car to the driver's side.

Tina followed her. "It makes me sick."

This time Bailey didn't answer. The thought of the boy beating the hell out of the girl and pushing her off the deck made her a little queasy, too, but she still didn't like being on Tina's side.

"When I think of that poor girl . . . You can't imagine. You don't have a daughter."

Bailey opened the car door. "You don't have to have a daughter to feel sorry for the girl."

"Of course, she wasn't exactly innocent," Tina said.

Bailey turned back to her. "Of what?"

"There are rumors the sex was kinky. Maybe he didn't beat her up. Maybe they were into S and M, and it got out of hand."

"You mean she got what she deserved."

Tina straightened her shoulders and lifted her chin a fraction of an inch. "That's not what I meant, and you know it. All I'm saying is if you play with fire, you stand a good chance of getting burned."

"I'll pass that on to the Marquis." Bailey slid onto the seat, turned the key in the ignition, rolled up her window, and sat waiting for Tina to move her cart so she could back out of the space, but she was angry at herself for getting sucked into the conversation. She understood her prurient interest; that was only human. But she couldn't forgive her lack of sympathy. Though she didn't think Juliet Mercer had been a slut or asking for it or any of the unfair calls that were being made, she couldn't seem to work up much compassion for the girl. God knows her own youth hadn't been spotless, but she couldn't help thinking there was a difference. They'd broken rules for causes, not kicks, marched instead of hung out, and used harmless drugs to get mellow instead of hard drugs to get high. Even the sex had been innocent. At least, it had been unsophisticated. She and the boy with the ponytail, who'd been the only boy for a long time, had been so amazed by the pleasure they'd stumbled upon that they hadn't had to jazz it up. They'd been so scared—of getting caught, of getting pregnant, of the sheer momentousness of what they were doing— that they hadn't needed to manufacture an air of danger. But the real difference, she knew, was that it had happened a long time ago. That was the reason she could defend the girl, but she couldn't feel for the girl.

The boy, she thought as she pulled out of the parking lot and turned east on 27, was another story. She hated the boy. Even if he hadn't killed the girl in some strenuous sexual practice or thrown her off the deck in a homicidal rage, he had a lot to answer for. She knew that from the pictures in the papers—image after image of a tall, loose-limbed boy-man with a greedy smile that looked as if he'd already chewed up half the world and spit it out. She imagined him cruising the streets of town in the succession of overpriced cars his parents would have provided for him over the years, or sailing into some local bar or club, the Talkhouse, taking up too much space and air and attention, hedonistic, exploitive, lethal to the less beautiful, the less blessed, the less bored. To Nell.

She turned off the highway onto a back road and told herself to stop it. She'd never even seen Charlie Prinze in the flesh. Unlike his parents, he didn't seem to buy books. One more mark against him.

She really had to stop this. The newspaper reports were probably exaggerated. She was sure Tina's gossip was. Come to think of it, there was no reason to assume any of Tina's story was true. Tina had been carried away by her infatuation with misfortune before.

She swung off Abraham's Path onto a narrower road. As she passed an old frame house on the corner, her eyes automatically slid beyond it to the small, sagging bungalow that Mack rented. The cracked and graying paint gave both buildings a faintly disreputable air. The yard was brown and balding. The only thing missing was a rusting washing machine or a stripped-down car frame on cinder blocks, though Mack's pickup came close.

Two figures were getting out of the truck. After she'd passed the house, she slowed the car and watched them in the rearview mirror. Mack walked to the back of the pickup. His son slouched behind, his eyes on the ground, his scrawny neck exposed to the world's wrath. The last thing she saw as she turned the corner was Mack struggling to get a large cardboard box out of the truck while his son, hands jammed in his pockets, eyes still on the ground, pretended to be somewhere else.

For once Tina hadn't exaggerated. That night the local news showed a clip of two beefy detectives leading Charlie Prinze in handcuffs from an imposing granite apartment building to a police car. There was also a shot of the house on the pond, a still of Juliet Mercer, and past footage of her weeping mother and grim-faced father going from a car to a public building on some cruel errand of tragedy.

Bailey watched with a practiced eye. The segment was good, brief and briskly paced with a variety of visuals. Of course, this was only the beginning. In a couple of days they'd run out of new footage and stills, though the story would linger for months. It had all the ingredients—wild sex, big money, and two good-looking kids. And it had enough moral resonance to allow the media to exploit the wild sex, big money, and two good-looking kids in the guise of social commentary. Each morning and evening the public could open their newspapers and turn on their televisions to a lurid world most of them were too poor or timid or God-fearing to enter. And a few minutes later they could close the newspaper and turn off the television with a sense of glee or at least consolation. They might be trapped in lousy marriages and dead-end jobs and crummy houses with mortgages they'd never pay off, but at least their kids, pains in the neck, admittedly, were alive and not on their way to prison.

She switched channels. She was just in time to see the perp walk again. The boy was wearing khaki trousers and a polo shirt, and despite the handcuffs, he sauntered along easily between the two detectives in ill-fitting suits and shiny ties knotted low on collars they couldn't quite button. His grace was lethal. She bet he was a killer on a tennis court or a dance floor or, apparently, in a bedroom. On either side of him the arresting officers were wearing identical just-doing-my-job scowls, but there was something unusual about Charlie Prinze's expression. Then she realized it wasn't the expression, it was the fact that she could see it. He wasn't hanging his head or holding up his cuffed hands or trying to hide. Just before he ducked into the police car, he stared straight into the camera. She could swear that handsome, greedy mouth was twisted into a grin.

Another still of Juliet Mercer, looking heartbreakingly young and promising in a cap and gown, flashed on the screen, but Bailey was still thinking about the footage of Charlie Prinze and the arresting officers. It said a lot about class distinction. It said even more about moral turpitude.

"I can't believe that's, like, the only TV in this dump." It was the longest sentence Will had strung together all day.

Mack glanced over at him. He was sprawled on his spine in the big chair in front of the television, the chair Mack usually sat in, with his chin on his breastbone and his legs stretched out to block any passage across the cramped room. His feet were huge, way out of proportion to his undeveloped body, and the tongues of the state-of-the-art sneakers Mack had bought him for his birthday stood at obscene attention. Mack didn't know why the shoes bothered him so much. It wasn't the money. He didn't care about money, though Donna insisted that anyone who had to get rid of it as quickly as he did must have a deep antipathy for it. Maybe it wasn't the shoes but the way Will wore them. The kid was young for his age, thirteen going on ten or eleven, but he must know how to tie his laces.

"Believe it," Mack said and stepped over the big, annoying shoes.

Will held up the remote control, pointed it at the set as if it were a gun, and clicked. The channel changed. He clicked again and kept going until he was back where he'd started. "Man, where's the cable?" he groaned.

"Right there. You just went through it at break-neck speed."

"That's just the shit they give you. Not the good stuff."

Mack sat on the couch. He could use a beer. He could always use a beer, but now he needed a beer. He looked at his watch. It was a little after six. He'd been with the kid for about four hours. He had two and a half months left. Boy, could he use a beer.

"You want to get some pizza?"

Will went on switching channels.

"Or I can throw some burgers on the grill." Irish

stout. He'd sell his soul for an icy bottle of Guinness right now.

Will was still racing through the channels.

"Maybe if you'd slow down, you'd see what was on."

Will accelerated the clicking.

"So what'll it be, pizza or burgers?"

Half a dozen channels shot by. Mack reached over and wrenched the remote control out of his hand. "Don't do that!"

Will slid down another couple of inches in the chair and jammed his hands in his pockets.

"If you're going to watch the damn thing, watch it."

"I was just seeing what was on."

Mack leaned over and put the remote on Will's chest. "Then for Christ sake, see. Don't just keep going around in circles."

Will went on lying there with his chin on his chest and his hands in his pockets. Mack turned back to the television, though he wasn't watching it. He hadn't meant to grab the remote like that. He glanced at Will out of the corner of his eye. His chin was still on his chest, but his eyes were on the screen. Mack looked at the set. It was another arrest, but at least this one wasn't violent. There was no footage of cops swarming into a building or breaking down doors or spread-eagling suspects against a wall. Two detectives were leading a kid in handcuffs out of a building, that was all. He heard the name Prinze a couple of times and, of course, the word *alleged*. There was also something about marks on the victim's neck, which might indicate a struggle or—the announcer was trying to sound dryly objective, but his mouth was watering so badly he could barely keep from drooling—"rough sex."

Beside him in the cramped room, Will didn't move, but Mack could feel the kid's interest quicken. It was nice to know something could catch his attention.

They sat through the segment and several commercials.

"Can I switch now?" Will mumbled when the news came on again.

"I didn't say you couldn't switch. I asked you not to keep switching so fast you couldn't see anything." But he knew he shouldn't have answered. The kid was just baiting him, and he'd risen to it. Christ, he'd even settle for a lite, though the few times he'd tried a lite beer he'd found the experience profoundly unsatisfying. It was like those vocabulary drills he had to give the kids who were going to take college boards. Lite beer is to stout as a dry hump is to a good lay.

He asked again what Will felt like eating. From the depths of the chair Will didn't answer.

Mack stood, went through the kitchen out to the yard, and started a fire in the grill. Then he went back into the kitchen and took a package of hamburger patties out of the refrigerator. They looked a little brown around the edges. He sniffed them. They smelled okay, or at least not rancid. He'd just be sure to cook them well done. The kid ate everything charred to a crisp anyway, except french fries. Those he liked limp and greasy.

As he went back and forth between the yard and the kitchen, he could hear the sounds of canned laughter and gunshots and loud music following one another in quick succession.

When the burgers were finished, he put them on the rolls he'd toasted, put the rolls on plates, and carried them with a jar of mustard and two bottles of Snapple to the living room. He put the plates and the jar on the stacks of books he used as tables and the bottles on the floor, one beside Will's chair, one next to the couch, and sat.

Will looked at the spread. "Where's the ketchup?"

He hadn't thought of ketchup. He always put mustard on his burgers.

"There isn't any."

"Man, no ketchup!"

"I'll get some tomorrow."

Will mumbled something into his shirt. It sounded like *dickhead* but Mack couldn't be sure.

He picked up the plate and held it out to Will. "Try one with mustard. They're better that way."

"Mustard sucks."

"I'll alert the culinary establishment."

"You got any mayonnaise?"

Mack got up, went into the kitchen, and came back with a jar of mayonnaise and a knife. Will lifted the top of a bun off a burger and slathered a thick layer of mayonnaise on the skinny patty. Then he opened his mouth and shoved in as much of the concoction as he could. Meat and bread and mayo oozed between his teeth as he chewed. Mack turned back to the screen. A guy on a tiny island with a palm tree was hallucinating a sweating bottle of beer. He took a burger from the plate and bit into it. Seventy-five more nights of gracious dining, give or take a few.

Will went on eating. Three hamburgers and rolls disappeared into his mouth within the space of ten minutes, without his taking his eyes from the screen or one hand from the remote control. Mack watched him out of the corner of his eye. It was a kind of talent, he supposed.

Will spoke twice more that evening. He asked if Mack had any ice cream. Mack had a freezer full of ice cream. Most people who were on the wagon for something did. He listed the flavors. Will asked for vanilla. It was one of the few Mack didn't have. Christ, what kind of kid liked vanilla anyway? A five-year-old, sure, but not a prepubescent.

"How about Rocky Road or pistachio or rum raisin?" Mack ran the list again.

Will said he'd settle for Rocky Road. Mack went

into the kitchen and came back with a half-full pint and a spoon and handed them to Will.

When he'd finished the container, he spoke again. "What did he do?"

Mack didn't understand the question. They'd actually been watching the same channel for more than sixty seconds, and he thought Will was asking him about the game. "What do you mean, what did he do? Valdez walked him."

"No, I mean the dude they arrested. Before. On the news. What was he, like, doing to her?"

Mack hesitated, debating the phrasing. Fucking, the first word that came to mind, and in this case probably the most accurate, somehow didn't seem right with Will. The term making love was sure to confirm his standing as a dickhead. He could go for the adolescent vernacular, doing the nasty, but he knew Will hated it when he tried to sound like one of the kids.

"They were having sex."

"No shit!" Will pulled a face and rolled his eyes. It was the most energy he'd expended all day. "Man. I know he was fucking her. But why were there marks on her neck?"

Again Mack debated the answer. Donna was always after him to talk to Will about sex, but he'd never been able to. How the hell could he talk to the kid about sex when Will wouldn't even hear him out on the weather? Besides, Will knew about sex. Maybe not the stuff he needed to, but a lot else. Still, he'd given Mack an opening. It wasn't what Donna had in mind. It wasn't what he would have chosen. But it was an opening all the same.

"He was probably trying to cut off her supply of oxygen."

Will still wasn't looking at him, but for the first time since the boy had walked into the house, Mack knew he was listening to him. "It's called a carotid sleeper. Because pressure is applied to the carotid arteries." He knew he sounded pedantic, as if he were lecturing on *The Scarlet Letter* or *Ethan Frome* but that was okay. In all the years he'd been teaching he hadn't turned a single kid on to Hester Prynne or Mattie Silver. With any luck he'd make snuff sex sound just as dull.

"You mean so she'll come better?"

Maybe Donna was right, and all the teachers were wrong. Maybe Will was a quicker study than they gave him credit for.

"Yeah," Mack admitted.

Will turned back to the television.

"Don't let it give you any ideas."

If Will heard him, he gave no sign.

"Guys have been known to off themselves that way. By accident."

Will went on staring at the television screen, but he wasn't changing channels.

"While they're jerking off."

Will slid a couple of inches down on his spine and fired off several channels in quick succession.

Nell wouldn't have seen the arrest on the news if her dad, who was in the living room, hadn't called to her mom in the kitchen to come quick because the police in New York were arresting that kid from the house south of the highway who was mixed up in that business with the girl who was found dead on the patio. Nell followed her mom into the living room, but she stood a little away from her parents as she watched the boy she'd met that night in the Talkhouse being led across the big color screen. It was weird. He'd come on to her, not big time, not even serious, but she had talked to him. For a split second he looked right into the camera. Even being arrested he looked cool. She wondered what would have happened if he'd really come on to her that night. Nothing. She wasn't crazy, like Tiffany. Last summer Tiffany had taken a ride from some summer guy who was so old he was practically bald. Besides, she'd been with Kevin that night. But still, you had to wonder.

Her mom clicked her tongue against her teeth. "I feel sorry for the parents. His as well as hers."

Nell couldn't believe it. What was it with grown-ups anyway? All they could think about was themselves.

"You don't have to feel sorry for him or his parents," her dad said. "They'll get some smart shyster lawyer, and he'll come out smelling like a rose."

Six

Nell had asked Maude if she could take the Saturday following Kevin's prom off. There was a party at someone's house after the dance, and breakfast at someone else's after that, and then they were all going to the beach. "The whole idea is to stay up for twenty-four hours and then crash."

Maude got Roger Brady, a real estate agent who was too honest to be successful and as a result had to moonlight at Livres of Grass, to come in, so it wasn't until Sunday that Bailey got to ask whether Nell had had a good time. She'd thought the question was rhetorical. She should have known better. In her own youth she wouldn't have been caught dead at anything as politically irresponsible and socially conventional as a prom, but there'd been other events she'd looked forward to with exaggerated expectation.

"It was okay," Nell muttered.

"Just okay?" Maude asked.

Nell shrugged her thin shoulders.

As the week progressed, and Nell remained silent and sullen, and Kevin's hulking frame didn't loom outside the store window even once, Bailey began to think that something more than unfulfilled expectations was bothering Nell. Then the weekend after the prom she turned up at Bailey's house early on Sunday morning in shorts, a T-shirt, and running shoes. Bailey was sitting on the deck brooding about the unhinged woman from the black-market search agency. The woman had to be unhinged to call at the crack of dawn on a Sunday morning to report a lack of progress. As soon as Bailey saw Nell coming across the yard, she waved and indicated she was going upstairs to change. When she came down, Nell was stretched out on the deck on her back with Edward on her stomach. That was the way with Edward; one minute he was a feral hunter, the next he thought he was of humans born.

When Nell pushed Edward off her and stood, Bailey noticed the large white button with red lettering on her shorts. JUSTICE FOR JULIET was written in an arc around the top, DON'T BLAME THE VICTIM around the bottom. In the middle was a clenched fist with the biological sign for a female superimposed on it.

"Where'd you get that?" Bailey asked as they started down the driveway.

Nell looked down at her shorts as if she'd forgotten the button, though if she'd put it on before she'd left home, her mother must have had something to say about it. "Main Street," she said as she broke into a run. "NOW has a table with petitions and stuff."

It had been a long time since Bailey had worn her passions on her sleeve, though she did have those bumper stickers on her car, but some of the recent coverage of the case almost made her want to again. As the flow of real news began to dry up, stories about how Juliet Mercer had "flirted with death" and died in a "night of kinky sex" were becoming more common. She was glad Nell had taken a button.

"I guess…that means…" her breath was shorter than Nell's "…you don't think…she was…a…slut… after all."

Nell didn't bother to answer. She probably didn't even know what Bailey was talking about. After all, the conversation had occurred a couple of weeks ago, the equivalent of an eon on an adolescent time line.

When they got back to the house, Nell went into the kitchen, opened the refrigerator door, and stood studying its contents. The small interior light illuminated the droplets of sweat on her arms and chest. She asked if Bailey minded if she took the last container of yogurt. Bailey told her to take whatever she liked.

They went out on the deck. Nell settled on one of

the chaises and opened the yogurt. She ate slowly and thoughtfully, taking tiny amounts from the spoon, then holding it up and licking the underside like a Popsicle. At this rate she could easily make it last for most of the morning. Bailey didn't mind. She didn't have to be at the store until noon, and she wasn't uncomfortable with the silence, but she was curious. Something was definitely up.

She picked up the paper and began reading the front page. After she'd worked her way through the entire first section, she looked at her watch and said she'd better go up to shower. She stood and collected the papers. She might as well have delivered a cue.

"Can I ask you a question?" Nell said.

"Sure."

"It's really personal."

"I said you could ask it. I didn't promise to answer it."

Nell was silent again. Bailey went on waiting. The only noise came from the wrens who'd set up housekeeping in the birdhouse beyond the deck. When Nell finally spoke, she kept her eyes on them rather than Bailey.

"When did you, you know, when did you do it the first time?"

Bailey stood hugging the stack of papers to her. "What makes you think I have?"

Nell swiveled her face from the birdhouse to Bailey, then she caught on. "Come on, Bailey. I'm serious."

"You mean how old was I or what were the circumstances?"

Nell thought about that for a moment. "Both."

"The spring I graduated from high school."

"So you were a year older than me."

Bailey put down the papers and sat on the end of a chaise. "I could have been two years older or a year younger. There's no rule of thumb. What's right for one person isn't necessarily right for another." She knew she was running off at the mouth, but this was important. "You could be ready now, though my guess is that if you have to ask me about it, you're not. Or you could wait for another year, or ten or fifteen."

Nell groaned. "Color me pathetic. I'm already behind schedule."

"That's what I'm trying to tell you. There isn't one."

"Tiffany's been having sex since seventh grade."

Poor Tiffany. "In that case, how does she get around the so-called slut issue?"

"Tiffany's really popular. The only time guys call her a slut is when they get mad at her."

It figured.

Nell sat examining a fingernail. For a couple of days after the prom her nails had been a disheartening grape color. Now they were back to milky white. She picked at one of them. "Did people think you were a slut?"

Bailey remembered the church basement with the mimeograph machine and the paper coffee cups and the posters. There were always posters: war is not good for children and other living things; make love not war. She saw the sweet toss of ponytail. *Wanna fuck?*

"It was the early seventies, which was when the sixties happened for a lot of people. We thought we were changing the world." She didn't add that until recently, until she'd heard Nell's rumors of sluts and studs and double standards that would have warmed the heart of any self-respecting Mrs. Grundy, she'd thought they had, at least in some ways.

"You mean peace marches and stuff?"

Bailey nodded.

"Cool."

Bailey admitted it had been cool, for a while.

"But afterward, were you glad, or sorry, or what?"

"Then?" Stupid question. There was only then, or rather now for Nell. There was only the immediate morning after. She'd never be thirty or forty or even twenty.

How had Bailey felt then? Glad was scarcely the word. Thrilled. Proud. Euphoric. Besotted. And even later, sorry wasn't the word. Miserable. Terrified. But nothing as pallid as sorry. She remembered standing on the street outside the clinic. *This is mine. I am its. I am all it has.* And she knew even then that she wasn't enough.

"Happy. For a while."

"What happened?"

She thought about the rest of it now. The big problem had been money. They'd always been so disdainful of it, but now suddenly they needed it, because in those days the safest thing to do, the thing the few people they knew who'd been in the same predicament had done, was to fly to Puerto Rico. He'd said he'd go to his parents, and she could tell he liked the idea. "They'll be apoplectic," he'd said. But she hadn't wanted him to tell his parents, because she'd known enough about grown-ups to know they might not want the neighbors to know, but they would want her parents to, and she couldn't do that to Gilda. She couldn't break Gilda's heart. So once again they'd decided not to trust anyone over thirty. Except the doctor in Philadelphia whose name, a false one, of course, he'd finally come up with. The doctor hadn't been cheap, but he hadn't been as expensive as Puerto Rico. They'd borrowed from friends. It had been a communal age. *Got some bread, man?*

He'd dropped her off on a corner in Center City. They wouldn't even let him wait with her. The directions had been explicit. She had to be standing alone on the corner.

It was early on Sunday morning. There was no one else around. She saw a car cruise by. A man was driving with a woman beside him in the passenger seat. They could have been anyone, a normal couple going to church, even. Only she knew they weren't. They were the people she was waiting for.

The car turned the corner, disappeared, then appeared again. This time it stopped. The woman got out, told her to get in the back, and climbed in after her. She tied a scarf over Bailey's eyes and made her scrunch down so no one could see her.

They drove around for a long time. At least, it felt like a long time to Bailey. She wondered where they were taking her. Then she realized that was the point. They were driving around because they didn't want her to figure out where they were taking her.

When they finally stopped, she heard the front car door slam and heard the man's footsteps going away from them. The woman helped her out and led her across a sidewalk and up a few steps. The steps were stone, not wood. She figured it was one of the old row houses. She could hear the man hurrying on ahead of them. The woman hustled her into the house.

Inside the woman took the scarf off her eyes. They were in a dim room, homey in a shabby kind of way. It could have been someone's living room. It probably was. The woman told her to wait there until she came back for her.

She sat on the couch. In front of it was a chipped wood-veneer coffee table with magazines. A few were recent, but most were old. The magazines were spread out in a fan shape, as if someone took pride in the place. For some reason that made her angry. There was a year-old copy of *Time* with a picture of Ted Kennedy in a neck brace on the cover. She was staring at his face and trying to think about Mary Jo Kopechne rather than herself when she noticed the subscription sticker in the lower left-hand corner. The name on the sticker said Mr. rather than Dr. The address was plain. They'd driven her around forever, but they hadn't thought to take the tag with the name and address off the magazine. She was dealing with cretins.

She picked up the magazine, peeled off the small white sticker, and shoved the scrap of paper in the pocket of her jeans. She imagined the police going through the clothes of the abandoned corpse for identification. She wanted the police to find them. She wanted them to pay.

"Nothing happened," she told Nell now. "We were young. He went back to school. I went off to school. It fizzled out."

"No bang, just a whimper?"

"I wouldn't say that exactly."

Nell picked up the empty yogurt container, scraped the spoon around the side, and licked it thoughtfully. "Kevin isn't stupid. Just because he doesn't get good grades doesn't mean he's not smart."

Bailey didn't say anything to that.

"Einstein flunked ninth-grade math."

"I know. I'm the one who told you that."

"Not everyone can go to Harvard."

"True. But you just might be able to. If you want to."

"Kevin says he'd rather go to a community college anyway. He says people there aren't so stuck up. He says he wouldn't go to Harvard if they paid him."

"Now I'm beginning to think he *is* stupid." She saw the look on Nell's face. "Only kidding."

She stood. Nell did, too. They walked around the deck to the steps.

"About Kevin," Bailey said.

Nell waited.

"In view of this conversation, I hope he's smart about one thing. I hope you both are."

Nell made a face and raised her eyes to the cloudless sky. "Now she's gonna go, 'safe sex, safe sex.' "

"You got it."

Nell hooked her hands in the back pockets of her running shorts. The gesture tightened the fabric so the white button with the biological symbol superimposed on the clenched fist blazed in the sun. "You and my mom."

Bailey was surprised. "Your mom talks about safe sex?"

"Hello? The only sex she thinks is safe is no sex. She goes to church and prays to God to give me the strength to resist. But she didn't have the strength to resist. I mean, look at me. And I bet you weren't this poster child for safe sex back then either."

"As a matter of fact, I was."

"You guys used condoms?"

"It wasn't the dark ages. They had been invented." What Bailey didn't add was that they hadn't always worked.

Nell was walking home along the grassy shoulder of the road when she noticed the turtle making its way across the pavement. The shell was about the size of her hand span, and the markings were clearly defined. She stopped and stood watching its slow progress. It had just crossed the white dividing line when a car whizzed by. The turtle lumbered around and began coming back toward her. Another car went by in the other direction. This one wasn't going as fast, but it still set up a backdraft. The turtle turned again and began crawling away from her. It made a couple of inches before another car came by. It turned again and started back toward her. It was really pathetic.

She walked to the middle of the road and picked it up between her thumb and longest finger. The head didn't disappear, but the legs churned as if it were swimming through the air. She carried it to the side of the road and put it down in the grass. It stayed there for a moment while she admired the markings and tried to remember what kind of turtle it was.

One summer when she was about Hughie's age her dad had made her a big wire pen in the backyard. At first her mom had been glad, because he'd had to clean up the yard to do it, but then when Nell began bringing the turtles home, her mom had complained that she wasn't running a shelter for wayward animals. Nell had just kept collecting. Every time she'd found a turtle she'd put it in the pen. By the end of the summer she'd had about a dozen turtles, Eastern painted and diamondback terrapins and a red-bellied. She knew because she'd gone to the library and taken out everything she could find on turtles and read it all. For a while there she probably knew more about turtles than anyone on the east end of Long Island. At least that was what her mom used to say, though you could tell she didn't mean it as a compliment. You could tell she thought it was weird. But her dad had told her mom to leave her alone. Her dad had liked the turtles, or at least the idea of her and the turtles. He was always saying knowledge was a priceless and powerful possession because once you had it, no one could take it away from you. The statement sounded good, until you remembered that there were times when her dad didn't even know where he'd been the night before.

Another car was speeding down the road. It slowed as it came abreast of her. There were two guys in it. They weren't old like her dad, but they weren't kids either.

The one on the passenger side leaned out the window. "Lose something?"

She started to tell him she was just saving a turtle—for Pete's sake, there were signs about watching for turtles all along the road—then remembered she wasn't supposed to say anything at all. She started walking. The car purred along beside her. The guy on the passenger side asked if she wanted a lift. She turned her head away. What was wrong with them anyway? Couldn't they see she was just a kid?

"There's plenty of room," he said.

She turned off the road onto a side street, though

it wasn't hers. The guy behind the wheel said something she couldn't hear, then they both laughed, and the car sped off.

They made her sick. She turned around and walked back to where she'd put the turtle on the grass. It was gone. She took a few steps to the edge of the woods, but there was no sign of it.

Her dad was wrong about never losing what you knew. She'd forgotten a lot about turtles. All that information had just disappeared. She wondered where knowledge went when you died. If it was energy, could it just stop? Maybe it evaporated and became part of the atmosphere. She liked that idea.

She started walking again. Bailey always said there was knowing and there was knowing. Actually, she didn't always say it. She just said it after she'd said something else, something Nell knew and didn't need to hear again, and Nell would tell her she knew that, and then Bailey would say there's knowing and there's knowing. Sometimes she didn't even say it, but Nell knew she was thinking it.

Sometimes she wished she were fourteen again, or better yet, ten. She'd known everything about turtles then, and about a lot else. And strange grownups never used to offer her rides then. Sometimes she wished Kevin would just disappear.

Ohmygod! She didn't mean that. She'd have to be

crazy to mean that. Kevin could have any girl he wanted. Everyone said so. But he wanted her. So what was wrong with her anyway?

Seven

Though no public official or member of the chamber of commerce would dare to go on record saying as much, the girl's death, or rather the boy's being charged with it, was turning into an economic boon. Reporters and camera crews and writers who already had contracts in negotiation came by train and jitney and rented car and television van looking for places to stay, and bars and restaurants to congregate in, and scraps of information, no matter how far-fetched or unsubstantiated, to inflate into news. If Annie Fenton was among them, she didn't call Bailey for dinner, or lunch, or a drink.

Someone, either on the scene or back in a newsroom or broadcast studio, even came up with a name. The Preppie Murder had been used, and the Hamptons Murder sounded too much like an Agatha Christie novel, but newspeople are a resourceful lot, and someone put together the logo on the shirt Charlie Prinze was wearing in one of the photographs, and another picture someone had turned up of a very young Charlie on a pony with a small helmet shadowing his tiny beaming face and an undersized mallet in his hand, and christened it the Polo Murder. Someone else ran it past legal to make sure Ralph Lauren couldn't sue, and the case was launched.

Then Charlie Prinze's parents hired Howard Iselin, and things really began to heat up. Iselin, Bailey knew from her days on the news front, was a sound-bite-and-photo-op-stealing ex-hippie who'd turned his early hatred of authority in general and government in particular into a multimillion-dollar career as a defense attorney. Wherever a prosecutor brought charges against financiers for bilking investors, or athletes or rock stars for raping groupies, or elected officials for subverting the constitution, Howard Iselin was there to defend them. The only thing he hated more than district attorneys was anonymity. The first thing he did was hold a press conference to declare Charlie's innocence—he referred to his client throughout as Charlie, never Charles and never Prinze, just Charlie, the boy next door—and decry the state's attempt to besmirch a blameless young man in the interest of pandering to the scandal-hungry media and making political capital. And that was just the initial salvo.

On the East End no one talked about anything but the case. People stopped speculating about the weather, the usual all-consuming topic in a resort area. They stopped complaining about traffic, which everyone agreed every summer got worse every summer. They even stopped talking about stopping the ferry and the new A & P. In the farmers' market and the hardware store and Mrs. Sam's Bait and Tackle, the consensus of opinion was that the boy should be punished, even if the girl had been asking for it.

A handful of dissenters pointed out that this was still America and the boy was supposed to be innocent until proven guilty, but most of the television-watching, tabloid-reading public knew better. Some of the locals who waited on the summer kids in stores, and cleaned up their messes at home, and were forced off the road by them in their flashy cars, knew best of all. They'd seen the excesses and depths these kids could go to. Besides, the police said the boy had done it, and while the local force wasn't perfect—there were several lawsuits pending against it—they weren't the LAPD either. And surely the DA's office wouldn't bring charges if it didn't have sufficient evidence. The cynical pointed out that, as the attorney for the defense had said, the district attorney had political ambitions. The truly cynical said that was a given, and all the more reason he wouldn't try the case unless he thought he could win it.

Though Bailey liked to think of herself as a rational woman who weighed evidence, deferred judgment, and believed in due process of law, she listened to the innuendo about the girl and got furious, and looked at the pictures of the boy and couldn't help but agree. He was guilty. As sin. She remembered a legal term from her days on the crime beat: "depraved heart murder." The phrase had to do with intent and didn't apply in this case, but she couldn't help thinking as an image it was right on the money.

"The girl was pregnant," Tina announced before she'd closed the door behind her. She wasn't even pretending she'd come in for a book.

"What girl?" Maude asked, though she knew what girl from the thrill in Tina's voice.

"The girl the Prinze boy pushed off the deck." So kinky sex was out, and unwanted pregnancy was in. "That must have been why he did it."

"You've been reading too much Dreiser," Maude said. "These days boys do not push girls out of boats or off decks because they're pregnant."

"Maude's right," Bailey added. "Kids like that stop at their local ATM, make a withdrawal, and head for the nearest clinic. Unless they've got really good medical coverage."

"Not everyone is as cavalier as you about abortion."

If it had been someone else, someone Bailey took seriously, she would have fought back. She would have explained that while she'd marched and signed petitions and contributed money to protect a woman's right to choose, she'd never for a moment thought the choice was easy.

"Maybe the girl didn't want an abortion," Tina went on. "Maybe she wanted the baby."

"Which in this day and age," Maude said, "would lead to a search for good day care, not murder."

Bailey drifted back to the table where she'd been arranging books. It wasn't as easy as she and Maude were making it seem—again, that was the effect Tina had on people—but it wasn't as hard as it had been. The row house in Philadelphia had given way to clinics, even if these days the clinics were being bombed. The decision was no longer shameful, but it could still be agony.

Out of nowhere she'd begun crying, then the cries had turned to sobs that had howled and shuddered through the unpeaceful quiet, and she hadn't been able to stop. The woman had come running into the room, and the man had been right behind her, and when he'd realized what was happening, he'd slapped Bailey, hard and more than once. She'd stopped sobbing then, but she'd kept saying that she couldn't, she couldn't, she couldn't go through with it. They hadn't argued with her. They already had their money. They'd just yanked the scarf over her eyes, and knotted it tight, tighter than before because now they were angry, despite the money. Then they'd shoved her into the car, driven her, without all the detours, back to the corner, pushed her out, and sped off. She'd had to wait a long time until Andy had come back to pick her up. They'd told him it would take a while and warned him not to be seen hanging around the corner all afternoon.

The next day she'd gone to Gilda, and Gilda had taken over. She'd made the decisions and the arrangements and even told Bailey's father. At least, Bailey assumed her mother had told her father. Her father had never mentioned it. Neither had Gilda, once it was over. She hadn't imposed an oath of silence exactly. She'd merely laid the incident to rest in a tiny grave of secrecy, not callously, but with reverence for the small death it was, then made it clear that it was time to get on with Bailey's life.

And Bailey had, more or less. She wasn't obsessed. Whole days, even weeks went by when she didn't think about it. But it always came back. *He* always came back. She'd pass a boy, or these days man—she'd always kept track of his age—on the street, or see a picture in a newspaper, or shake hands with a friend's child, and suddenly imagine she recognized a fragment of her own face, or a feature she barely remembered from that sweet boy with the ponytail. That was why, despite Gilda's warnings that she was looking for trouble, despite her own fear of it, she'd begun to search. But her mother's apprehension and her own concern were turning out to be unfounded. The agency that prided itself on its probity had said they were sorry. Her son wasn't looking for her, so they couldn't help her find him. The angry, unhinged woman had hit a dead end, though she'd told Bailey, actually she'd shouted at Bailey, that under no circumstances should she give up. She still had the list of resources Gilda had given her, but the one or two she'd called had sounded even less efficient and more off-the-wall.

Tina was still talking about the poor pregnant girl and the rich spoiled boy and the tragedy of it all. And once again, Bailey found herself in unwilling agreement.

Eight

The thunderstorm came out of the west abruptly and crashed through town swiftly. In the blink of an eye the air turned black as soot and big hot drops pelted the store window. Then just as suddenly the darkness lifted, and the rain turned to mist. Mack came walking through the door as the sun burned a hole in the clouds and sent steam rising from the pavement.

"How's that for timing?" he asked, his arms outspread, palms up.

"Moses couldn't have done it better," Maude said.

"Or at least Charlton Heston," Bailey added.

He put his hands in his pockets and moved into the store. His wet T-shirt clung to him. Despite his trimmed-down state, it was a couple of sizes too small.

"Snappy tee," Bailey said. "I didn't know tie-dye was in again."

Mack looked down at himself. He seemed surprised at what he saw. "I filched it from my kid. It was the last one in the house. I seem to have fallen behind in the laundry department."

"You ought to turn that job over to him," Maude said. "Children should earn their keep."

"You're a good woman, Maude. Marry me and straighten the Reese men out."

"I'd sooner move in with my children," she sniffed, but her voice, thick as whipping cream, gave her away. She was pleased.

He wandered across the store. "What about you, Bailey? Want to marry me and shape us up? Before you say no, remember I may be your last chance."

"Gee, I haven't had that romantic a proposal in years."

"Okay, if you're not interested in going hand-in-hand through life, how about one afternoon? Come out on the boat with the kid and me tomorrow."

She should have known. He was feckless but not aimless.

"On that boat? Not bloody likely."

"I fixed it up. It's in great shape."

"I bet."

"Come on, it'll be good for you. Think of the tan. You'll look like summer people."

"Think of the melanoma."

"I'll get sunblock. Thirty-five, fifty, you name it."

"I've got sunblock."

"Great! Then we're all set."

She started to tell him there was no way he was going to get her out on that boat with him and his son. Somehow the words came out as yes. "But I warn you, if that engine conks out, I'm going to make your life a living hell."

"Get in line."

"Wuzza, wuzza—poor Mack."

"You're right. The blues ain't nothing but a school of fish. It's going to be great. You're going to have the time of your life."

The next morning she was glad she'd said yes. The sky was a pale, freshly laundered sheet hung out to dry. The air was clear as Saran Wrap. And though she'd never admit it to Mack, like the character in *The Wind in the Willows* she liked messing about in small boats, even his small boat.

She didn't have to pack sandwiches or even make iced tea. Mack had said he'd take care of everything. He was obviously a desperate man. After she disposed of Edward's dead mouse, she took her coffee out to the deck and sat paging through the papers.

Charlie Prinze had been arraigned, then released on two hundred thousand dollars' bail. The amount seemed high to her, but the prosecution had cited the

instance of a Connecticut youth charged with rape
who'd skipped bail and, thanks to periodic and gen-
erous checks from his parents, spent close to a decade
enjoying himself in various European ski resorts and
watering holes. Besides, the Prinzes weren't likely
to put the same value as Bailey on two hundred thousand dollars.

There was a photograph of the boy coming out of
the hearing. He was wearing a blue blazer, rep tie,
and the casually lethal smile. Bailey went on studying the picture. His forehead was high and his eyes,
wide and set far apart, weren't stupid, but there was
a callousness to them, as if intelligence had atrophied to shrewdness. His hand was raised in a
thumbs-up sign. She thought of the dead girl and the
unborn baby. She wanted to slap him. She bet his attorney wasn't too happy about the picture either.

By the time she finished the paper, she was beginning to think Mack had changed his mind, or
merely forgotten. Reliability wasn't his long suit. She
was debating whether to call him when the phone
rang. A man who identified himself as Bob Leonard
said he was returning the message she'd left on his
machine two weeks earlier. "You didn't leave an
e-mail address, so it took me a while to get back to you."

Bob Leonard, she remembered after a moment,
was one of the names on the list Gilda had given her.
He did searches on the Net. He also sounded about
twelve years old. She wondered what he was doing

in this strange subculture—in the past few weeks she'd realized that it was a subculture—but she wasn't going to ask. She told him she'd already tried several sources without success.

"Never say die," he sang into the phone. "When you get to the end of your rope, tie a knot and hang on." Then he asked what she had. She heard him typing in the information as she gave it to him. He told her he'd be in touch. She was just hanging up the phone when Mack's pickup came groaning up the driveway.

She went back out on the deck. He left the engine running as he climbed down and walked across the yard to her.

"I had a little trouble getting the truck started."

"I must be out of my mind going out on the open water with a man whose life is one long mechanical failure."

"Don't worry about the boat. The boat is cherry."

"That's what you said about the truck."

They walked back across the yard to the pickup. The sun hit the windshield and bounced back off it, and all she could see of his son was a dark shadow slouched in the cab. Mack opened the door on the passenger side and introduced them, though Bailey knew the boy by sight. She said hi. Will grunted. She climbed up into the cab. Like a crab, he scuttled closer to the driver's side. As they bumped their way to Three Mile Harbor, she clung to the door to keep from jostling against the boy and again began wondering what she was doing here.

When they got to the boatyard, Mack parked the pickup, and they carried fishing rods and an ice chest and canvas satchels and an electronic fishfinder down to the dock. At least she and Mack did. Will skulked along behind them. She wondered why he didn't help. More to the point, she wondered why Mack didn't tell him to help.

The boat was a floating monument to good intentions, imperfectly realized. On the starboard side a lovingly varnished teak hatch cover gleamed in the morning sun, but its mate on the port side was gray and cracked. A broken radio antenna hung limply from the stern. One of the leather-upholstered seats was obviously new, but it hadn't been bolted to the deck. Bits of last autumn's foliage clung nostalgically to the shabby carpeting. On the transom she could see the ghostly outlines of a *P, H,* and *O* where the letters had peeled off. Now the name of the vessel was *ENIX*. One more season of neglect and Mack would be making a philosophical statement.

He tugged on one of the dock lines, and they went aboard. She helped him cast off while Will sat slumped against a bulkhead with his hands in his pockets and his eyes on the water. He stayed like that all the way out of the harbor, and it was a deep harbor. At one point Mack pointed out a flock of diving birds. Will muttered something. She thought she made out the word *sucks* but she missed the rest of it. He could have been talking about fishing, or his father, or life in general.

He was even impervious to the surefire adolescent aphrodisiac, speed. He didn't seem to notice when Mack opened the throttle and raced flat out from one part of the bay to another, and he did that a lot because the fish just weren't biting. Again and again he killed the engine and they drifted and cast, off Sammy's Beach and Cartwright Island and the Ruins. All around them birds dived for fish, and in the boat electronic fish swam across the screen of the fishfinder, but nothing took the hook, though Mack kept putting on different lures. Again and again he cast and reeled in, cast and reeled in. Bailey cast a few times. Will sat in the bow and stared at the water. After a while he came to the stern, opened the cooler, and took out a sandwich. He unwrapped it, gave it a baleful look, crushed the aluminum foil back around it, and opened the cooler again.

"They're all the same," Mack said.

"Where's the tuna fish?"

"Last time I made tuna fish you said you hated it. You said you wanted ham and cheese."

"Ham and cheese sucks."

"I'll pass your compliments on to the chef," Mack said.

"I'll take a ham and cheese." Where on earth had she picked up that voice, from Debbie Reynolds?

Will took the sandwich he'd unwrapped and rewrapped and shuffled back to the bow of the boat. Bailey opened the cooler, took out two sandwiches, and handed one to Mack. After a while

Will shuffled back and took another sandwich and a can of soda from the cooler and carried them back to the bow.

Around four Mack said they were skunked and might as well call it a day. That was when he got his first hit. In the next twenty minutes Bailey caught three blues and Mack caught two.

"Beginner's luck," he said, as he flipped her third fish from the net into the boat.

"Superior technique," she insisted, but she let him wrench the hook out. It was, he'd convinced her by showing her the fish's teeth, no work for an amateur.

They cast again.

"Come on," Mack called to the bow of the boat. "Get a line in."

"It's fun," Bailey said—either her or Debbie Reynolds.

Will raised his eyes from the water and gave her the same look he'd given the ham and cheese sandwich.

"Got one!" Mack said and began reeling it in. He reeled and stopped, reeled and stopped, playing the line to keep tension on it. "It's a big mother," he crowed. "This baby could eat all three of yours."

She felt a tug on her own line and started reeling.

"Get the net," Mack shouted.

Will looked at him uncertainly. Mack had netted her three fish, she'd netted his two.

"Get the fucking net," Mack shouted again.

Will stood but didn't do anything else. "Over there!" Mack gestured toward the long-handled net with his head.

Will picked up the net, took a few steps with it, and stood there.

"Get it in the water!"

Will bent and put the net in the water. Mack struggled to play the fish into it.

"Reach for it, goddammit! Reach for it!"

The fish swam past the net.

"Fuck!" Mack howled. He grabbed the net from Will with his left hand and, with the rod in his right, managed to play the fish into the webbing; then he hauled the net in, flipped out the fish, and moved to Bailey's side of the boat.

It happened a moment later while Mack was trying to net her fish. It wasn't anyone's fault. Mack had lost his temper, but you couldn't really blame him. You couldn't blame Will either. He'd blown it with the net, but that was the point. Now he was trying to prove himself. That was why he tried to take the hook out of Mack's fish. Only he didn't know how to. He'd never even bothered to watch Mack do it. And the fish was, as Mack had predicted, a big mother. It still had a lot of fight in it. At least that was the way it sounded from Will's howl.

Mack sprang toward him and kicked the fish to the other side of the boat. Will stood holding one bloody hand with the other.

"Are you okay?" Bailey shouted, but no one was paying attention to her. Mack was trying to look at Will's hand, and Will was trying to pull it away from him, and their bodies were going back and forth in a ludicrous tug of war. There was blood all over both of them, but she couldn't tell if it was from Will's hand or the fish.

"Let me see it," Mack shouted and reached for Will's hand again.

"Get the fuck away." Will pulled his arm back.

Mack tried to grab it again. Will pulled it away again. Then he began to scream. "Fuckhead. Asshole. I hate you. I hate you. *I hate you.*" His face was red from the sun and the rage and the blood that he smeared every time he tried to wipe his eyes, and there was more blood on his shirt now, and all over the boat. The fish was thrashing and thumping, and Will was sobbing and shouting, and Mack was trying to get hold of Will's hand. He reached for it again, and Will pulled it away again, and then he started swinging. His face was screwed up, and he couldn't possibly see through the tears and the blood and the fury, but his hands were balled into fists, and he was pounding and punching and flailing at Mack, going for his head and his face and his chest and his stomach. And Mack was standing there taking it.

When Will finally stopped swinging, Mack produced a first aid kit that could belong only to an accident-prone man and cleaned the wound, which was, miraculously, not a bite but a cut that had probably come from the other hook on the lure. Maybe the hook had got in the way of the fish. Or maybe Will's reflexes were too fast. Whichever, it was a miracle because, as Mack kept insisting, a blue that size could take off a man's finger without any trouble at all.

"Talk about fluke accidents," he muttered while he bandaged.

"Or blue accidents," Bailey said, but no one was listening to her.

"Don't ever do that again," Mack said. "Not unless you know how." He lowered his face into Will's line of vision. Will turned away.

"Do you hear me?" Mack shouted.

Will didn't answer.

"You could have lost a finger," Mack yelled though he was only inches from the boy. "Don't ever do that again."

Will refused to get in the cab of the pickup with them. He insisted on riding in the back of the truck. He sat slumped in a corner holding his bandaged finger erect as if he were sending an obscene message to the world.

"What I want to know," Mack said to Bailey on the way back to her house, "is how come when goddamn Hemingway takes his goddamn sons fishing, they learn the meaning of life and he comes home the revered Papa. When I take my kid fishing, he almost loses a finger and I'm a fuckhead and an asshole."

"He didn't mean it."

"Bullshit."

"Anyway, he didn't lose a finger. Fortunately. And it's a nice fish. A Hemingwayesque fish. Go home and sleep and dream of lions."

"That's *The Old Man and the Sea,*" he grumbled. "I was talking about *Islands in the Stream.*"

"Don't take it out on me."

They drove in silence for a while. His eyes, bleached and watery and hopeless behind the dark glasses, kept darting to the rearview mirror. Finally he reached up and twisted it so he could see the back of the truck rather than the road. Will was still slumped in a corner holding his finger up to the world.

"Fuck," Mack muttered.

She slid down a little in the seat, just the way Will did when he was trying to disappear.

The first thing she did when she got home was take off her bloodstained shorts and T-shirt and put them in the machine to soak. Then she went around the deck to the outdoor shower and stood for a long time beneath the clean sky and swaying trees and let the water pound her into peace.

Maybe Gilda was right. Maybe she ought to forget this search business and leave well enough alone.

Nine

A few days later the computer hacker called again. "No luck," he sang into the phone.

She wasn't surprised. She hadn't expected him to turn up anything. Clearly the gods, or Gilda, were sending her a message. She really should give up.

"There is one more possibility," he said.

It occurred to her that he hadn't yet asked her for money. So the preliminary computer search was a come-on. She got ready for the pitch.

"Do you have a birth certificate?"

She thought of the worn piece of paper that was coming apart at the folds. She'd been surprised they'd let her take it from the hospital. They hadn't let her get away with anything else. Gilda hadn't wanted her to, but she'd insisted, though she hadn't known why or, for that matter, what to do with it. For years she'd moved it around with her, from college dorm to graduate school room, first apartment to second, tucking it in the back of underwear drawers and beneath scarfs and within journals. Finally she'd locked it up in a safe deposit box in town, then moved it to this one out here. She told him she did.

"Terrific!"

She didn't see why.

"They told you when the adoption became final, they'd issue a new birth certificate with the baby's new name and the adoptive parents, and seal the old one, right?"

"I think so."

"They said there'd be no connection between the two. No way for anyone to trace them, right?"

"Right."

"They lied!"

"What do you mean?"

"There's one connection. The original certificate and the adoptive one carry the same number."

"I don't see how that helps. I mean, if I thought I was onto someone, that would prove it, but I don't see how just knowing the number can help."

"It can if you're willing to spend a couple of hours if you're lucky, or a couple of days if you're not. I could get the whole thing in a database with a scanner in a lot less than that, if they'd let me at the stuff, and then it would be a cinch, but they won't. The thing is, you can go through the records for that year. They've got them in books"—his voice was heavy with disgust—"at the Forty-second Street library. If you luck out, you might be able to match up the numbers. That would give you a name. Which might or might not mean something. If John and Mary Smith adopted your baby and named him John Junior, fageddaboutit. But if the name's far out and if they stayed in the area, you could be onto something. It's a long shot. And the method's practically preindustrial, but you could give it a try. If you really want to find out."

She thought about it for close to a week. The image of herself as a glassy-eyed bag woman spending day after day in the library poring over public records wasn't encouraging. On the other hand, there was no reason she shouldn't go into town on a day off. She hadn't been to a museum in months. And she could drop in at the library first. Just for a look.

She stopped at the bank on the way into town. Sue Anderson, whose reading tastes ran to surprisingly gory mysteries, waved to her from behind the teller's cage. Ed Farrell, who'd made her life a living hell when she was trying to get a mortgage, observed that it was a nice morning. She made her way to the safe deposit vault. Old Mr. Ames opened the iron grille, took her key, and shuffled off. He returned a moment later carrying a long metal box, led her into a small closet-sized room, put the box with her key on top of it on the table, and closed the door behind him. It was all routine. She could be taking out a piece of jewelry or clipping a coupon, if she had coupons to clip.

She pulled out the chair, sat at the table, and stared at the box for a moment. She didn't have to open it to know what was inside. The contents were meager at best. One diamond-and-emerald engagement ring, one matching wedding band, the deed to her house, a birth certificate. Not the story of her life, maybe, but a pretty good sound bite.

She slid the metal catch open, lifted the top, and sat looking at the contents. The small black velvet box was on top. She took it out and put it on the table without opening it. She didn't have to look. She knew the rings were inside. She took out the manila envelope and put that on the table too. She wasn't interested in legal documents now, at least not in legal documents about real estate.

The birth certificate lay in the bottom of the box. No envelope, no protection, just the yellowing piece of paper. She lifted it out of the box and unfolded it, careful not to tear it where it was separating along the creases, and sat studying the information, though she knew it all in her sleep, literally. Sometimes she dreamed about it.

"Name of child. David Bender." She hadn't given him a middle name. That would have been excessive. "Sex: Male. Place of birth: New York Hospital. Date

of birth: June 24, 1972. Father: Andrew Snyder."
Gilda hadn't wanted her to enter that, but Andy had,
and Bailey had been adamant. She was giving the
baby so little, nothing really. She had to give him
that. "Mother: Bailey Bender."

Her eye moved to the number. 17274. As Bob the
hacker had said, it was a long shot. The chances of her
finding its match were small, unless she wanted to
spend the rest of her life poring over old records. And
she didn't. Even if she found the number, the hacker
had also warned her, what then? John Smith. Or, because in those days agencies had automatically placed
babies born of one denomination with parents of the
same denomination, as if faith were a genetic charac-
teristic, Mark Schwartz or Stephen Samuels or
Michael Gold. How far would that get her? Still, it was
worth a try, as long as she didn't get her hopes up.

She put the rest of the things back in the metal box,
tucked the birth certificate into her shoulder bag, and
left the cubicle.

She'd forgotten how handsome the library was, all
coffered ceilings and restored gilt and long marble
hallways. She'd forgotten the rest of it, too: the
homeless and inebriated and unbalanced, dozing
over Burke and Montaigne and bound volumes of
Popular Mechanics the signs warning her to hold on
to her handbag and keep an eye on her possessions;
the surly staff who knew she was up to no good.

She filled out the necessary slip, handed it over, and sat waiting. A boy returned with several huge volumes. Clutching her handbag under her arm as directed, she lugged them to a table in a far corner of the room. She sat and opened the first volume: *Births Reported City of New York.* She turned the page. The entries were arranged alphabetically by the baby's last name. They skipped all over the lot, from January to June, Manhattan to Brooklyn, low numbers to high. She could be here all year. Only she wasn't going to. She'd sworn to herself she'd be reasonable about this. As if there were anything reasonable in what she was doing.

She debated her options. She could go through systematically. That way if she did decide to come back and make a real search, she'd know where she'd left off. But that way was also an invitation to the unhealthy obsession she was trying to avoid. She'd dip in and out of the books. If she found something, fine; if not, she'd heed the message from the gods and Gilda.

The numbers were listed on the far right of each large page, after the baby's name and date of birth, and the mother's maiden name and father's given name. She began running her finger down the numbers. All she was looking for were five-digit numbers beginning with the numeral one. Logic told her there couldn't possibly be a million, but it felt as if there were.

After an hour, her eyes were bleary and her hands filthy. This was no way to spend her day off. She'd give it another half hour, an hour at most. She closed the first book, opened another, flipped to the middle. She was in the *M*'s now. She skipped through the MacDermotts and McCarthys, though a MacKinley did catch her eye. She thought of Mack and his son. Maybe it wouldn't be so terrible if she didn't find anything. Still, she'd give it a little more time. She began going down the numbers again when she got to Marmelstein.

She was going faster now, because she knew it was hopeless, and because the numbers were mind-numbing. Every once in a while she came across a 1-7-something and stopped, but the rest of the number never jibed. At the beginning of the *P*'s she even came across a 1-7-2. Her heart did a tiny somersault. The rest of the number was 1-8.

She glanced at her watch. It was almost three. She was getting hungry. And if she didn't leave soon, the museum would be closing by the time she got there. Ten more minutes. Fifteen at the most. She combed one column of numbers, then another. She turned the page. Her finger caught on another 1-7. The rest of the figure was way off. Halfway down the page there was a 1-7-2. Her finger stopped. She looked at the number: 17274.

She dragged her finger back across the page, from right to left.

"Father's given name: Eliot.

"Mother's maiden name: Vickers.

"Date of birth: 6/24/72."

She'd stopped breathing. Her finger kept going.

"Name: Prinze, Charles."

It couldn't be. At least, it couldn't be the same Charles Prinze she'd been reading about for the past month. Things like that didn't happen. It was too outrageous. It was too coincidental. And that Charles Prinze wasn't adopted.

She moved her finger to the right again. "Father's given name: Eliot."

How many Charles Prinzes could there be whose fathers were named Eliot? She tried to think about it logically. Not a lot, certainly, but surely more than one. Even in the greater metropolitan area, assuming this Prinze, Charles—her Prinze, Charles—had remained in the greater metropolitan area. And there was no reason to assume he had. These Prinzes, her Prinzes, could have moved to California, or Europe, or Timbuktu.

She looked at the page in front of her again. The letters and numerals were like small black insects writhing on the paper. She blinked several times to put them in focus. The number was the same. And the date of birth was right. She wished she knew Caroline Prinze's maiden name. She tried to picture her charge account at the store or the credit cards she'd used on occasion. She couldn't.

It wasn't the same person. If Charlie Prinze, the other Charlie Prinze, the notorious Charlie Prinze, had been adopted, some enterprising journalist would have unearthed the fact. It was the kind of story the media loved to run with. Early rejection. Feelings of inadequacy. Other children asking why his mommy had thrown him away. She knew the scenario. She'd done her share of reading on the subject, more than her share.

She ran her finger across the page to the father's given name again. Eliot. Not the most common name, but not unusual either.

Maybe no one had unearthed the fact the boy was adopted because the Prinzes had buried it so well. Maybe their lips, like the official records, had been sealed. Maybe they were old-fashioned. It didn't seem likely. Caroline Prinze was a family therapist. But it was possible. She thought of an old movie that kept running on one of the cable channels. Ann Blyth's sister goes to the mother's desk for something and stumbles across, *gasp* the papers proving Blyth was adopted. All hell breaks loose, until the final credits.

She sat staring at the page in front of her. She'd tamed the letters and digits back into place, but now the insects in the form of beads of perspiration were running down her sides and the small of her back. What was wrong with the library anyway? They'd polished the gilt and restored the moldings, but they couldn't even keep the damn air-conditioning running.

It was just too much of a coincidence. She probably stood a better chance of getting run over by a car or winning the lottery than of being the biological mother of Charlie Prinze, the sociopath. Only, she'd covered enough bizarre news stories to know that coincidences did happen. And the more she thought about it, the more she realized it wasn't a coincidence. It was demographic and social logic. Gilda had taken her to a prestigious agency, exactly the kind Eliot and Caroline Prinze would have turned to. That had been the first connection—not coincidence, but connection. Then there was the religious link. Next came similarity of values, or maybe only value. The Prinzes were connoisseurs. They liked good goods. Gilda had made sure that everyone concerned knew this was no ordinary baby; this was the baby of the valedictorian of her high school class, the recipient of an impressive scholarship, an achiever. The father, a pre-med student at an academically rigorous men's college on the Main Line—Gilda wouldn't say which one, but how many Haverfords were there?—was no slouch either. And finally there was the geographical inevitability. Where else would New Yorkers like the Prinzes build their country house? Where else would someone like Bailey go to drop out or give up or find the courage to search for that missing part of herself? Coincidence, hell. This was predestination.

She sat in the handsome room among the homeless and derelict, sweating the possibilities. It wouldn't be hard to find out for sure. She hadn't forgotten what were euphemistically called her investigative skills. But she had to be careful. If Charlie Prinze didn't know he'd been adopted, this was no way for him to find out. She wanted to protect him, even from her. She thought of the pictures of him swaggering in and out of police custody. Who was she kidding? The boy could take care of himself. She was the one she wanted to protect.

There was another way to find out, more discreet, absurdly easy. All she had to do was walk down the hall and make a phone call. One of the advantages of having a checkered professional past was a tangle of old friendships, acquaintances, and owed favors. She could think of half a dozen people who would look in a file and give her basic information like the notorious Charlie Prinze's date of birth. Annie Fenton for one.

She had the number in the small leather book she still carried in her shoulder bag, though it was no longer the lifeline it used to be. Only, now it was.

She found a pay phone and dialed Annie's number. A recording answered. She was about to hang up. There were other people she could try. Then she remembered Annie's habits. She started to leave a message. As soon as she identified herself, Annie picked up the phone.

"Just screening out the deadbeats, losers, and general nuisances."

"Glad to hear I don't qualify."

"I'll always pick up for you, luvey."

Bailey didn't know about that, but she did know as long as Charlie Prinze was in the news, and she lived in the area, Annie would take her calls.

Bailey said she had a favor to ask. Annie's voice dropped a few degrees in temperature. Friendship went only so far, especially to an out-of-work freelancer.

"Not about a job," Bailey reassured her. "I told you, I'm out of the business."

"You name it."

"Remember when you called me about Charlie Prinze?"

"You said you didn't know anything about him."

"I didn't. I still don't. That's why I'm calling you."

"You doing a piece for the local paper?" The condescension in Annie's voice was tinged with sympathy. Bailey remembered why she'd liked her.

"Possibly. I'm still in the preliminary stages. I thought you might be able to give me some background."

"Some? Want me to drive a truck up to your house and start unloading the files?"

"All I'm looking for is pedigree. Age, date of birth, the really basic stuff."

"Jesus, Bailey, it sounds as if you're living in the dark ages. You could get this on the Net. But hang on."

She heard the keys of Annie's computer begin to dance. She felt the perspiration running down her sides again.

"Speaking of pedigree," Annie said as she typed, "did you know he was adopted?"

It took her forever to get home. She must have been out of her mind to drive into town on the eve of a Fourth of July weekend, especially a Fourth of July weekend that was predicted to be hot and sun-drenched. The traffic inched along the Long Island Expressway. It came to a halt on Route 27. She sat in the silent, air-conditioned isolation booth of her car and looked around her at the other vehicles, stuffed with kids and toys and clothes and pets, groaning under the weight of bikes and windsurfers and boogie boards and Sunfish. The pulse of the entire East End throbbed in anticipation. Her own felt weak by comparison.

As soon as she got home she went into the living room, sat on the floor next to the wicker baskets full of old newspapers—the Collyer Brothers' revenge on Martha Stewart—and began going through them, flinging aside national and international news, politics and finance, arts and opinion. What were public events compared with her personal drama?

By the time she'd got to the bottom of the third basket she'd separated out close to a dozen stories on Charlie Prinze and as many photographs. She went to her desk in the small study and came back with a magnifying glass. One after another she lifted the pictures close to her face and examined them under the lens. The lethal smile hadn't come from her, or from that sweet boy with the ponytail. Neither had the shrewd, calculating eyes. She studied the picture of him coming out of the bail hearing, his hand raised in a thumbs-up sign. Surely that callous stranger couldn't be her flesh and blood. Surely if he were, some umbilical cord of memory would connect her to the knowledge. She'd borne him. She'd even held

him. The nurse hadn't wanted to let her. She'd said
Bailey didn't deserve to hold him. She'd said the
sooner Bailey forgot about him, the better, for her and
for him. She'd said to another nurse, "These girls
have no maternal instincts." But the other nurse had
come over and put him in Bailey's arms. For how
long—five minutes, ten, sixty seconds?

He'd been a miracle, wondrous, mysterious, terri-
fying in his helplessness. And she'd known she wasn't
going to be any help. She'd kept touching him,
running her finger over his surfaces and examining
his specialness. The wizened red face all screwed up
against the world, and the downy head still showing
the forceps marks, and the tiny hands and feet with
the miniature nails. The nails had made her cry.

She stood and began stacking the newspapers. It
took her three trips to get them all out to the car. She
would have driven them to the dump then, but the
dump closed at five and it was after eight. She'd get
rid of them first thing in the morning. On the way to
the store. Before that, before she even had her coffee.

The next morning she awakened to a sky that looked
like the side of a battleship and an ocean wind that
couldn't be expected to blow much good. So much for
the predictions of sunny days and balmy nights. Mist
drifted across the highway, turning the legendary clar-
ity of the East End light into a murky myth. The dump
lay like a foul-smelling wasteland under a sodden sky.

She flung her newspapers into the receptacle for recyclable paper, got back in the car, and drove like hell.

By late Sunday the sky still pressed down on the area like a sheet of metal, but rain no longer threatened, and word went out that the fireworks would go off as scheduled. Nell asked Bailey if she planned to go. Bailey said she didn't think so.

They were closing up when Tina came into the store. She said it certainly had been a washout as holiday weekends went. Maude just smiled. Predictions of bad weekend weather could wreck business, but unpredicted bad weather could be a boon. Thousands of people had been trapped in damp houses and soggy motel rooms. The bell above the door hadn't stopped ringing all weekend.

Then Tina asked if they'd heard the latest, and Bailey knew she hadn't come in to gloat, at least not only to gloat. "About the Polo Murder, I mean."

Maude said that depended on what the latest was. Nell said she had to run because Kevin was waiting. Bailey didn't say anything.

"Charlie Prinze is adopted."

So the news was out.

"I don't see what that has to do with anything," Maude said.

"It's ironic, that's all."

"What's ironic about a couple not being able to have a child and adopting a baby?"

"Not them, him. Here's this boy—who knows who his parents were? They could have been drug addicts or a prostitute or anything."

"They could also have been two perfectly nice young people who got into what we used to call trouble," Maude said.

"Are you saying blood will out?" Bailey asked Tina, though she'd sworn she wasn't going to get drawn into the conversation. "The boy's a bad seed?"

"I'm saying," Tina went on, "no matter who his parents were, his life was up for grabs. He could have ended up in a foster home. Being abused, even. He could have ended up on the street. Even if the parents were two clean-cut kids, in high school or something, and they decided to keep him, he could have ended up in a trailer park somewhere. Instead he gets adopted by this couple who have everything. They take him into their home and send him to the best schools and give him all kinds of advantages. The irony is incredible."

"What irony?" Bailey asked.

"He could have had nothing. Instead he was handed everything on a silver platter. And he still managed to throw it all away."

Ten

Mack wasn't looking forward to the fireworks. For years he hadn't been able to go. Even now the crackling noise sounded too much like incoming fire, and the staccato light was an incendiary nightmare. The worst part of it was there was no getting away. All over town dogs scrambled under beds and whined in fear. If he stayed home, he'd feel just like them. He might as well go. You could even say he was setting an example by going, he thought as he turned the truck off the road and into his yard, though he wasn't sure there was anything particularly exemplary about spending an evening lolling about on soggy sand, surrounded by people eating food that was probably hazardous to their health and working up to states of inebriation that were definitely harmful to the communal fabric, while dangerous explosives went off overhead.

The first thing he saw as he came through the door and his eyes adjusted to the gloom—Will always kept the shades down, the better to watch the ever-changing channels—were the big Nikes with the untied laces. Propped up on the ottoman, they loomed in Mack's line of vision like an infuriating *V* for victory. Attached to them by pale skinny legs— the kid hadn't been outside in days—Will lay sprawled on his spine in front of the flickering screen. Mack's spirits shriveled. Until then he hadn't realized how much they'd expanded during the past few days.

Will had refused to go clamming with him that morning, but he hadn't been sullen or snide about it. In fact, for the last week or so he'd been almost civil. The night before they'd watched a video of *Get Shorty* and actually laughed together, at least once or twice, though Will's maniacal *he-haw, he-haw* at the more violent scenes had been like a fingernail down the blackboard of Mack's spine. He knew that violence, violence and sex, were the staffs of adolescent life. He knew that he was overly squeamish about the first subject. But sometimes Will's ghoulishness scared him. Still, it had been something of a father-son first, not exactly the Cleaver household, but an improvement. Only, looking around the room now, Mack knew he'd been too optimistic. When he'd left this morning, he'd mentioned that it might be a whole new experience if, when he came home this evening, he could see the floor. Will's clothes lay like a crazy-quilt wall-to-wall carpet. He'd also said it might be novel to return to a sink that wasn't full of dirty dishes, not to mention potato chip bags and soda cans and ice cream cartons on every surface in sight. Will had said he'd take care of it. Mack should have picked up on the phrase. It was one of those things kids say when they mean exactly the opposite.

His first instinct was to kick the clothes aside—he wasn't winning any awards in the neatness department himself—and go to work on the dishes. It was the fastest solution. God knew, it was the easiest solution. He told himself he was taking a stand for the sake of Will's character. That was what Maude was always telling him to do. He knew he was merely pissed.

"I thought you were going to pick this stuff up."

Will kept his eyes on the television screen.

"I said, I thought you were going to clean up before I got home."

Will didn't move a muscle.

"Jesus, am I a tree falling in an empty forest? Earth to Will, earth to Will. What about this crap?"

"I'll get to it."

"Good. As soon as you do, I'll get to your allowance."

Will lifted his scrawny shoulders and dropped them, an eloquent statement of what he thought of Mack's paltry dole. Of course, in all fairness to the kid, he was merely following in his mother's footsteps there.

Mack picked up a bag of taco chips from one of the chairs and sat. "Look, why don't we clean this up together? Either that or have it declared a national disaster area. Then we can go to the fireworks. Don't worry, I'll drop you off before we get to the beach. Nobody will see us together."

"You're going to the fireworks?" Will's eyes were still on the screen, but there was a nasty undercurrent to his voice. Something must have happened since Mack had left the house that morning. Or maybe nothing had happened. Last night, the past week had been the aberration. This was the way things were.

"Sure I'm going. It's the Fourth of July. I'm an Amurrican."

"Yeah."

"Hey, I vote. I pay taxes. I even served my country in its time of peril."

"It figures. The only war we ever lost was the one you were in." Will was still staring at the screen, but Mack had the feeling he wasn't watching the screen.

Where in hell was this coming from anyway? Will could be sullen and silent, but except for that afternoon on the boat when he'd got hurt, he didn't go on the attack. Especially about this. Mack hadn't even realized Will knew what Vietnam was. To the kids Mack taught, "the war" was the Gulf War.

He glanced at the shelves of books. The volumes on the war hadn't been touched. He knew because they were the only books in the house that were neatly shelved, and if Will had bothered to look at them, he wouldn't have bothered to put them back. Besides, the kid didn't read. Something he'd seen on television? He never watched anything long enough to find out what it was about, let alone get an overview of American military history. His mother? Donna carped about money, and complained about Mack's irresponsibility, and said he was an unavailable father, just as he'd been an unavailable husband, but she'd never hit him here. So where the hell had this sudden patriotic fervor come from?

"What's this 'we,' *Kemo Sabe?*"

"You know what I mean. The only war America ever lost."

Mack told himself to let it go. Will was a kid. Hell, he'd been a lot older than Will, and he'd still gone. He wasn't about to let Will do the same thing, but he had plenty of time to worry about that.

He bent and picked a T-shirt up off the floor. That was what this was about, not the war, not Mack, just this mess that Will didn't want to clean up. Well, fuck that, and fuck character building too. They could sit here fighting about it for the next hour, or Mack could pick up the junk and wash the dishes before Miss Havisham's fucking cobwebs took over and the fucking mice began lining up for fucking handouts.

He stood. "Yeah, well, as they say, war is hell."

"Not if you're the dude torching the villages and killing the babies."

Will's eyes were still on the television screen so he didn't see Mack's hand coming. It caught him across the cheek. He turned away from the screen, finally. Mack saw his face. His eyes were wide with surprise. Then his mouth curled into a grin.

Will sat on top of the closed toilet and turned on the bathtub faucet full force. He'd won, and he wasn't going to spoil it by letting the asshole hear him cry. Cocksucking motherfucking dickhead homo asshole. He hated Him. The way He just sat there all the time. No matter what he did, He just sat there and stared at whatever he was watching or read His fucking books or made some dumb joke He thought was hilarious. Like He was Jim fucking Carrey. Like He was so fucking cool. Once when he was little, he'd heard his mom call Him the coldest man in America. Like a fucking dweeb he'd got out of bed dragging his Batman quilt with him and gone into their room to give it to Him. Talk about dumb. Talk about assholes. But not tonight. Tonight he'd kept his cool, but He'd lost it. He'd made Him lose it.

He gave the air a high five. *Ladies and gentlemen, the heavyweight champion of the world.* He just wished he could stop fucking crying. Not that he had to worry. If he were home, his mom would be banging on the door by now, asking if he was all right, yelling what was he doing, complaining about the fucking water. But here he could spend the whole

fucking night in the fucking bathroom, and the asshole wouldn't even notice.

But He'd noticed tonight. He wiped the tears and
snot with the back of his hand, then gave the air another high five. The winner and still champion.

Nell sat on the end of her bed staring at herself in
the mirror above the dresser. Go on down, she told
her reflection, but she couldn't move. Go on down
and stop sitting here in your room staring at your
dumb dorky face like some geek. From downstairs
she could hear her mom's voice in that squeaky register it climbed to when she was trying to be nice, and
Kevin's low, uneasy sentences, and louder than both
of them, the sound of the television. She had to go
downstairs. Pretty soon they'd begin to wonder what
she was doing, and then her mom would come upstairs to find out what was wrong.

Like excuse me, if she knew what was wrong,
would she be sitting up here staring at her dumb, ugly
face? She couldn't still be mad about last night. That
was something else that was weird about her. Once
she got mad, she couldn't stop being mad, even when
she found out she had nothing to be mad about. Kevin
was right. She'd freaked out over nothing. Made a
mountain out of a molehill, her dad would say.

There'd been a whole bunch of kids, just hanging.
Someone had said, Hey, man, let's hit the beach, and
all of a sudden everyone was driving to the beach and

piling out of cars and running around acting crazy. Someone threw Tiffany in the water, and when she came out they all started making retard jokes about wet T-shirt contests. Nell hadn't walked away, exactly, but she'd kind of started inching back to the parking lot real slow, and pretty soon the rest of them did, too, and that was when it happened. Usually in Kevin's car she sat up front next to Kevin, but not always. Sometimes she liked to sit somewhere else, as if she were just part of the gang and not part of Kevin, and last night she wouldn't have cared where she sat, if that geek Jimmy Tate hadn't started in. He wanted to sit up front—riding shotgun, he called it, like they were going to do a drive-by shooting instead of just hanging out. She still didn't care, and she was about to get in the back, but then Jimmy had to make that dumb crack about her getting into the bitch seat, where she belonged. That was what they called the middle seat in the back, because there was no way you could sit there without getting all scrunched up and looking really geeky. At least, Jimmy called it that when he wanted to sound like some *baaad* rapper and not some skinny kid from the East End who had a curfew. Then he said it again, and gave her a slap on her bottom, and she just flipped out and started screaming at him about what a retard he was and how she better not do that again, and Kevin was like "Chill out, it's just an expression." And then Jimmy, who thought he was so cool because Kevin was on his side, had gone, "That's right, bitch, bitch seat is just an expression." So Kevin had to get mad at him too, only later Kevin said he hadn't really been mad at Jimmy, because Jimmy was just kidding around, but he'd had to act like he was mad at Jimmy to defend Nell. So it was all her fault. That made her even madder, but she knew that was dumb, because how could she be mad at Kevin for sticking up for her? But she couldn't help it. The harder she tried to stop being mad, the madder she got, so by the end she could barely look at Kevin without wanting to scream at him, which isn't exactly the kind of feeling you're supposed to have when you're going to do it, and to tell the truth, she hadn't wanted to, but Kevin said once you did it the first time, you were at a new level, and you had to do it all the time, and then they had a fight about that too, and it was just like the business with the bitch seat all over again, just like she knew that was only an expression and she was making too much of it; she knew Kevin was right, everyone else who did it the first time went on doing it, so if she didn't want to do it all the time, there must be something wrong with her.

She looked in the mirror. She wondered if other people could tell how weird she was.

Her mom was calling her from the bottom of the stairs now. "What are you doing up there?" Like what could she be doing?

She stood. Her legs weighed a ton. She could barely drag them along. Her whole body was stiff, like she was some robot that needed oiling.

Her mom was standing at the bottom of the stairs looking up at her as she came down. Kevin was sitting in her dad's chair. He did that when her dad wasn't home, and it really bummed her out. It was like that thing Mr. Reese said they did in books. He called it foreshadowing. He said writers did it in suspense stories to scare you, and if Kevin was trying to scare her about what was coming by sitting in her dad's chair watching television with her mom, he was doing a good job of it.

He waited till her mom turned away and gave her an eyes-rolled-up-in-his-head-so-only-the-whites-showed look and cocked his head toward the television set. Her mom had one of her religious programs on, the one where they called in to ask the minister for advice on how to run their lives. Nell's worst fear was that one of these days her mom would call in to ask about her or her dad or Hughie. Nell would kill her. She really would.

Kevin hadn't made a move to get out of her dad's chair. He was supposed to be in such a hurry to get to the fireworks, but they were taking a new call, and sometimes people called in to ask about sex, which they called sin. He wouldn't want to miss that.

The television minister was leaning forward and looking serious to show the audience how carefully he was listening.

"My name is Martha and I'm a mom," the call-in voice said.

The audience applauded.

The minister smiled. "God bless you, Martha," he said.

"I have five little ones. The oldest is six."

The audience cheered.

"What are they getting so excited about?" Nell said. "It isn't like she saved the rain forests or found a cure for AIDS."

The minister made a thumbs-up sign. "Jesus loves you, Martha."

"Watch your tongue," her mom said.

"Come on, Mom, AIDS isn't a dirty word."

Normally that would be the signal for her mom to start lecturing her, but Martha had begun to tell her problem, and her mom wasn't about to miss that. Martha wanted to stay home and raise her children, and her husband wanted her to stay home and raise their children. The minister said he wanted her to stay home and raise them to be good, Jesus-loving Christians, and Jesus did, too.

"The problem is," Martha said, "money. My husband works in the meat department at the Publix. He's a hardworking man, but it still isn't enough to take care of five children. So what we want to know is what does the Lord want me to do? Does He want me to get a job, or does He want me to stay home with my children?"

"The Lord wants you to trust in him, Martha."

"I do. That's why I'm asking. My husband says the

Lord wants mothers to stay home with their children, but I think He might make an exception in this case."

"Trust in the Lord, and He'll show you the way," the minister said.

"Retard! She's asking *you* the way," Nell told the set.

"Don't be disrespectful," her mom said.

"Every child is the Lord's blessing," the minister said. "Each human life brings its own grace."

"Christ!" Nell shouted at the screen.

"Watch your mouth!" her mother yelled at her.

"But he's pathetic, Mom. I mean, she's got five kids she can't even feed, and he's just blah-blah-blah, trust, blah-blah-blah, faith. The guy isn't just dumb, he's dangerous."

Her mom turned from the screen to her, finally. "That's not you talking. That's Bailey Bender."

Nell started to say it wasn't, she could think for herself, only she knew the more she talked to Bailey, and the more she listened to her, the more Bailey's ideas got mixed up with her own, so her mom wasn't really wrong after all. She clamped her mouth shut.

"Pray for guidance," the minister urged.

"Come on, squirt," Kevin said.

"Don't be late," her mom warned.

Bailey heard the truck in the driveway, went to the sliding doors, and flicked on the outdoor lights. The illumination didn't carry to the clearing at the end of the driveway, but even in the shadows she could make out Mack's pickup. He climbed down from it and started across the grass toward the house. As he stepped into the circle of light, he squinted against the glare, then reached up and smoothed his hair. She'd never seen him do that. His hairline wasn't receding an iota. It occurred to her as she stood watching him cross the yard that he was a man who'd been meant to age better than he had.

She couldn't decide whether she was glad to see him or sorry. Since she'd got home from the store, she'd been prowling the house, edgy as Edward when the birds were in full cry. She didn't want to be alone, but she knew she wasn't fit company.

Mack came up the steps to the deck. "I've run away from home."

"I think that's Will's line," she said from the other side of the screen door. This was okay. She could deal with someone else's problems. They floated on the surface of her consciousness, barely making a ripple.

"Are you kidding? The kid's got a full refrigerator, a couple of thousand cable channels, and a remote control clicker. He's not budging." He walked around to the side deck.

She took her yellow foul-weather jacket off the coat stand, pulled it on, and followed him. "You want coffee or some of that stomach-turning beer or something?"

He sat in one of the chairs facing out to the yard, put his feet up on the railing, and shook his head no.

She sat in the chair next to him and put her feet up beside his.

"I hit him."

Her head swiveled to him. A slight ripple, but still on the surface, still not sinking in.

He went on staring out into the darkness. "I lost it and hit him."

"Is he okay?"

He turned to face her. "Christ, Bailey, I didn't slug him. My hand was even padded. I was holding one of his goddamn T-shirts."

"What happened?" she asked, though she was still having trouble fathoming what he was saying.

He told her about the video the night before and the clothes all over the floor and the food on every surface and the dishes in the sink.

"And?"

"And then he started needling me."

"What do you mean, needling you?"

Mack repeated the crack about the only war we ever lost. Bailey was surprised. She'd always thought the ability to go for the jugular was an acquired adult taste, like brussels sprouts or scotch.

"So you slapped him?"

"Not for that."

"Then, for what?"

Mack went on staring out into the yard.

She waited.

"I shouldn't have let him get to me."

She was still waiting.

"I said war was hell, and he said, 'Not if you're the dude torching the villages and killing the babies.'"

She heard her own sharp intake of breath. The boy knew how to go for the jugular, all right.

"I didn't even know I was doing it."

She reached out and put her hand on his arm. She'd never known a man who didn't tense his muscles in response to that gesture, but his arm was already so tight she thought it was going to snap.

"To think I'd ever long for the good old days," he said after a while, "when I was an asshole and a dickhead."

She took her hand away. "He was just trying to get a rise out of you."

"Yeah, well, he succeeded."

She tried to think of something to say, but she was out of her depth. They sat in silence for a while. Not even the katydids were singing. Somewhere in the distance a firecracker went off. Mack flinched.

He said he ought to go, and went on sitting there. She hugged her jacket to her and tucked her hands under her arms.

He asked if she was cold. She said she was fine, though she was beginning to shiver. She'd put on a jacket but was still wearing shorts. She rested her head on the back of the chair. Thin clouds raced overhead, watering the moonlight to a skimmed-milk thinness and turning the yard into a ghostly, surreal dream. Beneath pale leaves shimmering in the wind, tree trunks melted like wax into the bleached earth. The world was a figment of her imagination. Maybe the last few days were too.

He reached over and put his hand on her thigh. She looked down at it. The ghostly light drained the sunburned color from the skin and accentuated the bones. It was a white skeleton, an X ray of a hand, an eerie shadow of the real thing. He left it there for a moment, without movement, without pressure, a gesture suspended, a possibility waiting to happen.

She'd thought about it. On and off since the night of last year's fireworks. Probably for longer than that. But not now, not when he really was the walking wounded, a casualty bleeding from too many hits, badly in need of a transfusion. Not tonight, when she was running around trying to slam the doors she'd had the false courage to open.

Another firecracker went off. His hand clenched. His pain went through her flesh. Then he relaxed his fingers, took them from her leg, and stood.

She walked him around the deck to the steps and down to his truck. They stood beside it for a moment.

"What now?" she asked.

"I go home. He should be there. I told him he's still got a curfew. If he's not, I get back in the truck and drive around town until I track his skinny ass down." He shrugged. "In other words, it's back to normal, or what passes for normal in the Reese household." He climbed into the truck, started the engine, and backed down the driveway.

She stood in the moon-thinned darkness watching him. Despite the way he talked, and what his former wife and Tina and a lot of other people, including her at times, believed, he really was trying. He'd always taken care of Will financially, and these days he was doing his best to keep house for him. He picked up after him, and did his laundry, and kept the refrigerator stocked with things Will said he liked—that week. He stayed home so Will wouldn't be alone, sat alone worrying because Will was out, and drove around town trying to head off trouble when he was late. He'd relinquished his freedom and rearranged his schedule and changed his life. As she stood listening to the sound of the truck fade in the distance, she realized Mack had done more to care for his son than she ever had for another human being. She was a dutiful daughter, and she'd been a fairly accommodating wife; she'd made compromises and even an occasional minor sacrifice, but she'd never spent day after day, week after week putting someone else's needs before her own in a thankless stream of consistent self-subordination.

Book Two

Eleven

Bailey leaned closer to the mirror in the cramped bathroom at the back of the store to apply her mascara. It reminded her of the old days, when she used to put on makeup and even change clothes in various ladies' rooms after work. She and the other young women who'd had not just evenings but whole lives ahead of them had complained about juggling cosmetics bags and jewelry rolls and briefcases filled with belts and scarfs and extra pairs of panty hose on sinks and radiators and window ledges, but they'd loved every minute of it. The cold tile bathrooms had simmered with expectation. Success and adventure and love had lurked in the shadows of the evening ahead like benevolent muggers.

She felt the same jittery anticipation now, though she tried to curb it. Gilda had tried to do more than that.

"You're asking for trouble," her mother had warned her.

"You said that before."

"And I was right. You found it. Let it alone. Walk away while you still can."

But Gilda was wrong. It was already too late.

The night of the fireworks, after Mack had left, she'd sat down and written to David. Charlie. It wasn't the most direct approach, but it was, she'd decided, the kindest. She didn't want to burst in on his life. She wanted to give him a choice.

He called a few days later. His voice on the phone was low and diffident. She could barely hear him from the pounding in her ears. It was hard to believe something she'd played out in her mind so many times was actually happening.

After he identified himself, there was a silence. He said he didn't know what to say. She told him that made two of them and asked if he was willing to meet her.

"Yeah," he said slowly, and she wondered whether the hesitancy was the result of shyness or reluctance. "Sure," he said finally. She decided he was shy.

"Would you like to come here?" She glanced around her living room as she spoke, trying to see her house with his eyes. *So this is how she lives. So this is what she gave me up to attain.* It wasn't much. Then she remembered: She didn't have to justify herself. Only apparently she did.

"Where's here? My movements are kind of restricted these days."

She hadn't thought of that. Bail provisions kept

him from leaving the county. The media kept him even closer to home.

"Why don't you come here?" he said. "My mom and dad—" He stopped suddenly. She heard the discomfort that hung in the silence. "What am I supposed to call you anyway?"

"Whatever you want. Bailey would be fine," she added, and took the directions to the house, though by now everyone in town knew where it was.

Gilda was appalled. Again. "You're going to that house! You're going to be alone with him."

"He's my own flesh and blood."

"He's a stranger."

They were both right.

"What do you think he's going to do?" Bailey asked. "Beat me up and hurl me from the deck?"

"You're trying to be funny, but the district attorney doesn't think it's a joke."

"He says he wasn't there when it happened."

"You talked to him about it?"

"I mean that was his story in the papers. And according to the system, he's innocent until proven guilty."

"Tell that to the legal scholars. I'm your mother."

"And I'm his."

That stopped Gilda, but not for the reason Bailey thought.

"All right," Gilda went on. "Let's say for the sake of argument that he's guilty. Just for the sake of argument," she repeated when Bailey started to protest. "Let's say that either intentionally or by accident he killed the girl. What does that say about him?"

Bailey didn't answer. She knew where her mother was going, and she wasn't going to help her get there.

"I'll tell you what it says about him. This is a boy who does not have a healthy attitude toward women. And you don't have to be a board-certified psychiatrist to figure out who the first woman he was angry at was."

Bailey told her mother she didn't want to discuss it and got off the phone. Gilda was wrong. She didn't know Charlie. Bailey didn't either, but at least she'd spoken to him on the phone. And it wasn't just her opinion. There'd been an article in the paper right after the news that he'd been adopted broke. She'd been surprised to see him on the front page of the *Times,* even the lower left-hand column of the front page, though she shouldn't have been. She'd been in the business long enough to understand the rationalization. Television and the tabloids had shown that the story had legs. Now it was time for the paper of record to ring in with a responsible, in-depth article about the implications of the incident for society at large, though it wasn't entirely clear what those were.

The article had continued in the second section, a full page of Charlie's life. Her eyes had gone up and down the narrow columns of type. Her spirits had ridden a roller-coaster with them.

As the only child of a prominent, socially responsible couple, Charlie Prinze had been given every advantage, but according to various teachers, coaches, and administrators at the exclusive schools he'd attended, he hadn't been spoiled. At least, no more spoiled than other children of his background and blessings. His mother, a family therapist, believed in discipline, which in the vernacular of the day she called tough love. His father, though more easygoing, set high standards of public service. Both parents, a variety of their friends and colleagues insisted, preached the doctrine of giving something back to society. At Andover, Charlie had done community service with the elderly. At Brown, he'd tutored inner-city children. His summer jobs had ranged from congressional internships to a student volunteer program in Myanmar. A few weeks earlier she would have been skeptical. This Charlie Prinze ought to be canonized, not indicted. Now her maternal pride soared. Even if there was a PR firm in the wings, and she knew there had to be, Charlie had given them plenty to work with. Several people who knew him spoke pointedly of his gentleness. A professional who'd never met him, but claimed an expertise in psychological profiling, found none of the obvious signs of a criminal or even violent temperament. No one mentioned any childhood incidents of putting cats in washing machines or setting fires for fun.

She checked herself in the mirror one last time. She was so busy judging Charlie. What about his take on her? What if he thought she was ugly or frumpy or blowsy? What if he was ashamed of her? Most kids, at some point in their lives, thought their parents were hopelessly dumb or achingly embarrassing or simply too grotesque to be seen with. But most parents had the years before, the childhood love affair with Mommy and Daddy, to hang on to through the years of rejection. Most parents had memories to sustain hope. All she had was her own guilt and, though she'd never admit it to Gilda, his presumed anger.

She put her makeup back in her handbag and came out of the bathroom into the store.

"Hey, you look nice," Nell said.

"Don't sound so surprised."

"You know what I meant. That's a cool outfit. Where're you going?"

"It's none of your business where she's going," Maude said, though Bailey knew she was as curious as Nell.

Mack, who'd come into the store while she was in the bathroom, looked up from the book he was leafing through. She hadn't seen him since the night of the fireworks.

"Must have a heavy date," he said.

"That's what I love about small-town life." She started out of the store. "No one pays attention to what anyone else is up to."

The heated pavement of the parking lot felt soft as sand beneath her feet. In the car she started the engine, turned on the air conditioner, and twisted the rearview mirror to check her image once more. This was crazy. She'd interviewed for jobs she'd wanted desperately, gone out with men she'd thought she could love, even got married with less trepidation than this.

She pulled out of the parking lot and started down Main Street, stopping for pedestrians, giving other vehicles a wide berth, yielding the right-of-way at every intersection. She was driving with such exaggerated care that anyone following her might think she was under the influence.

When she reached the pond, she turned left into the more desirable terrain of sprawling houses and ocean views and beach access—south of the highway, as it was known in the real estate ads. Surely, that should count for something. If she hadn't given him up, he never would have ended up here. If she hadn't given him up, he wouldn't have had the advantages.

Ah, so you did it out of altruism. She shook her head. This was crazy. She was going to meet him, not plead her case before him.

Maybe she should have brought along a third person after all, not to protect her, merely to ease things between them. She shook her head again. They didn't need a buffer. He must have felt the same way, because he'd mentioned that his parents would be in town and the housekeeper was off. There wouldn't be anyone else around.

She pulled up in front of the house. No name or even number gave it away, but she knew it from the photographs and news clips, and from the handful of cars and vans parked in front. The story had quieted down for the moment, the peaceful hiatus between the aftermath of the arrest and the beginning of the trial, but a shot of Charlie coming or going or ten seconds of him taking a dip in the pool or whacking a tennis ball around the court still rated as news.

She parked the car on the street, locked the three doors from the inside, got out, and locked the driver's side. There was nothing of value in the car, only the registration and insurance cards in the glove compartment, but her name was the one thing she didn't want the reporters to have, though she knew a search of the license number would give it to them. Her name would come out eventually, but not yet, not until she and Charlie had a chance.

She felt the inhabitants of the cars and vans watching her as she walked up the driveway. It was odd to be on the other side of the story. She imagined them speculating on who she was. A friend of Caroline Prinze? A personal trainer? She couldn't be one of the team of attorneys; she wasn't carrying a briefcase. Clearly, she wasn't anyone closely connected to Charlie Prinze. A shred of nostalgia for her earlier life made her want to give them a break. Her sense of survival kept her walking straight ahead.

The house, a large white frame in what the real estate ads would call mint condition, sat far back on a manicured lawn. Topiary hedges made a neat hem around the grounds. Red geraniums, so hearty they looked plastic, bloomed from window boxes and hanging baskets and massive urns. In a Hollywood movie, set in the early years of the century, the property would belong to a middle-American middle-class family with a stern but loving father, adoring, addle-brained mother, and passel of mischievous yet lovable kids. On the East End of Long Island, a stone's throw from the ocean and overlooking a pond, on the eve of the millennium, it could belong only to a CEO or investment banker or entertainment celebrity. Or to Eliot and Caroline Prinze. They didn't earn as much as any of those breeds. Liberal pundits were not exactly at the top of the financial food chain, and Caroline Prinze's income as a family therapist would barely cover the upkeep of the grounds. But the Prinzes lived in a world, at the epicenter of a world, where you didn't have to earn large amounts of money to make large amounts of money. All you had to do was say yes when someone who did have vast amounts of money suggested you invest a small sum or, better yet, offered to invest it for you. Money rained down on the Prinzes like ticker tape in an old-fashioned victory parade. There was nothing they could do to avoid it.

He'd told her to go around to the back of the house. "It isn't as bad as it was in the beginning, but there's usually someone watching. And they have telephoto lenses." She knew that. She also knew, they both did, that coming face to face with each other would be awkward enough without having the event recorded for posterity, or at least the evening news.

She made her way around the side of the house. The tennis court was off to the left, the pool directly ahead of her. He was sitting on the end of a chaise with his back to her, his elbows on his knees and his shoulders hunched forward.

These girls have no maternal instincts.

The words came back to her the moment she saw him, and she knew the nurse had been stupid as well as cruel. Just the sight of him made her heart ache like an atrophied muscle that has had a sudden workout.

She stopped on the grass so he wouldn't hear her footsteps. She needed time to take him in.

He was tall, she could tell that even though he was sitting, and rawboned, and thinner than he'd looked in all the pictures. The shape of his head beneath his smooth dark hair was elongated, Grecian, unimaginably elegant. Her hand curled at the need to reach out and cradle it. His hair halted abruptly at the razor-sharp line of a recent haircut to reveal a long tanned neck. The smooth brown skin struck her as shockingly vulnerable. His shoulders were wide but so bony that his T-shirt hung from them as if from a hanger. She knew she wasn't seeing him clearly. Objectivity had fallen away the moment she'd found him sitting there—before that probably. She also realized that Gilda had a point. He could hurt her, all right, but the violence wouldn't be physical.

She went on staring at him. The T-shirt and shorts left his arms and legs exposed. A growth of fine dark hair covered his forearms and calves and thighs. He was a man, not a boy. The knowledge made her hang back for another moment.

He turned, saw her, and stood. The sight of him, face to face, was like a physical blow. It was like falling. It was like falling in love. She put her hand out to steady herself, though there was nothing to grab on to. She closed her eyes for a split second. She opened them. He was still there. And he was beautiful. His brow was high and smooth and intelligent, and his face was long, though not as long as her own, and his mouth—how had she ever thought that mouth was greedy?—was wide and wonderfully mobile. She was dying to see his eyes, but he was wearing sunglasses.

They stood, staring at each other across a few feet of unforgiving afternoon glare. She took another step toward him, then stopped.

"You're..." his voice trailed off. He held himself stiffly, like Edward on the lookout. He was the one who didn't trust her. Why should he?

"Yup, I am," she said. Her laugh was so nervous it sounded like a shrieking seagull.

She took the few steps toward him and held out her hand. He took it. Then, at exactly the same moment, he ducked his head toward her and she lifted her face to him, and they brushed cheeks.

Oh, God, she thought, oh, God, it's going to be all right.

He let go of her hand and took a step back. "Hi," he said.

"Hi," she said.

She asked him if he minded, if it wouldn't be too embarrassing for him, if he took off his dark glasses. He took them off, then ducked his head, because after all it was embarrassing, this tentative dance, this terrified sniffing out of each other. He lifted his face to her again. She'd always assumed his eyes had changed color afterward. He'd been born with a full head of shaggy dark hair. Surely the birth blue wouldn't last. They were dark blue now, almost violet. Whom had he got them from? Not her. Not that sweet boy with the ponytail.

He slipped his glasses back on. She knew she had to stop staring at him this way, as if she were trying to ingest him.

They executed an awkward dance that brought him back to the end of the chaise and her to the chair beside it.

"So," he looked down at his big bare feet, then back at her, "tell me about me." He gave her a small, cautious smile. As far as she was concerned, it had more wattage than the ball of sun sitting behind his shoulder.

She'd sworn she wasn't going to stay long. She'd be brief, as if she were making a hospital visit. Mustn't tire the patient. Mustn't let the patient tire of her. She wanted to see him again. She wanted him to want to see her again. She couldn't lose him a second time.

After forty-five minutes she glanced at her watch and said she really ought to go. He said casually, as if they were two ordinary people, as if, more important, he liked her, "Oh, come on; stay a little."

Half an hour later she said she really did have to go. This time he didn't protest. She cursed herself for having overstayed her welcome.

She stood. He did, too. The sun was behind him. She shaded her eyes with her hand as she looked up at him. "Maybe we could do this again. I mean, if you'd like to."

"Yeah," he said, "sure."

"We don't have to. I mean, if you'd rather not, I'll understand." It wasn't exactly a lie. She'd understand. She'd be heartbroken, but she'd understand. She already did. Why would he want to see her?

"It's not that."

"Then what?"

He put his hands in the pockets of his shorts and shrugged his bony shoulders. "You sure you know what you're getting into? Some people aren't exactly eager to know me these days."

"You mean because of..." She hesitated. Suddenly she didn't know what to call it.

He laughed. There wasn't a lot of joy in the sound. "Yeah, because of that. You haven't asked about it."

She went on staring up at him. He was a fathomless shadow against the glare of the sun.

"There are a lot of things you haven't asked me either. We don't have to cover everything the first time."

"Yeah, but this is pretty major. I mean, it must make a difference to you."

She didn't know what to say. That more than anything she wanted him not to have done it? But that if he had, she'd stand by him? That was the party line of motherhood, and it was true, though she wasn't a card-carrying party member.

"I guess I've been trying not to think about it."

"In other words, you believe I did it, too."

She didn't know what she thought anymore, because she didn't know him, she merely loved him. It was an instinct, an atavistic pull, a force she didn't even want to resist, but it wasn't knowledge or understanding or perspective. She couldn't see him clearly now, and she had no compass points from the past. It would have been different if they had a history, if she remembered the way he hadn't been able to meet her eyes when he'd said he wasn't the one who'd filched the stuff from the five-and-ten or had gone on the offensive when she'd had him on the rug for smoking dope. She might not have had more confidence in him, but she would have had more ability to read him. That particular history, however, existed only in her fantasies. She had no precedents, nothing to go by except her own lust for his innocence.

"Why don't you tell me about it?"

He sat on the end of the chaise again. This time he took off his glasses without her asking. She sat across from him. Then he told her how they'd gone out with some friends and come back here and ended up arguing. She'd read it all in the papers. She'd read more in the papers, because he didn't dwell on the sex.

"Then what?"

"I drove back to town."

"At that hour?"

"I was pretty pissed. I didn't know what else to do. Besides, I like to drive. Especially late at night when the roads are empty. It's a good way to mellow out."

She pictured him, temper frayed, reflexes slowed, judgment impaired, careening around curves at unsafe speeds. *Mellow out?* she wanted to scream. *More like check out.* She kept her mouth shut. This wasn't the moment for a lecture on motor vehicle safety.

"What about her? What did she do?"

"I don't know. Maybe she sat on the deck and kept drinking. Maybe that was how she fell. Or jumped. Or decided she could fly."

"Do me a favor. Don't say that to anyone else." She stopped. When had she become a partisan? More than that, a conspirator?

"All I meant was that anything could have happened. But I wasn't here so I don't know what did. All I know is we had a fight and I left."

"What did you fight about?"

He sat staring at his big feet, set solidly on the stone patio. The patio, it occurred to her suddenly, where Juliet Mercer had fallen.

"The fact that she was pregnant?"

He looked up at her. "I didn't even know she was until the police told me."

His face was earnest. Too earnest. And the story was absurd. No wonder no one believed him.

"Look," she said, "this is practically the twenty-first century, and I'm relatively hip for a woman who's old enough to be your mother. Pregnancy isn't exactly a deep dark shame anymore." She hesitated. *The way it was when I was young. The way it was when I got pregnant with you.* But he was looking at his feet again. If he made the connection, he wasn't going to show it. He probably hadn't even made it. Maybe Gilda was right. Maybe he was angry as hell at Bailey. But he had more immediate problems on his mind. "It just seems unlikely that she wouldn't have told you."

"Now you sound like the police."

"I'm sorry. I'm just trying to make sense of what happened."

"Yeah, well, as soon as you do, clue me in."

"Why wouldn't she have told you she was pregnant?"

"How would I know?"

"Did she think you'd be angry?"

"Why would I be angry? I mean, it's not like she pulled it off alone."

How had she suspected him, even for a moment? "Then, what did you fight about?"

He was leaning forward with his elbows on his knees again, and he hunched his shoulders further and went on staring at the pattern of stone beneath his feet. "Nothing. Everything. I mean, I know that sounds crazy, but that was the way it was with Juliet. Afterwards I never knew what the fights were about."

"But you must remember something."

He glanced at her, then away. "Nothing that would make any difference." He dragged his eyes back to her. "Listen, maybe I'm not supposed to say this. I mean, not speaking ill of the dead and all that."

"She's dead; she isn't necessarily a saint."

"The thing of it is, Juliet was a real HMW."

"HMW?"

"High-maintenance woman. I'm not saying the fight was all her fault or anything, but she had a lot of what my mom calls needs."

The portrait wasn't particularly flattering, but that didn't mean it was inaccurate.

"I take it this particular fight was pretty major."

"With Juliet there wasn't any other kind."

"Did it get violent? Physically violent, I mean."

He'd been staring at the ground again. Now he looked up at her, his eyes an honorbound navy blue. "No."

"The papers said there were bruises."

He stood so abruptly he knocked over the wrought-iron end table. "If you fell from there"—he squinted up at the deck above their heads—"to here, you'd have bruises, too." He bent and righted the table, but didn't sit again. She could feel him standing behind her. That was all right. She didn't particularly want to look him in the eye when she asked the next question.

She tried to pretend she was back in her old life. Forget feelings, disregard niceties, just get the story. "The news reports said the marks on her neck were from choking."

"That wasn't a fight," he said quietly.

She waited for him to go on. He didn't.

"From sex?" she asked finally. This wasn't right. This was none of her business. Only, suddenly it was.

Again he didn't answer. She twisted around to look at him. He nodded.

"But she was okay afterward? I mean, she had the marks, but you hadn't hurt her or anything."

"She was fine. Hell, she thought it was great."

She hesitated. She didn't want to ask this either. It wasn't the kind of thing a man should have to tell anyone, let alone a birth mother he hadn't seen for a couple of decades, but she had a feeling it was important. She told herself again to pretend he was a stranger, and she was just doing her job. "Does that mean you didn't?"

He took a moment to answer, then the words rushed

out of him in a single breath. "It scared the shit out of me." He glanced at her for a split second, and she caught the expression in his eyes. He was ashamed. Not of what he'd done, but of the fact that he hadn't enjoyed doing it. And at that moment she knew, or at least made up her mind, that he was innocent. She realized she wasn't being entirely logical. Just because he hadn't enjoyed choking a woman into an admirable orgasm didn't mean he hadn't flown into a rage when the woman taunted him about not enjoying it. Men had been known to. But she didn't think this particular man had. She'd met her share of insecure males determined to prove themselves on the playing fields of women's bodies: the quantity boys, who kept track of the number of women they bedded in a day or a lifetime, and the quality boys, who ticked off acts as if they were following steps in a do-it-yourself manual or chanted silent mantras to set personal bests in the endurance heats. She'd heard them brag about women and boast about sex and, if you were foolish enough to get mixed up with them, wheedle compliments about their prowess. And there was one thing she knew for sure. A man like that, a man fragile enough to fly into a homicidal rage at a sexual slur, would rather die than admit to a woman, even his mother, that there was an erotic act he didn't enjoy.

She stood. "Tell me one more thing. If Juliet was such a high-maintenance woman, such a demanding pain in the neck, why were you mixed up with her?"

He went on staring at her. A small tic of embarrassment tugged at his lower lip. "She was a ten. Face and body."

She should have known. He was her son, but, as she'd realized as soon as she'd seen him sitting there with his long hairy arms and legs, he was a man.

"So," he said, "now that you know the story, you sure you want to get mixed up with me?"

As if she had a choice.

Twelve

She was surprised at how long the news took to break. The morning after she met Charlie she awakened expecting the worst, and she knew just how bad the worst could be—reporters, cameras, obscene offers from talk shows and tabloids, threatening phone calls from anonymous evil-wishers—and again the morning after that. If she hadn't known better, she would have been lulled into thinking she was going to get away with it, but she did know better. Five days after their first meeting, a woman who came in to do the heavy cleaning in the Prinze house told a reporter, who'd camped out in front of it and offered her a lift, that she'd heard from the regular housekeeper that Charlie Prinze's real mother had turned up. After that it took fewer than twenty-four hours to finger Bailey.

The calls started that afternoon. It was her day off, so she was there to get them. She answered the first call, admitted she was Charlie Prinze's birth—not *real,* she corrected the reporter on the other end of the line, but *birth*—mother and said she had no further comment. Four more calls followed in quick succession. Annie Fenton rang in on the sixth.

"You certainly put one over on me," Annie said.

"I wanted to tell you," Bailey lied, "but I had to be sure. Thanks. For your help, I mean."

"If you think I'm going to say it was nothing, you're wrong. You owe me, luvey. When can I come out and see you? I can be on the road in fifteen minutes."

Bailey heard the indecent eagerness in her voice. Was that the way she used to sound? "The road? You mean you won't spring for airfare?"

"Sure, if you think it'll be faster, but by the time I get out to La Guardia and catch a flight—I don't know how often they run on weekdays—it'll be just as fast to drive."

"I was joking."

Annie didn't say anything to that, but the silence was eloquent. She didn't think this was a joking matter. Bailey was beginning to wonder how they'd ever been friends, or if they'd ever been friends, only she knew. She was the one who'd changed, or at least was in a new position.

"You can laugh, but I'm really excited. This story

could do a lot for both of us." Annie was always looking for a story with what she called resonance, which meant something that she could inflate into a book contract.

"Come on, Annie, what good could this story possibly do me?"

There was another silence, and for a moment Bailey thought Annie was actually chastened. Then she spoke, and Bailey knew she was the one who was being chastised. "If you're talking about money, you know I can't pay for a news story."

"I wasn't talking about money. I was talking about privacy."

"Listen, Bailey, this isn't just about you. It's about larger issues. Adoption and motherhood, for one. Men's violence and women's vulnerability, for another."

"Charlie's innocent."

"That's it! Exactly what I'm after. A woman torn between feminist convictions and motherly love.

"It's more than motherly love, it's—" She caught herself. The old newsroom joke: *But his mother swears he didn't do it.*

The phone rang again as soon as she hung up. This time she took it off the hook and left it that way. A little while later a car pulled into her driveway, and a man got out, came up on the deck, and knocked on the frame of the sliding screen door. Before he could identify himself or produce his credentials, she said she had no comment and told him, politely, that he

was trespassing on private property. He said all he
wanted to do was talk to her. Still polite, she told him
if he didn't get his car out of her driveway, she'd call
the police. He assured her he'd take only a few minutes of her time. She picked up the phone. The man
went down the steps from the deck and back to his
car. She stood behind the screen watching to make
sure he got into it and drove away. She should have
known better, but she was out of practice, and dis-
tracted. He managed to get a few seconds of film before he started the car and backed it out of the driveway. There'd be a line of cars and trucks parked
along the road in front of her property before the day
was out, and a picture of her on the evening news.

Nell could tell from the way her mom was slapping
the chopped meat into patties that she was wishing the
patties were something or someone else. It reminded
her of the time she'd gone with Bailey to the dump,
and they'd stood above one of the recycling bins flinging glass bottles into it and cheering as they exploded.
Bailey had said it was a form of therapy, but her mom
didn't look as if she was getting much benefit from it.

What was she mad about anyway? Nell was the
one who ought to be angry. She'd come home and
found her mom had opened her mail, again. Her
mom had said it was only a college catalog. Nell had
said that wasn't the point; the envelope was ad-
dressed to her. Her mom had said Nell was a minor,

and it was her responsibility to make sure she didn't get anything funny in the mail, just as it was her responsibility and not some electronic V-chip's to make sure she and Huey didn't watch smut and violence on TV. *Excuse me, Mom, like Yale is sending me pornography in a plain brown wrapper.*

But by then they weren't fighting about anything; they were just fighting. That was why her mom had started in about the catalog, and how she didn't see why Nell was sending all over the country when there were plenty of good colleges close to home—if the local community college was going to be good enough for Kevin, it ought to be good enough for her—and they couldn't afford any of those expensive private schools anyway, and before Nell started talking about scholarships, she better remember she might be the smartest girl in her class—*Not* girl, Nell wanted to scream; *I'm smarter than the boys, too*—but it was a small class and there was a big world out there, and it wasn't like she was black or Hispanic or any of those minorities who had it easy these days, so she was just setting herself up for a fall. She didn't want to spoil Nell's dreams or anything, she just didn't want Nell to be disappointed.

Her mom picked up another handful of meat and started pounding. The problem, Nell thought, was that her mom couldn't make up her mind. Go to college so you can get a good job, but don't go to too good a college so you forget who you are. Like her mom had any idea who she was. Don't end up like me, but just who do you think you are, young lady? That was why her mom hated Bailey. She said she didn't, but Nell could tell. Because Bailey gave her what her mom called ideas. And to tell the truth, her mom had a point, because Bailey didn't care about a lot of things that everyone else Nell knew said were important, and could get really worked up about one or two things no one else even thought about. Sometimes she found that exciting, but sometimes she just felt scared and angry and kind of guilty, and then she'd come home and try to be extra nice to her mom. Except like now, when her mom wouldn't let her.

Sometimes she felt sorry for her mom. At least she did when her mom wasn't working over a bunch of helpless patties that were supposed to be dinner. It was almost enough to make Nell get serious about being a vegetarian. She wasn't going to be like her mom, no way, but just standing there thinking that made her feel really mean. She wanted to tell her mom she was sorry, but she couldn't very well apologize for thinking something she couldn't admit in the first place, and anyway it didn't matter because now her dad was shouting from the living room the way he did when there was something important, something he thought was important, that he wanted them to see. His voice was practically shaking the house, and it never did that anymore. It hadn't since he'd begun going to his meetings again.

He was shouting at her mom to get in there, and that he didn't believe it, and that she better hurry before she missed it. Her mom put down the patty, but didn't stop to wash her hands. Nell followed her.

Her dad had turned up the sound, and the voiceover was shouting about the Polo Murder, for a change. You wouldn't think her dad could still get so worked up about it. But then she saw the screen and knew why he was shouting. There was a picture of Bailey. She was standing in her kitchen peering out of it, just as Nell had seen her do dozens of times.

"What is it?" her mom asked, then she saw the screen, too. "That's Bailey Bender!"

"Shh." Her dad turned the sound louder. And he yelled at Nell about her music.

Now there was a man on the screen. You could tell he was standing outside because there were trees in the background, and he was saying he was speaking from outside the house of Bailey Bender, the birth mother of Charlie Prinze, and those were the latest developments from the East End of Long Island. Then some guy in a studio was thanking him, and her dad was turning the sound down.

"I don't understand," her mom said, though any retard could understand. What Nell couldn't do was believe. She couldn't believe Bailey had never said a word to her.

"Did you know about this?" Her mom wasn't exactly shouting, but her tone made Nell feel as if she were about to be worked over like one of those hamburger patties.

"How would I know?"

"What do you mean, how would you know? You spend half your life over there. It's always 'Bailey says,' and 'Bailey thinks,' and 'Bailey this,' and 'Bailey that.'"

"I didn't know."

"I don't understand. I don't understand how a woman could do that. Her own child."

Neither did Nell, but she wasn't talking.

"I always knew there was something funny about her."

Part of Nell wanted to scream that the only thing funny was that Bailey had found one solution to the problem while her mom had found another, but she couldn't because for once she agreed with her mom. There was something weird about what Bailey had done.

"I don't want you going over there anymore."

Nell didn't answer, though she had no intention of going over to Bailey's, not after the way Bailey had lied to her. That morning a few weeks ago when she'd accused Bailey of being a hypocrite, just like her mom, and Bailey was like, no, not me, I'm different. It made her sick to remember it. Maybe her mom knew something after all. At least her mom had kept her.

She started for the stairs. Her mom followed her. "Did you hear me?"

She climbed the first few stairs.

"Nell!"

"I heard you."

"I don't want you going over there."

"You don't have to worry about that."

Mack was surprised that Will didn't change the channel when the news came on. The kid had a habit of sitting through the commercials, then switching when the program started, especially if the program was news. But this time he hadn't switched. Then Mack realized the reporter had said something about the Polo Murder. Will was addicted to it. Well, why should his kid be any less prurient than the rest of the television-watching public?

"Hey!" Will said, and suddenly he was sitting up in his chair. "That's her." He waved the remote control at the screen. "The one who came fishing. What'shername. Bailey."

Mack looked at the screen. The picture was dark and grainy, but it was Bailey, all right. He was surprised. Tina Coopersmith had been on television giving her opinion about the case and everything else under the sun, and a couple of other people he knew, but he hadn't expected Bailey to step into that circus.

Will had pulled his legs up under him and was bouncing up and down on his haunches, chanting "Wow" and "Hey, man" and "Allll right." Mack wished the kid would shut up a minute so he could hear. Then even Will was surprised into silence, and Mack heard.

When it was over, he sat for a while staring unseeingly at the screen. He wondered why she hadn't had an abortion. Even then it wouldn't have been that hard. An abortion wouldn't have shocked him, but somehow the idea of having the baby and giving it up did. He wasn't blaming her or anything. He was just surprised.

And later, sitting on the steps watching clouds that looked as if they'd been stretched from a ball of absorbent cotton drift overhead, he found himself remembering all the dumb cracks he'd made about how it would serve her right if some day she had a problem kid of her own. From the other side of the screen door he heard the sound of gunshots and laughter and sirens in quick succession as Will surfed the channels. Problem kid, hell; he hadn't realized how lucky he was. He wondered if he ought to get in the truck and drive over to see how she was. She might want company. On the other hand, she might not. He thought of Tina Coopersmith rushing to the scenes of accidents with indecent haste. He tried to imagine what he'd say once he got there. He decided to keep his distance.

Thirteen

No one came out and said anything to her about Charlie. Actually, what people tended to do was stop what they were saying when they saw her, though some of them rearranged their faces into expressions of solicitude. Tina even brought a strawberry-rhubarb pie, which Bailey figured was one step down from a casserole on the condolence scale. The hell of it was, Tina made a mean strawberry-rhubarb pie. No one, however, went on record as saying she was responsible for what Charlie had done, assuming he'd done anything, and they did assume. And no one came out and blamed her for what she'd done, or rather hadn't done, herself. After all, this was the nineties. The politically correct among her neighbors championed her right to an alternative lifestyle vis-à-vis maternity. One woman with an MBA likened her to an outsource. Even the hard-liners had to applaud her reverence for life. But she knew. No matter how her fellow citizens dressed it up, they were in unspoken agreement. Overnight she'd become a unifying force. Overnight she'd become the one thing society abhors most—a bad mother.

Gilda told her she was imagining things. Bailey didn't argue because she didn't want to worry her mother, but she wasn't imagining the late-night calls telling her, alternately, that she was an unnatural woman for giving up her child, and some kind of a witch for having produced such a son. She wasn't imagining the trash piled at the end of her driveway, not the harmless heap of cans and bottles mischievous kids might dump, but a festering mound of meat bones and chicken gizzards and, on top, a dead chipmunk. And she certainly wasn't imagining the letter she got telling her she wasn't fit to keep a cat, let alone give birth to a child. That one got to her because that one was from someone who knew something about her life. Heedless of the implied threat, Edward made purring figure eights through her legs while she stood reading.

The harassment bothered her, but it didn't really frighten her. She'd received crank mail before, when her name had appeared in the credits for some show or other. Once after a special on the *Intifada* she'd got a letter saying it was self-hating Jews like her who were responsible for the Holocaust. And for half a year she'd received mash notes from an admirer who'd managed to decode the secret messages she was sending him in the news broadcasts. Unfortunately, whenever the news turned nasty, so did his letters. But that kind of thing came with the territory of being in the public eye, even its peripheral vision. Still, these new incidents did tend to make her less trusting of her neighbors, who smiled in the supermarket, and murmured words of support in the bookstore, and delivered pies to her door. She'd known she wasn't living entirely among friends, but she hadn't realized she had quite so many enemies. She and Charlie both. If the local population were this enraged at her, she could imagine how they felt about Charlie. And the local population was the jury pool.

A few days after the news about Bailey broke, Nell quit. Actually, her mother quit for her. Loraine called Maude to tell her Nell wouldn't be working in the store anymore.

Maude wasn't surprised, though she was annoyed. She told Loraine she wished Nell had given her some notice. Loraine said that Nell was only a child, and it wasn't as if it had been a real job. Maude pointed out that if this was the kind of irresponsible precedent Loraine wanted to set, Nell probably never would have a real job. The conversation wasn't productive, but Maude was angry, and not merely because she was left shorthanded at the height of the season. She'd noticed the way Nell had been avoiding Bailey. She'd even tried to talk to Nell about it, but these days Nell wasn't talking. She arrived for her shifts late, raced out the door to Kevin's waiting car the minute they were over, and wasn't winning any awards for salesmanship while she was there. The only thing she was good for was tearing the covers off unsold paperbacks to return them to the publishers for credit. It was a disagreeable job that all of them hated, partly because of the broken nails and paper cuts, mostly because they were all too in love with books to enjoy trashing any but the trashiest of them, but for the past few days Nell had gone at the job with a vengeance. One afternoon Bailey had walked to the back of the store while Nell was flaying a harmless biography with particular passion. "Where'd you get your training?" Bailey had asked. "Serbian-held Bosnia?" Nell hadn't even looked up from what she was doing.

Maude put an ad in the local weekly and told herself they'd be better off without Nell, though she knew Bailey wasn't likely to feel that way. Ignoring the gossip and stares and unspoken disapproval of acquaintances and the cowardly threats of strangers was one thing; enduring the disappointment of someone you cared for, even if you were enduring it because you'd rediscovered someone you cared for even more, was something else. That was the rest of it. Maude didn't want Bailey to get hurt. She wasn't suggesting that the boy was a bad seed, or even guilty, though she admitted to herself if not Bailey that things did look suspicious. She just didn't want to see Bailey investing too much in Charlie, though how much might be too much, she couldn't say.

Fourteen

Bailey had expected the call. Charlie had said his parents wanted to meet her, though he hadn't looked especially pleased when he'd said it. But she'd expected the call to come from Caroline Prinze. Tending the social fires was one of those instinctive things, like waking at the baby's first cry, that women just couldn't shake the habit of doing. Besides, Eliot Prinze was a busy man. Nonetheless, he was the one who called.

"I've been wanting to meet you for some time," he said on the phone.

"I've been wanting to meet you, too," she answered, though she wasn't sure that was true. She was curious to meet Charlie's parents, she'd been fantasizing about them for years, but she was also afraid to meet them. She didn't understand that. They couldn't do anything to her at this point in her life, except show her up for what she was, or rather what she wasn't.

"No," Eliot said, "I'm not just being polite. I mean it. I wanted to meet you even before you wrote to Charlie. Partly to thank you."

She didn't know what to say to that either. "You're welcome" seemed a little pallid for the magnitude of the gift. She waited for him to go on.

"But it's more than that. For years you were a ghost in our lives. I told Caroline it's time we laid the ghost to rest."

Now she knew why Eliot Prinze rather than his wife had called, and maybe even why Charlie had seemed uncomfortable about the meeting. Eliot was ready to lay the ghost to rest. Caroline was less eager. Bailey understood the sentiment. She wasn't sure how she felt about Caroline Prinze, the woman who'd saved her son, the woman who'd taken her place, but she did know how she felt about their relationship. Her connection to Eliot was artificial. Her relationship with Caroline was abnormal.

Eliot asked if she could come by for dinner or lunch or a drink that weekend. Unlike Annie Fenton, he didn't make it sound as if he were lowering the ante, merely as if they were eager to meet her. She was opening on Sunday, so she could get away early. She said she'd stop by late Sunday afternoon.

She wasn't as unhinged as she'd been the afternoon she'd driven to the house to meet Charlie, but she was still pretty anxious. She'd spent years imagining the people who'd become her son's parents. In her saner moments she'd speculated on what he did for a living, and whether she worked or stayed home and baked cookies and ran up Halloween costumes on the old Singer. She'd hoped they encouraged him to read and took him to the planetarium and believed in consistent discipline. In her more deranged moments, she'd imagined a martinet of a father who shook him out of bed at dawn so he could deliver papers and shovel snow and stoke the family furnace, or a neurasthenic mother who broke his spirit with irrational fears and coddling and enemas, or two narcissists who drove him to excel in school and succeed in sports and win trophies and kudos they could brag about to their friends. When her overheated imagination flagged, the real world kicked in. One holiday season she'd covered the story of a man who'd been fired from his janitorial job, gone home, and beaten his three-month-old son to death. The obligatory psychiatric expert they'd used for the segment had called it a classic case, and for days afterward she'd walked around with an anxiety that had burned like a low-grade fever. Another time she'd walked out in the middle of a lunch with three friends when one of them had confessed that, after years of unsuccessful fertility treatments, she'd decided to look at the upside of adopting a child. Now if she and her husband were too caught up with work to spend much time at home, they wouldn't feel as guilty.

As she turned south of the highway, she realized her fears hadn't been entirely irrational, merely unrealized. Charlie had lucked out. They both had.

This time she went to the front door. A housekeeper let her in and led her briskly through the house. She had a passing impression of pale, sunwashed colors and plumped-up furniture crouching like small fat animals on polished wood floors. They came outside onto the stone patio that skipped three steps down to the pool. Caroline Prinze, who was sitting at an umbrella-shaded table, stood as soon as she saw Bailey, came up the stairs to meet her, and said, of course, now she remembered her from the store.

Bailey said she remembered Caroline, too. She also remembered thinking the first time she'd seen Caroline, and on subsequent occasions that not only was she an extraordinarily good-looking woman—the looks were beginning to fade, but the cheekbones would go on forever—she was also one smart and sensible cookie. If she'd been less intelligent, she might have become a model. If she'd been more driven, she might have tried for a career as an actor. Instead she'd applied her sound values and those enviable cheekbones to making an impressive marriage and carving out a successful career in the helping professions. Bailey didn't know if she was going to like Caroline Prinze, but she couldn't help admiring her.

Eliot Prinze called from the tennis court that he'd be there as soon as he and Charlie finished this set, if Bailey didn't mind. She called back that she didn't Charlie waved and smashed a mean serve across the net. The serve thrilled her. She wondered where he'd got it. It couldn't all be expensive lessons. On the other hand, it certainly hadn't come from her.

Caroline asked Bailey what she'd like to drink. Bailey said iced tea would be fine. For some reason she had the feeling she had to keep her wits about her.

"I think you ought to know," Caroline said when they'd settled around the circular wrought-iron-and-glass table under the big yellow-and-white-striped umbrella, "that Eliot was encouraging Charlie to search even before you wrote."

The statement had a certain dull resonance, like the sound of the tennis ball going rhythmically back and forth in the distance. "Does that mean you didn't want him to?"

"I didn't want him to during adolescence. It's a difficult stage at best. I thought that would only complicate it more. Instead of having to work things out with me, he could just turn to the spare."

Again Bailey heard the echo of the comment. There was no reason to assume that Caroline was referring to anything more than the normal evolution from mommy-loving little boy through mother-hating teenager to adequately functioning adult male. But she couldn't help remembering Gilda's comment about a boy who obviously had a problem with women.

"There's also the issue of inflated expectations," Caroline went on, "and disappointments. Most adopted children are convinced their birth parents are either too good to be true, or too bad. Mommy's a glamorous movie star, unless she's a prostitute. Daddy's president, unless he's a pimp." Caroline gave her a tight smile, the kind she probably used to end a professional hour. "The truth, of course, usually lies somewhere between. In any case, I wanted Charlie to be ready to deal with what he found."

"And you think he is?"

Caroline shrugged. "As much as he's ever going to be. Though the timing isn't exactly ideal. Charlie said you and he talked about the accident."

"He told me what happened that night."

"Do you believe him?"

The question caught Bailey off guard. She wasn't sure whether Caroline was testing her or expressing personal doubts.

"I just wish we had some evidence that he really did leave." She realized her mistake immediately. The *really* made it sound as if she didn't believe he had. But before she could extricate herself, if she could, she saw Charlie and his father come off the court and start across the grass toward them. The similarity of movement, heads erect, shoulders back, legs as loose and lanky as Hollywood cowboys', was disconcerting. Walking a step behind, Charlie, who was a few inches taller, looked like a shadow elongated by the slanting rays of the setting sun. But as they drew closer, the resemblance faded and the differences became dramatic. Charlie's face was all long lines and lightning-quick mobility. Eliot's—square, strong-jawed, thin-lipped—looked as if it had been hacked off Mount Rushmore.

"Whipped again," Charlie said as he slumped into a chair.

Eliot stood behind it and began massaging Charlie's shoulders. Charlie shrugged off his hands. The rebuff would have cut Bailey, but Eliot didn't even seem to notice. He pulled a chair out from the table and sat. "You've got the game, Ace, but I've got the psychological edge." He winked at Bailey. "Every time he gets close to beating the old man, he freezes. A nice, old-fashioned Freudian phobia I plan to milk as long as I can." He leaned forward and held out his hand to Bailey. "I'm Eliot. Welcome to the family."

He poured iced tea from the sweating pitcher for Charlie and himself, leaned back in the chair, crossed one white-socked ankle over the other knee, and beamed at her as if he, as if all of them in this skewed parody of the modern nuclear family, didn't have a care in the world, and Bailey almost believed him. But a little while later, in the middle of one of his stories about Charlie—this one concerned holding a rope for each other in some Outward Bound demonstration of mutual trust that made Bailey's vital signs go weak—Charlie got up and disappeared into the house without a word. That was when Bailey knew that even a man with Eliot's public-confidence ratings couldn't paint a rosy glow on this.

Charlie returned a little later, and a little after that she said she had to go, though Eliot urged her to stay for dinner. Caroline did too, but Bailey had the feeling she didn't mean it. Caroline wasn't exactly chilly. *Restrained* was the word that came to mind. Bailey decided not to take it personally. Once or twice she'd turned and found Caroline watching her, as if she was trying to figure out who Bailey was and what she was up to. Once or twice she'd noticed her watching Eliot and Charlie the same way. Perhaps it came with the profession. Bailey preferred to think Caroline was clinical rather than suspicious, especially of Charlie.

Eliot walked Bailey to her car. The dusty gray Toyota with the earnest bumper stickers looked like a heap of cinders next to the red BMW convertible Charlie said he'd driven into town after he'd fought with Juliet Mercer, and a khaki Suburban, and a low-slung Jaguar XJS the rich deep color of Eton's playing fields. For the first time in her adult life Bailey was ashamed of herself for a possession; then, in quick succession, ashamed of herself for being ashamed. She and Maude always laughed at the summer people, who at the end of the season paid for the privilege of driving their pristine four-wheel-drives through a field flooded into a virtual-reality mud bog by some enterprising local. But that had been before she'd found Charlie. She could tell herself if that was the way his mind worked, if he'd bought into the world he'd grown up in, she didn't care what he thought. But she did.

As they stood in the deepening violet dusk, Eliot put his hand on the roof of her car to brace himself. She wanted to tell him not to. He'd get filthy.

"What do you think of him?"

He had to be kidding. Couldn't he see she was in love? "I think you did a good job."

"We had some pretty good material to work with. I wish you'd met him before all this happened, though. He wasn't so angry then. Or guilty."

The word went off like an alarm. "Guilty?"

"Not guilty of what happened that night. Though God knows he's torn up about Juliet. Guilty for letting us down. Me, in particular."

"Why does he think that? I mean, have you—" She stopped. Where did she get off casting parental stones?

"A couple of papers have dropped my column. And there's been a noticeable decline in the number of people clamoring to hear me speak, not to mention the number of sponsors eager to have me appear on their programs. Charlie, of course, has noticed. He blames himself. And therefore takes it out on me."

"That doesn't make sense."

"It makes perfect sense. Caroline calls it the law

of love. When we're mad at the world, or ourselves, we beat the hell out of our nearest and dearest. If for no other reason than that no one else would put up with it. Still, by now I ought to know enough not to provide grist for the mill. I could have kicked myself for that Outward Bound story." He banged his fist on her ash-gray car. "God, I wish this were over!"

The outburst surprised her. From the look on his face, it must have done the same to him. He rearranged his expression back into what he obviously believed it had to be for the good of everyone concerned, took his hand from the car roof, and put it on her shoulder. Now they'd both be filthy.

"Sorry. Just letting off steam. Listen, we're going to beat this thing. The prosecution hasn't got a case. That's not just my opinion. Iselin says so too."

When Bailey had worked on the news stories Howard Iselin had made, she'd been outraged by his choice of clients and offended by his self-promotion. Now she was prepared to forgive him anything, if he was only as smart and unbeatable as he claimed.

"Not that we're taking any chances. Let's face it, the days when Clarence Darrow could waltz into a courtroom and knock the stuffing out of creationism by sheer eloquence are long gone. So we're not sparing the specialists. Charlie's already met with a team of shrinks."

"You're not going for a plea of mental impairment!"

He smiled. "We aren't looking for what's wrong

with Charlie. We're looking for what people, in this case jurors, will think is most right. The psychologists do a workup to determine his most marketable traits. We match that against the demographic studies we've had done, then put it alltogether in a jury questionnaire. Meanwhile we have a PR firm working the press. We've got to humanize Charlie. Make him look less like the spoiled rich kid the DA's office has dreamed up." He hesitated, then shrugged and smiled again. "Okay, I admit it, with a little help from Charlie. He's not a saint, thank God. One of those repressed kids who gets up one morning, picks up an assault rifle, and mows down a couple of dozen innocent bystanders or three or four loved ones. He's not perfect, but he's not guilty."

She didn't say anything, but the doubt must have registered on her face, because he squeezed her shoulder. Years ago she'd told a photographer who'd done the same thing to keep his fucking hands off her if he wanted to keep his fucking job—that had been early in her career when she was still trying to prove she was one of the boys—but she kept her mouth shut now.

"I know Charlie," he went on. "He might have got angry at Juliet. Hell, he was probably furious. Juliet could be, shall we say, difficult."

"An HMW?"

His smile turned shamefaced. "I'm afraid that's my term. The point is, Charlie might lose his temper.

He might slam out. He did slam out. But he wouldn't get physically violent. I know him," he repeated.

On the way home she thought about Eliot's faith and the other more practical arrangements he was making. The fact that they were spending a small fortune on psychologists and PR firms and jury consultants didn't mean anything. As Eliot had pointed out, the days when you hired a good attorney and hoped for the best were long gone. These days a defendant might not be innocent until proven guilty, but that didn't mean he was guilty just because he was trying to appear innocent.

She was grateful Eliot had the money to spend. Years ago she'd produced a series of segments on the price of justice. The stories of rich and even middle-class citizens going free after murdering spouses and running over strangers and embezzling funds, while deadbeats and drifters and other have-nots served long sentences for committing, or sometimes only being convicted of committing, minor offenses had sickened her. The inequity of the system still made her queasy. She was just glad Charlie wouldn't get the brunt of it.

By the time she got home, a sliver of moon, stingy as a lightbulb in a French pension, had climbed overhead. It did nothing to illuminate the yard. Her headlights made two white tunnels in the night. When she turned them off, blackness closed in. She hadn't left on any lights because she hadn't expected to stay at the Prinzes' this late, and of course the flashlight that belonged in the car was in the house because she hadn't brought it out after the last time she'd used it.

She sat behind the wheel debating her options. She could turn the headlights back on, find her way to the house, and return with the flashlight to kill the car lights, but that seemed like more trouble than it was worth. Besides, it was humiliating not to be able to wander her own property at will. On the other hand, one night last summer when she'd come home late and tried to find her way to the house in the dark, her foot had come down on something slippery that had writhed under her weight. She'd screamed, dashed for the house, and tripped up the stairs. For a week afterward, every time she'd noticed the childish scab on her knee, she'd cursed herself for being afraid of a harmless garden snake.

She got out of the car and started across the yard. She couldn't even make out her house against the sky. The world was that black. She felt something damp and cold against her cheek, a leafy branch of the oak at the beginning of the path. At least, she hoped it was. She veered a little to the left and felt one of the paving stones beneath her foot. She was home.

Her eyes, recovering from the glare of her headlights, were beginning to adjust. She could make out her roof against the sky and even the outline of the deck. A shadow detached itself from the bulk of the house and loomed up over her.

She screamed.

"For God's sake," Mack said.

"How could you do that!" she shouted.

"I thought you could see me."

"How in hell could I see you? The place is pitch dark."

The shadow shook its head.

"Why didn't you put on a light?"

"I couldn't get inside. When did you start locking your doors?"

She didn't answer. She hadn't told him about the phone calls or the letter or the festering pile of trash. What was the point? In her former life she'd turned the crank letters over to management, and they hadn't done anything. Now she didn't even have that recourse. She had no one to report things to except the police, and she certainly wasn't going to bring them into it. The police had come up with the evidence, the so-called evidence, against Charlie. The police had taken him away in handcuffs. The police were the enemy.

She fumbled in her bag for the key, then fumbled the key into the lock. Her hands were still shaking from his stupid scare. The man was a menace. Though he had shown up the day after the news had broken on the pretense of having an overabundance of mussels. He'd even, as he was leaving, asked if there was anything he could do. "I'm not talking about cutting the grass or fixing a light," he'd said, and they'd both been so surprised by the offer that he'd had to make a quick getaway.

"You're late," he said as he slid open the door for her.

She stepped inside and switched on the lights. The world receded into docility. "I didn't know I had a curfew."

He followed her into the kitchen. "Eddie and I were getting worried."

She asked if he'd had dinner.

"The kid and I scarfed down some pizza about an hour ago, but I'll take something to drink."

She took one of the bottles of fake beer he'd left in the refrigerator and handed it to him with an opener and glass. He put the glass on the counter, opened the bottle, and began pacing the kitchen. He took a swig, moved on to the dining room, wandered through the living room, and came back into the kitchen.

"You trying to work that off while you drink it?"

He stopped and leaned against the counter. His shorts sat low on his hips. Fatherhood was keeping him in fighting trim. She noticed the rope of gnarled white scar tissue that ran up his thigh and disappeared into his shorts. The darker he got as the summer progressed, the more pronounced it became. She'd never asked him how he'd got it, though every time she noticed it, she imagined, or rather knew she couldn't begin to imagine, that part of his life. She dragged her eyes away from it.

"My ex-wife," he said, "and don't ask which one, the lovely Donna, Bella Donna, is getting married."

"Congratulations."

"This time she's marrying smart. A real go-getter, she says. An entrepreneur. An Israeli entrepreneur. How do you like that?"

She leaned against the counter across from him. "How do you?"

He took another swig of the beer. "I wish them every happiness."

"What about Will?"

"He thinks the guy's all right. Not a wimp like his old man. You know those macho Israelis."

"Watch yourself."

"As my son, the military historian, pointed out, they don't lose their wars. But he's not sure about Las Vegas."

"What does Las Vegas have to do with it?"

"They're moving there. According to Donna, and the entrepreneur, it's a happening place. Forget gambling; we're talking post-modern ranch houses, state-of-the-art sewage systems, and houses of worship that seat three thousand believers a pop. The Mafia meets family values, and gives way. Fertile ground for entrepreneurs."

"Maybe, but I still can't believe it's a healthy environment for developing forms of life, like teenage boys."

"Funny you should mention that." He took another swig and wiped his mouth with the back of his hand. "Donna thinks maybe he should stay here with me." His voice was even, and his face wasn't giving anything away.

She folded her arms across her chest, the classic stance, as any book on body language will attest, of noninvolvement. "What does Will think?"

"Hard to say. He doesn't want to go. He says he'll miss his fellow juvenile offenders. On the other hand, he doesn't want to live with me. I was thinking he could move in with you. You have all this space, and the kid's quiet. Except for the dulcet tones of the TV, you won't even know he's here."

"I assume that's a joke."

"Yeah, but I scared you, didn't I? As we speak, he's in the process of making up his mind."

He put the bottle on the counter and jammed his hands in the pockets of his shorts, his body hunched against the fear of what was going to happen and what had already, irrevocably, disastrously, happened; his face a battlefield of good intentions and discouraging experience; his heart, she suspected, pounding in fear that Will would go, or stay.

She felt sorry for him, more sorry than she ever had, because she knew how hard he was trying. As she stood watching him, she saw herself unfold her body, take the two steps across the kitchen, put her arms around him, and tell him it would be all right. Only, she knew it wouldn't. He'd be defeated if Will went, miserable if he stayed. There was no way this was going to work out, just as there was no way she was going to take those two steps across the worn linoleum. She hadn't been able to before, when her own child had been a ghost, spooking her life with no more than a shadow. And she wasn't going to now that the shadow had become substance, not to a cornered man bristling with need as thick and abrasive as a three-day beard.

Fifteen

The difficult thing, the damn near impossible thing was to keep her life spinning in its own orbit, limited as Gilda insisted that was. She had to resist the sheer gravitational pull of Charlie. She couldn't let herself begin to revolve around him. It wasn't easy.

She'd always dreamed about David. Now she began to dream about Charlie. Once she took him to kindergarten, but they couldn't squeeze his long, hairy legs under the small desk. Another time they were driving somewhere. She was supposed to be steering, but the car kept swerving out of control, and when she slammed on the brakes, he careened through the windshield and bounced on the hood like a rubber ball. The hollow *boring* sound battered her into consciousness. She came wrenchingly awake, her holey heart hammering in her chest, her blood thumping in her ears like a boom box.

The daylight hours were almost as threatening. Sometimes walking the aisles of the IGA or driving the local roads or waiting on a customer, she was suddenly standing outside herself watching and wondering what was wrong with this picture. She had what she'd always wanted, but not the way she'd wanted it.

She loved Charlie, but she didn't know Charlie. She kept up a running debate on the likelihood of his innocence and the possibility of his guilt, the absurdity of Charlie's beating a woman to death and the knowledge that people lost their tempers and accidents happened. Her mind ricocheted from one doubt to another like the steel ball in a high-scoring pinball game. She no longer knew what she thought, let alone what Charlie might have done.

One evening he stopped by on his way home from visiting friends who'd taken a group house in the neighborhood. She asked if he'd had a good time.

He was bouncing around the kitchen the way Nell used to, only more so, picking things up and putting them down, opening and closing cabinets, even, at one point, grabbing the door frame and chinning himself a few times. Now he stopped and looked at her as if she were either stupid or cruel. "A blast. More fun than the proverbial barrel of monkeys."

"I take it that's a no."

He took a bread knife off the magnetic strip and flipped the blade with his thumb.

"Be careful."

"Stop sounding like a mother." He looked at her, then shook his head and put the knife back on the strip. "I'm sorry. No, I did not have a good time."

"What happened?"

"Nothing happened. It just isn't much fun being the Claus Von Bulow of my generation. Either that or a het Jeffrey Dahmer. Like tonight. There's this girl who has a share in the house. I've known her for a while. Not well, but well enough for her to crash on my floor once. Just now she was going somewhere when I was leaving, so I offered her a ride. She freaked out. Like I was trying to lure her into my car to rape and dismember. Like she'd be taking her life in her hands just being alone with me. Fuck!" He slammed his hand down on the counter.

She jumped.

"It's all so weird. The only one I can stand to be around is Sophie."

"Who's Sophie?"

"Juliet's best friend. But nothing like Juliet."

"Not an HMW?"

"No way."

"Is she going to testify for you?"

He took the knife off the magnetic strip and began toying with it again. "What's she going to testify about? She doesn't know what happened that night. She wasn't even out here that weekend." He put the knife down. "Besides, she says she doesn't want to get involved." He picked it up again. "After it happened, people were practically breaking down her door. You know, all those sleazy magazines and talk shows." He thumbed the blade a few times. "And, she doesn't want to hurt Juliet's parents."

"Even if it would help you?"

He slapped the knife back on the magnetic strip. "Big help. She goes into court and says, 'Listen, everyone, I don't know what happened 'cause I wasn't there, but believe me, he's one great guy.'"

"There's such a thing as a character witness."

He stood looking at her for a moment, then shoved open the screen door, went out on the deck, and slumped onto a chaise with his hands jammed in the pockets of his shorts. His long, hairy legs hung over the sides. She remembered the minutes—or had they been seconds?—she'd held him, and the fragile milky-white nails. She slid open the screen door and followed him out on the deck.

"I'm sorry," he said without looking up at her.

She sat in the chair next to his. "It's just that I keep thinking there must be something more we can do, something we're overlooking, evidence or witnesses or I don't know." She stopped. He had the best counsel money could buy. He had a raft of backup experts.

And she was telling him they must be overlooking something. She was Gilda's daughter, all right.

"You want witnesses? How about the two guys who saw me come in that night."

Her head swiveled to him. "What?"

"Sure. The garage attendant says I dropped off the car around three-thirty. The doorman in my building says I got home around three. Obviously one of them has it backwards. Not that it matters. According to the medical examiner, Juliet could have died as early as one. At that time of night, it's no big deal to make it into town in under two hours."

"*Under* two hours?"

"I do it all the time. My dad's personal best is an hour and thirty-two minutes. Of course, that's my dad." The spin on the last few words reminded her of his returns when he was trying to beat his father at tennis. She decided to give it up.

They sat in silence for a while, and when he spoke again, she was surprised he was still on the subject. He usually disliked talking about the accident.

"That first afternoon you came to the house," he began, "you asked if I would've been angry if I'd known Juliet was pregnant." He hesitated. She waited. "Was he—the guy with the ponytail, I mean—was he angry?"

So he'd changed the subject after all. She wondered how far he was going to go with it.

"*Terrified* was the word. We talked a good game:

Make love not war. Let's do it in the road. But it was still a pretty uptight time."

He went on staring out across the yard, and when he spoke again, he didn't turn to her. "How come you didn't have an abortion?"

He was going all the way, as the saying had gone. "It was pre–*Roe* v *Wade*."

Now he turned to look at her. "And you were such a law-abiding citizen? Give me a break."

"I just meant it wasn't as easy then."

"It couldn't have been that hard. People did it. How come you didn't?" He didn't sound angry exactly, but he was egging her on, as if he already knew something, but wanted her to confirm it.

"I went for an abortion." She glanced over at him again.

He nodded. He even smiled, a small rictus reflex that made his large, milk-fed, orthodontically perfected teeth glint in the last light of the evening. "I figured. So what? They blew it?" He shook his head. "How do you like that? I owe my existence to sheer incompetence."

"They didn't blow it. I did. At the last minute I realized I couldn't go through with it. Call it an eleventh-hour epiphany."

"How come?"

She had to be careful. She didn't want to claim too much. Even after all these years she wasn't completely sure. In some ways she was less sure than she'd been then. She remembered being afraid of

what was going to happen to her. That was why she'd
torn off the magazine label and put it in the pocket of
her jeans. She'd wanted the police to find them and
punish them. But she hadn't been afraid only for herself. She'd sat clutching her stomach with both hands
in that soulless room decorated into a semblance of
respectability. There was no bulge. If anything, she'd
lost weight since the results of the test had come back.
Certainly there'd been no sign of life. Except in her
own mind. She knew it was there. She was the only
one. You couldn't count Andy. He was trying, he really was, but he had no sudden exhilaration of his own
body, no gut sense of his own responsibility. All he
had was a bad-news announcement that had hit him
out of the blue, an unjust blue at that, because they
had been careful. And you certainly couldn't count
those two cretins in the other room. She was the only
one who knew. And she was the only one who was
responsible. If she didn't protect it, no one would.

She hadn't thought all that through, of course. It had
just come to her. That was when she'd begun to scream.

"I was terrified," she said again. "For you as well
as me. That's why I couldn't go through with it. You
already existed for me."

He didn't say anything to that. He just turned to
look out across the yard again. But she knew he'd
heard her. More than that, she knew it was what he'd
needed to hear.

Neither of them spoke for a while after that, though

the conversation was still a palpable thing between them. But gradually she stopped thinking about the words she'd parceled out to him so carefully because she was afraid of making a mistake, and began to think about his question. He'd assumed she'd have had an abortion. Most women she knew who'd found themselves in her position had. She didn't blame them. She'd tried to have one herself. And afterward she'd marched on Washington and raised money and, once, been roughed up at a rally by a couple of pro-lifers so other women wouldn't have to take that blindfolded ride. And thanks to all that, Juliet Mercer wouldn't have had to. So why hadn't she told Charlie she was pregnant? He wouldn't have been angry. She wouldn't even have had to be ashamed. It didn't make sense. Only, suddenly it did. Things had changed since she was a girl, but not that much. Nell had taught her that. Time went by, but a kiss was still a kiss, a sigh was still a sigh, and a slut was still a slut.

She glanced over at Charlie. His face was only half turned away from her, and she could see his profile. He didn't look happy, but he didn't look as angry as he had when he'd asked why she hadn't had an abortion. She hated to ruin it.

"About Juliet," she began and saw his face harden again. "You said you didn't know she was pregnant."

"I didn't."

"You also said you had no idea why she hadn't told you."

"So?"

"Do you think it could have been because it wasn't your baby?"

He turned to look at her. Dusk had inched across the yard and up the deck, and his features were shadowy in the fading light.

"I'm not saying it wasn't," she went on quickly, "but it's a possibility."

He went on looking at her for a moment, then turned back to the darkening yard. "Nice theory," he admitted, "but there's one problem. Juliet loved telling me about other guys."

The more she heard about Juliet Mercer, the less she liked her. But that gave Charlie an excuse, not an alibi. "How did you feel hearing about them?"

He went on staring into the night. "In the beginning it used to bug me." He turned to her with a smile as lopsided as a fish hook. "Then I realized that was what she wanted."

Sixteen

The next afternoon Charlie stopped in at the store and asked if he could talk to her for a minute. She led him to the back, where there were no customers.

"Listen," he began, "I just want you to know you don't have to do this."

"Okay, what don't I have to do?"

"Howard Iselin wants to meet you. He said, and I quote, he's not going to play the adoption card, but he wouldn't mind letting it lie there on the table."

"If I pass muster?"

"He's a bastard. I mean, he's supposed to be this great legal mind, but the guy's an animal." He hesitated. "You might as well know, he checked you out."

"What did he find?"

He grinned. "Not much." He stopped smiling. "He said a jury will forgive you one mistake—he means me."

"You're right; the man's a bastard."

"But he couldn't take the chance that you had a whole bunch of mistakes, or were on a first-name basis with your local recreational-drug dealer, or something like that. I'm sorry, but I thought you ought to know what you're getting into."

"He's just doing his job."

"Yeah, that's what he says. He says he wants all the bimbos in this case on the other side. Nice guy, right?"

"Nice guys make lousy defense attorneys."

"Anyway, he's coming out tomorrow, and he wants to know if you'll be there."

"So he can check me out in person?"

"You don't have to."

It wasn't exactly her dream, more like one of the nightmares she awakened from with overactive vital signs, but unlike Juliet's best friend, Sophie, she did want to get involved. She said she'd be there.

Howard Iselin maneuvered his big, awkward body out of the wrought-iron chair to shake hands with Bailey. His broad face, deeply tanned and criss-crossed with lines, made her think of a mahogany bar scarred by generations of drinkers. His knit shirt and cheap cotton trousers hung and pulled on him as if they'd been bought from a mail-order catalog without consulting the instructions on how to measure for size. She had the feeling nothing about his appearance was accidental. Howard Iselin wanted people to dismiss or at least underestimate him. She hoped that was a sign of cunning rather than hubris.

He didn't waste any time getting down to business. "I got the results of Morris's poll. They're not bad, but I wish they were better. It's the economy, dummy. Even with this recovery, people are still worried about their jobs."

"I suppose that's Charlie's fault too," Eliot said.

Charlie slumped another inch lower in his chair. He'd barely said hello to Bailey when she'd arrived, and he refused to meet anyone's eyes now. He looked like a boy being hauled into the principal's office for a dressing down—sullen, shamed, suddenly younger, and dangerously guilty.

Iselin shrugged. "People are running scared financially. They resent anyone who isn't. The point is, this is one case where we'd be better off with a jury that isn't one payday away from welfare and has more than a sixth-grade education, but that's one animal we ain't gonna get. Anybody with even a half-baked job and an IQ over a hundred is going to take one look at the situation, figure that the trial won't be a one-night stand, and know exactly how to answer the questionnaire to get their asses challenged out of there. So we're left with the underemployed, the over the hill, and"—he rolled his eyes—"housewives. And that ain't good.

Show me a woman who calls herself a homemaker, and I'll show you a broad who's out for blood."

"You'll have to forgive Howard," Eliot said to Bailey. "Political correctness isn't his long suit."

"Screw political correctness, Eliot. I can show you half a dozen jury studies that prove housewives are more likely to convict than any other group, bar none. And we're talking about a county full of the broads. But not to worry. I've got shrinks toiling night and day on the jury questions, like a bunch of goddamn monkeys writing goddamn Shakespeare. We'll smoke out the real bloodsuckers. We're not going to get the jury we want, but I think we can finesse one we can live with. In the meantime, I've made up my mind." He looked around the table from one to the other of them. "I'm going to subpoena the diary."

Bailey hadn't even known there was a diary. The papers hadn't mentioned it. Charlie hadn't said anything about it. But she could tell from the frowns on Eliot's and Caroline's faces—small expressions of mourning, for Juliet, for good taste, for a safe, above-reproach world lost to them forever—that they knew about it. Charlie showed no emotion at all, except the yearning to be somewhere else.

"I still don't like the idea," Eliot said. "It's emotional trespass." He looked around the table, searching for support. "Okay, forget principles. Let's be practical about this," he went on, and Bailey was willing to bet that the jokes about uterus envy and how to tell the difference between Eliot Prinze and Mother Teresa had filtered back to him. "This is a young woman's diary. We can assume it contains personal reflections meant for no one's eyes but her own. I'm not talking just about hopes and dreams."

"Don't forget aspirations," Iselin said.

Eliot shot him a look that proved he wasn't such a nice guy after all. "I'm talking about crushes, romantic fantasies, sexual confidences." He glanced at Charlie. Charlie's eyes flashed up, then away. "What I'm trying to say," Eliot went on, "is I think it's pointless as well as wrong. We'll be sullying Juliet's memory without strengthening Charlie's defense. The media will smear her, then crucify us for using blame-the-victim tactics."

"Except," Iselin said, "we're not blaming the victim. Because there is no victim. Except Charlie. Because there was no crime. There was an accident, or maybe a suicide—which is one more reason I want the diary—but there was no crime."

"I agree with Eliot," Caroline said, and Bailey knew from the conviction in her voice that whatever fights Caroline might choose or disappointments she might nurse or concessions she might wring behind closed doors, in public she stood squarely behind her man, an admirable stance if you subscribed to the philosophy of country-and-western songs, a necessary place to be if you were married to a famous and powerful man and wanted to stay that way. "Subpoenaing a dead girl's diary from her grieving parents is going to do us more harm than good. Especially since we don't even know if there's anything in it."

"But what if there is?" Iselin asked. "What if after one of their fights—we all know this wasn't the first." He looked at Charlie. Charlie looked at the stones beneath his feet. "What if after another fight she went home and wrote, 'Dear Diary, I can't go on without him. I'm going to end it all.' Put that together with an expert witness who gets up on the stand and testifies that all over America kids are offing themselves while their parents are going on talk shows to say what a big surprise it was, because Johnny or Mary was such a sunny kid, and the suicide theory doesn't sound so off-the-wall after all."

He looked from one to the other of them again. No one came out and agreed with him, but no one disagreed either.

"There's something else," he continued. "This pregnancy business. Charlie says she never told him. Maybe a jury will believe him, maybe it won't. But maybe, just maybe, she mentions in the diary why the little bun she's got in the oven happens to slip her mind every time Charlie comes on the scene." He hunched his big body forward. "I know it's not nice, Eliot. I even know it could make us look bad. But we can't afford not to subpoena the fucker."

Charlie's eyes were still on the ground. Caroline was staring at Eliot.

"I think it's immoral," Eliot said. "I think it's immoral, but I know we have to do it."

Seventeen

Iselin subpoenaed the diary. Juliet Mercer's parents petitioned the judge to quash the subpoena. In an ordinary case the pretrial hearing would have been a nonevent attended only by attorneys for the prosecution and defense, but this was no ordinary case. The fact that no multimillionaire CEO had fired half his work force, no congressional aides had complained of sexual harassment, and no religious fundies or skinheads had bombed anything that week helped. The media were out in force for the hearing. Iselin was prepared for them. He'd even sent Charlie out to buy a new shirt for the occasion. No monograms, definitely no polo-player insignia, and half a neck size too large. "I want you to look vulnerable," Iselin had said. "I want you to look like you're fucking wasting away."

The tactics didn't surprise Bailey, nor did the fact that Iselin had insisted that they all attend the hearing. He'd even told her what to wear. "No red," he'd instructed.

"I don't own anything red."

"Yeah, I should have known. And no black. I'll have my secretary send you the list."

He was a man after her mother's heart.

She'd been prepared for Iselin's strategy, but not for Juliet's parents. She should have known better. Under other circumstances she would have, but there were matters she was learning not to think about, whole areas of her mind she was managing to close down, connections she was refusing to make.

Juliet's parents were standing in the hall outside the courtroom when she arrived. They might not have noticed her—she wasn't with Charlie; she'd driven over alone—if she hadn't stopped a few feet away from them and stood staring. Until then they'd been images of misery in the newspaper, symbols of sorrow on a screen, abstract suffering as distant as the heartbreak that came by satellite from Rwanda and Bosnia and Afghanistan. They hadn't been a man whose shoulders slumped under the smooth linen of his navy blazer—he'd once aspired to nattiness—and a woman whose facial lines ran so deep they looked as if they'd been hewed. They stood close to each other, immobilized by pain, stony with for-bearance. Then Juliet's father noticed Bailey over his wife's shoulder, and his face came alive with ha-tred. His wife turned to follow his gaze, but she had nothing left. Her glazed eyes stared out from her rav-aged face like those of the small dead animals Bai-ley sometimes came across in the road when she was running.

One of Iselin's assistants came over, took her arm, and steered her away from the Mercers. She didn't look at them again, though she was achingly aware of them across the aisle from her during the hearing. Once she heard a sniffle. She didn't turn to see where it was coming from. She just went on staring at the back of Charlie's beautifully shaped head, wonder-ing what was going on inside it.

Iselin spoke of his client's right to full disclosure of the evidence. Across the aisle Juliet's father shifted position and shuffled his feet. Bailey could hear the rage in the movements. She looked at Charlie again. He didn't move a muscle.

The arguments went on for some time. At a little after four the judge ordered the Mercers to hand over their daughter's diary. A small, tragic moan escaped from Juliet's mother. Her father muttered. Bailey re-fused to look at them. She sat staring straight ahead. Iselin's face was stretched into a grotesque frown, like a child who's trying to keep from laughing. Eliot and Caroline looked grim. Charlie's eyes were on the floor, and his face was so impassive he might not have heard the ruling.

Iselin and his assistants stood and began packing up their laptops and briefcases. Bailey hung back to let Charlie and his parents leave the courtroom ahead of her. She stepped into the aisle just as Juliet's mother did. Their eyes met again. Mrs. Mercer's flared to life just long enough for the hate to dart out at Bailey, then they went dead again. Bailey stepped back to let the Mercers go ahead of her.

The hall was packed with men and women shoving cameras and microphones and their big, noisy, intrusive faces at them. Her former colleagues. She even recognized several of them. They jockeyed and jabbed and pushed and surged. They howled questions. They demanded a full face for a photograph. *Come on Charlie look this way Charlie how'd it go Charlie give us a smile Charlie what's in the diary Charlie hot stuff Charlie what's the skinny Charlie come on Charlie over here Charlie this way Charlie give me a break Charlie Charlie Charlie Charlie.* And still they kept surging around them, surrounding Charlie, engulfing Iselin, pushing them together, driving them apart, trampling Caroline, shoving Bailey, demanding to know what Eliot made of it all, though never giving him a chance to say.

Charlie was trying to look calm, but the lights made him squint and the faces pushing into his made him grimace until his mouth was curled into the cruel, callous smirk. The harder they drove, the calmer he tried to appear, the meaner he looked. Bailey caught glimpses of his head, cresting the wave of inhuman curiosity, and couldn't believe this scowling public enemy was the Charlie she knew.

Then somehow Iselin surfaced above the crowd. Half a dozen microphones shot up before his face. A dozen voices demanded to know what was in the diary. Iselin, a little rumpled, a little tired, more than a little grave, leaned into the sea of mikes. He opened his mouth and waited for quiet. The shouts died. He began to talk. His tone was reasonable, measured, stripped of every emotion except concern for the memory of a dead girl and the future of an endangered boy. The defense, he explained, was not interested in the more lurid passages of the diary. They had no desire to expose sexual excesses, drug and alcohol abuse, or any of Juliet Mercer's other secrets, if in fact there were secrets. Unless, of course, those secrets had some relevance to the accident. In short, the defense demanded the diary be admitted as evidence not to sully the memory of Juliet Mercer, but to establish the innocence of Charlie Prinze.

That was all he had to say. The television news that evening and the papers the next morning would carry the same story with varying degrees of innuendo. Juliet Mercer had kept a diary of her sexual excesses and drug and alcohol abuse.

* * *

The crowd inside the courthouse had been after a story. The mob outside wanted blood. Bailey heard the shouts before she came through the doors into the searing afternoon sunshine. She saw the sea of placards before she could read the lettering on them. They went up and down on the other side of the police line, stabbing the white-hot sky with rage.

The chanting grew louder as their group drew closer. The crowd howled at Charlie. They begged for his blood and bones. They demanded justice. They swore revenge. They heaved their signs into the air, and shook their fists, and hurled their hate over the police line.

A phalanx of cops tried to steer Charlie past the demonstration. The crowd surged forward. The police pushed back. The howls grew savage. It was like running past a pack of wild animals that had smelled blood. Bailey had seen it all before, she'd even got it all on film before, but she'd never been on the receiving end of it. Even in the demonstrations of her youth, she'd been the one hurling the anger. Her body began to fold in on itself, as if it remembered the air-raid drills of its formative years. Her pace slowed. One of Iselin's assistants grabbed her elbow and shoved her along. "Just keep going," he hissed. "Keep moving and don't make eye contact."

She tried to follow directions. She averted her face. She lifted her feet. She moved forward. They were almost past the mob when something whizzed past her face and hit Charlie's shoulder with a thwack.

She saw the stain spread over his jacket and begin to drip down his back, red as blood, or a ripe tomato.

They were in reach of the cars now. She turned back for one last glimpse, though Iselin's man was still dragging her along. A grandmotherly woman with a halo of frizzy gray hair and a pair of dentures bared in hate held another tomato aloft, ready to fire. And there beside her, thin arms going up and down with a sign that demanded JUSTICE FOR JULIET, face smeared with bloodlust, was Nell.

The girl wasn't Nell, of course. The more Bailey thought about it, the more certain she became. Even if Nell had wanted to make the trip to the county seat for the demonstration, Loraine wouldn't have let her. She was merely the ghost of Nell. Bailey knew because for weeks now she'd been running into her all over town. Sometimes she spotted her from a distance, others she came right up behind her. She'd recognize the delicate high-waisted body, and the long seabird legs, and the curtain of silky brown hair, until she got close enough to see or the ghost turned, and Nell became someone else.

Only that night as she sat alone in her house trying to shut out the images of Juliet's parents and the echoes of the bloodthirsty crowd and the memory of the bloodred stain on Charlie's back, she found the ghosts of Nell crowding in on her. They were everywhere she looked, inside the house and out, staring back from the sliding glass doors, lurking in the shadows of the deck, taunting her from the trees that hung heavy and still in the suffocating night. And like the ghosts she came upon all over town, they were a shifty, mercurial lot. Sometimes they looked just like Nell, others like Juliet Mercer.

Eighteen

Iselin hadn't been entirely wrong. There was a single piece of evidence in the diary that didn't prove Charlie's innocence but did corroborate some of his story. "Sophie is the only one who knows," Juliet had written in the last entry. Unless she'd told Charlie the night she'd died, which of course was possible, he really hadn't known she was pregnant.

The hearing also had repercussions. The first occurred a few days later. Sophie called Charlie to tell him how much she hated him. Halfway through the conversation she broke down and began to cry. He did, too. They ended up consoling each other.

The second had a less happy ending.

Bailey was late getting home from work again, but

this time she'd remembered to leave a light on. The halogen flood positioned under the eaves made the yard look like a day-for-night movie set. That was why she saw it as soon as she came out of the clearing.

The body lay on its side at the foot of the steps to the deck, the soft brown coat encrusted with blood, the four legs already stiffened with rigor mortis. She didn't scream. She was curiously calm, as if she'd been expecting it. Every time there was a new development in the case or Charlie even made the news, her neighbors remembered how incensed they were at having her in their midst, though she still couldn't tell from the letters and calls whether they were incensed at her for being Charlie's mother or for not being his mother.

She forced herself to approach the stiffened body. Two dead eyes glinted up at her, shining with accusation in the reflected light of the overhead flood.

She stepped over the carcass, went into the house, and called the police. They were still the enemy, but now they were the necessary enemy. It took almost half an hour for a car to arrive. She couldn't complain. She hadn't dialed 911. This wasn't an emergency.

She recognized the cop, though she didn't know his name. He looked about twelve—it seemed to her most of the force on the street did—and was doing his best to appear older. He merely succeeded in looking as if he had a chip on his shoulder. Sometimes when he passed on the street as she was opening or closing the store, he said hello. They were friends then, on the same side of the law. But once when she'd come across him chalking her tire to make sure she didn't overstay her two hours in the public lot, he'd given her a look that said, One word out of you, lady, and you're up against the wall for a weapons check. She hadn't said a word. She hadn't planned to. Town parking was a problem, and the poor kid was just doing his job. Now he pretended not to recognize her, though he had to know who she was, not only the woman who ran Livres of Grass and sometimes parked in the public lot, but also Charlie Prinze's birth mother.

He came up the path and stood staring down at the bloody carcass. "Roadkill," he said.

"Roadkill? In my backyard?"

"Somebody hit it and kept going, and it staggered in here to die. Sometimes deer do that."

The scenario struck her as unlikely, but then, what did she know about the habits of the local fauna? She looked at the cop. His face was impassive. He and his cronies could have done it themselves. As Charlie's birth mother she wouldn't be high on their list of favorite citizens. Then the moment of total paranoia gave way to ordinary distrust.

"Or maybe somebody killed it and dragged it here."

He looked from the dead doe to her. It wasn't the up-against-the-wall stare, but it was skeptical. "You have any reason to suspect that?"

She told him about the phone calls and letters and

trash dumped in her driveway. He asked if she'd reported any of it. She said she hadn't. He frowned and shook his head. She couldn't tell if he thought she was foolish for not reporting it before, or for making so much of it now. She thought of telling him about the anti-Palestinian fanatic and the code-breaking admirer, but decided not to muddy the issue.

She glanced at the bloody carcass. Though she cursed the deer when they ate her tomatoes and shrubs, she still had a soft spot for them, especially the does watchfully herding their fragile fawns through her yard.

"Who would do a thing like this?"

He looked up from the notes he was making. "You tell me." He went on staring at her as if he was waiting for an answer.

"I have no idea. I don't even recognize the voices when they call." She remembered the letter telling her she wasn't fit to keep a cat. "Some of the threats are from people who know me, though, or at least that I have a cat." She told him about the letter.

He wrote the information in his book, then looked at her again. "I got news for you, ma'am. If this isn't roadkill that wandered in here to die, if this is connected to the letters and the calls and the trash, it isn't just someone who knows you. It's someone who's got a serious thing about you." He raised his eyebrows. His forehead practically disappeared under his cap. "So you sure you don't have any ideas?"

She told him she didn't. He shrugged, flipped his

notebook closed, and said someone would be around to pick up the deer. "Unless you like venison." He winked. She was surprised. They must have bonded again. Then he walked down the path, got into his car, and backed down her driveway.

He was gone by the time she thought of it. Edward was usually waiting for her on the deck when she got home in the evening. At the least, he'd turn up a few minutes later. The call of the wild was all very well, but there was something to be said for supermarket chicken liver or even a can of Little Friskies. He hadn't turned up yet.

She began calling him. The more she called, the more shrill her voice became. She wasn't going to jump to conclusions. He usually showed up, but he didn't always show up.

She walked down the driveway crooning his name. *Edward, Eddie,* Every time a leaf rustled or branch snapped in the darkness, she whirled around in the direction of the sound, sure that Edward would come slinking out of the underbrush, unaware and unrepentant. He didn't.

She turned back and made a couple of tours of the house and yard. Her voice had become a croak in the night. She went back down the driveway and started down the road. There were no streetlights, but there were plenty of shadows. Each one that moved was a potential Edward, though none of them turned out to be. She went on calling. She could hear the desperation in her voice, she could see herself as she'd look to others—a hysterical woman shrieking terms of endearment into the night.

She decided to go back, get into the car, and canvass the neighborhood. She wasn't panicking. She was merely facing facts. He wasn't an outdoor cat, no matter what his genetic memory whispered to him. His front claws had been surgically removed. His instincts had been blunted. If her human enemies, or, according to the cop, enemy didn't get him, his natural ones would. There was a fox in the area, and raccoons, some of them rabid.

She'd left the car keys in the kitchen when she'd gone in to telephone the police. She crossed the yard toward the house. The dead deer still lay at the bottom of the steps. And there, sniffing around it as serious and systematic as a coroner, was Edward, the little ghoul.

Nineteen

The first thing she noticed when she drove up that evening was that the hammock was strung between the two oaks again. She was surprised because one of the hooks had got twisted out of shape the past winter and she hadn't been able to get the hammock ring on it this spring. The second was that Mack was lying in it.

He swung his legs over the side and started for the car. "You need a handyman," he said.

"Not as long as I have you."

"I meant me." He locked his hands behind his head.

"Shakes my ashes,
greases my griddle,

churns my butter,
strokes my fiddle,
my man is such a handy man."

He executed a mean bump and grind.

"I was wondering who'd inherited Alberta Hunter's mantle." She went around to the back of the car and opened the trunk, which was full of cartons because she'd stopped at the cut-rate beverage store on the way home. It had been crowded with a few summer people loading up on designer water and tonic, and a mob of locals in fishing boots and foul-weather gear, joking and laughing and slapping one another around in demonstrations of muscular affection and Friday-night euphoria. She'd found the atmosphere heady, until she'd remembered these hale, high-spirited fellows were the same great guys who kept the women's shelter full all winter long. At least some of them were. For all she knew, they, and their wives and girlfriends, were also the same solid citizens who, drunk on their own self-righteousness and a couple of six-packs, called her house and made menacing references to her poor, unsuspecting cat and dumped deer carcasses on her property. She'd made her purchases and got out fast.

Mack leaned in to get a case of seltzer and noticed the six-pack of nonalcoholic beer she'd picked up— as a gesture of hospitality, she'd told herself, not an open-door policy.

"What are you doing with that?"

She reached for it. "What do you mean, what am I doing with it? You don't need a diploma from the Betty Ford Clinic to buy the stuff."

He lifted the case of seltzer out of the trunk and started for the house. "You know," he called back to her without turning around, "in some societies buying a man's nonalcoholic beer is tantamount to commitment."

"But not in this one," she said as she followed him up the path.

Inside the kitchen he put the case of seltzer on the counter and took one of the bottles of fake beer he'd left the last time out of the refrigerator. "I wanted you to be the first to know. The kid made up his mind."

She waited.

"He's decided to stay with me."

She leaned against the counter opposite him. "Congratulations."

"That's one way of putting it."

"Come on, you must be doing something right."

He shrugged. "Let's just say neither of us has taken a swing at the other for a while." But it was no good. He was having a hard time hiding the pride.

Later that night after Mack left, she sat alone on the deck thinking about Will's decision. She was glad for Mack, though she knew there were times ahead when he wouldn't be glad himself. There were times in the near future when both he and Will would regret the decision, and rage at each other, and swear they were going to call the whole thing off.

She didn't envy Mack. Only, suddenly she did. As she sat alone in the darkness on the deck of her house in the middle of the woods in the middle of the night, the knowledge of how much she'd given up went off in her head with the sudden blinding intensity of a camera flash. And then, because there was no other way she could live with it, went out.

She was on her way up to bed when she noticed the mark on the wall at the top of the stairs. It was a dark smudge in the shape of a palm print on the pristine, white surface high up near the ceiling. The fingers of the print were spread-eagled, and the span was too big to be her own. She wondered whose it was and how it had got there. No workmen had been in the house. She certainly hadn't thrown any wild parties. Then she remembered. Several months earlier the light over the stairwell, which was beyond her reach even with a stepladder, had gone out. She'd bought one of those long-handled gadgets that turn at one end to rotate the bulb at the other, but had only succeeded in breaking two bulbs. After that she'd lived in a semi-darkened hall for several weeks until Mack had been over one night and noticed it. He'd climbed onto the railing in the up-stairs hall and balanced himself against the wall with one hand while he'd changed the bulb with the other.

It was funny she hadn't noticed the mark before. She was scrupulous about washing Edward's paw prints off surfaces. Mack's fingers weren't long but they had a wide grasp. She'd noticed that when she'd watched him fish and cook and try to fix the various things in his life, and hers, come to think of it, that were broken.

She stood staring at the print, remembering the night. She'd held on to his legs to steady him, though God knows what good it would have done if he'd begun to fall. Her face had been only inches from the clenched teeth on the zipper of his worn khakis. She'd told him to hurry. He'd told her to cultivate a little patience.

She thought of going back downstairs to get paper towels and the bottle of spray cleaner and the stepladder, but it was late, and she was tired. She promised herself she'd do it first thing in the morning.

Twenty

He turned the car off 27 and headed for the beach. He wasn't ready to go home yet, though it was almost midnight and he had no place else to go. He hated being alone in that house. It wasn't fear. There was nothing to be afraid of, except the damn trial and what would happen after it, but that was something else. He just couldn't stand wandering around the empty house. He kept thinking of that night, imagining what would have happened if he'd played things differently, if they hadn't got into a fight, if they hadn't come out here for the weekend in the first place, like a kid who keeps going back to the moment he held the ball in his palm, before he rotated his arm back, before the momentum began to build, before the ball left his hand, before he saw it sailing toward the window he'd been told not to play in front of a hundred times, before he heard the crash and saw the glass shatter and knew he was in big trouble. And he kept picturing Juliet.

The police had made him look at the photographs again and again. They hadn't played good cop, bad cop. It had been more complicated than that. The same cop had been nice sometimes—*So who d'ya think's gonna win the pennant this year, Charlie?*—and a real prick the next, shoving those damn pictures in his face, asking him about the sex, telling him he might as well admit it, because they already had proof, and it would be better for him if he just told the truth. And there'd been more than two of them. Once he'd counted seven in the room at the same time, laughing with one another, joking with him, looking at one another, ignoring him, shoving their faces in his face, playing weird mind games. Like the time thing. He hadn't had a watch, but every time he'd got a look at one of the cops' watches the time had been different, not different like two-thirty, then three, then four, but two-thirty, then one, then four. And they kept coming back to the pictures and the sex. *Tell us about getting it on, Charlie. Hot stuff, right, Charlie? I bet she drove you to it, Charlie.* Sometimes he thought they were really getting off on it. Sometimes he thought that was exactly what they wanted him to think. Then they'd pull out the pictures again.

He stopped the car in the beach parking lot and covered his eyes with his hands. The prints were black and white. Black bruises, white skin, black blood. There must have been a couple of dozen shots from every angle. A close-up of a leg bent the wrong way. Hair, that long silky hair she used to toss around like a whip, matted with dried blood. A mouth opened into a dark hole—of what: pain, fear, surprise? Black bruises on her neck blown up till they looked like skid marks. He'd almost thrown up when he'd seen those. One of the cops had leaned over him to get a better look at the pictures. "Great tits," he'd breathed in Charlie's ear, an obscene parody of a come-on, and Charlie had felt the rage twist his stomach like nausea.

He took his hand from his eyes and sat staring straight ahead of him. Ribbons of fog curled in front of his headlights. The moon was a dull haze behind a sheet of ghostly clouds. All that was visible of the ocean was an occasional breaking wave that foamed corpse white in the darkness.

He saw the lights in the rearview mirror and watched the car approach. He could see the outline of the light on the roof though it wasn't flashing. The car pulled up beside him. The cop sat looking at him for a minute, as if debating how much trouble he wanted to give him. Charlie had the feeling he'd like to give him plenty.

"Beach is closed."

A few months ago Charlie would have told him there was no sign about the beach closing at any hour and anyway, he wasn't on the beach, but that had been another Charlie in another life. He told the cop he was just going, put the car in reverse, backed around, and drove slowly, not so slowly that he seemed to be looking for trouble, but not so fast that he was exceeding the speed limit, away from the beach.

At the top of the hill, he turned left toward home. The pictures of Juliet loomed out of the fog again. White skin, black blood, her mouth open in a silent scream that would go on forever. There must be somewhere else he could drive.

He cruised up one street, down another, past the houses, or the privet hedges in front of houses, of people he knew and people he used to know and people he didn't know at all but who probably knew of him. He passed places where he'd played tennis and swum and partied. He slowed in front of the house where Sophie was staying with her dad and stepmother. The lighted windows glowed like amber in the damp night. Behind the screen door, the front door was open. He thought of going in. It wasn't that late. He and Soph could hang out for a couple of hours. Only there were a lot of lights, so her dad and stepmother were probably home, too. "It's not that they blame you or anything," she'd lied. "It's just that they don't want all the publicity." Like her stepmother didn't pay big bucks to one of those PR types who called themselves social secretaries to get her picture in the paper at all those revolting parties for all those good causes.

He kept going, then made a right, and passed the house where Sophie had lived with her dad and mom before the divorce. Poor Soph wasn't having a good summer.

When he reached the highway, he turned east, past the restaurant where he'd helped organize a picket line of Guatemalan workers who'd been stiffed for back wages a couple of summers ago, hooked a right toward the water again, and cruised past the house where he'd smoked his first joint and, farther down toward the ocean, another house that some sleazy Aussi banker had rented the summer before. The guy had been bucking for the title of born-again Gatsby, because every weekend he'd given huge parties where out-of-work actors turned suckling pigs on spits, or made fake clam bakes in seaweed, or passed out baby scallops or infant shrimps or prenatal godknowswhats that had been flown in from Scotland or up from Chile or over the goddamn polar cap from the goddamn Sea of Okhotsk. He'd hated the parties, but he'd gone because the women had been real knockouts. He remembered one he'd finally got the guts to go up to. Her eyes had just about glazed over, until she'd picked up on his name. Then you could practically hear the fucking bells going off in her fucking gorgeous head. *Ding dong ding dong.* Only it hadn't been his name she'd recognized but his dad's. He bet she'd recognize his name now.

The obscene pictures flashed in the dark again. Blood ran out of her nose and down her upper lip like two black worms. He closed his eyes, then opened them wide to make the image go away.

He took a right and another right and headed away from the ocean. He didn't know where he was going, but he knew he couldn't go back to that house. He crossed the highway and started down the road to the point. Halfway there the car veered off it onto a smaller road. The car, not him. He hadn't planned to come here. But somehow he'd ended up here. Then he did something really dumb. A little way down the road, before he even reached her driveway, he turned off his lights and killed the engine so she wouldn't know he was there. He didn't want her to think he was some kind of weirdo, skulking around in the night, lurking outside her house, practically stalking her, for Christ sake. He coasted to a stop at the edge of her property and sat, though he didn't know what he was waiting for.

The cop turned up a few minutes later, the same fucking cop from the beach. He must have been following him, though he hadn't noticed the car behind him when he'd been cruising around.

This time the cop got out of his car and came around to the driver's side of the convertible.

"We gotta stop meeting like this."

Charlie didn't say anything.

The cop asked for his driver's license and registration. Charlie handed them over. The cop took out a flashlight, studied them, then handed them back.

"You know I could take you in."

The old Charlie would have demanded to know for what and done a quick monologue on due process and a few other legal niceties. This Charlie didn't say anything.

"Do I have to follow you home?" the cop asked.

Charlie said he didn't and started the engine.

The doorbell didn't wake her—she was still reading—but it did startle her. It had the same effect on Edward, who'd been asleep at the foot of the bed. He sat up, suddenly alert. She got out of bed, pulled a bathrobe on over her T-shirt, and made her way downstairs, flicking on lights as she went.

A policeman was standing on the other side of the sliding glass door, the same policeman who'd come when the deer had died, or been dumped, in her yard. She unlocked the door and slid it open.

"Just checking, ma'am," he said through the screen.

That worried her a little. As long as the police hadn't taken the threats and vandalism seriously, she hadn't had to.

He asked if she'd had any more trouble. She said she hadn't.

He stood with his legs apart and clasped his hands behind him. He was trying to look official. He managed to appear uncomfortable.

"You know a Charlie Prinze?" It wasn't really a question. And it certainly wasn't a time for him to come interrogating her about Charlie.

"Of course I know him."

"I just found him parked in front of your house."

"What do you mean, parked in front of my house?"

"He was just sitting out there. Watching."

He made Charlie sound like a Peeping Tom. "Watching?"

"Watching. He was sitting out there in his car. No lights, no engine, just sitting there in the dark watching your house. At least what you can see of it from the road, which isn't much."

She leaned around him, as if she could see to the road. "Is he still there?"

"I sent him home." He stood on the other side of the screen door staring at her. Suddenly, he didn't look like such a child after all. And suddenly she knew what he was thinking.

"Look," he said, "I can't do anything unless you file a complaint."

"For what?" She hadn't meant to bark at him.

"Harassment."

"He was sitting in his car. That's not harassment."

"There's all that other stuff."

"That wasn't Charlie. Besides, you said the deer was roadkill."

The cop didn't say anything, but again she knew what he was thinking. He'd taken his sensitivity training. He was up on his domestic violence statutes. For all she knew, he read the same psychology books Gilda did. And he knew a classic case when he saw one. *She'll scream bloody murder when he comes at her with a knife or a gun. And if he's successful, the media will pick it up, and the pols will run with it, and her next of kin will sue the force. But just try to get her to file a complaint against the son of a bitch when it'll do any good.*

She didn't argue with him. Once again, he was only doing his job. She thanked him for keeping an eye on the house, but told him he didn't have to worry about Charlie.

Twenty-One

A few days later Bailey ran into Nell, not the ghost of Nell, but the real thing. By the time Bailey got to the beach, mothers had dragged red-eyed, salty-skinned children from the surf and bundled them into cars, and vacationing couples had gone back to their rooms to make love, and only a few compulsive volleyball players and a handful of solitude seekers were left. It used to be her favorite time of day, when the long rays of the sun spilling down the sand warmed rather than burned, and the water took on the colors of an Impressionist palette. But lately she was more likely to notice the chill in the afternoon breeze and see the slick, oily surface of an ocean that stretched too far for comfort. The scale of the deserted beach struck her as too vast, the space beneath the pale dome of sky as too hollow. She felt as if she could easily float off.

She dug her chair into the sand like an anchor and took a fat hardcover book, heavy as a stone, from her canvas bag. She even managed to lose herself inside it for a while. Then she looked up and saw Nell and Kevin coming along the beach. His arm lay heavily on her shoulders, as if he were leaning on a crutch, and her arm circled his waist, as if she were propping up an invalid. A cigarette dangled from his soft, slightly girlish lips. To Bailey's horror, another smoldered in Nell's free hand. As they went by, Nell pretended— Bailey was fairly sure it was a pretense—not to see her.

Several days later she saw Nell, the real one not the ghost, again, though this time she almost didn't recognize her. Bailey was driving down Main Street, and as she passed the movie theater, her eye instinctively combed the crowd of kids hanging out in front of it. She recognized the familiar seabird silhouette immediately, but surely the metallic orange hair that stood out in spikes couldn't belong to Nell. Only Bailey saw, as she drove by, that it did. She couldn't believe it. She'd thought she knew Nell, or could at least predict her behavior. But suddenly she had no idea what silly, or not so silly, thing she'd do next.

Mack told her she was making too much of it. Kids came into school with a different color each day. Brain Stain. Shock Locks. It was a form of self-expression.

Bailey knew he was right. All Nell was doing was trying to look as much like her peers and as little like the enemy, adults, as possible. It was a necessary rite of passage, only Bailey couldn't get over the feeling in this case it was more than that. Or maybe it merely seemed like more than that to her because this time she was the enemy adult.

"All right," she said, "forget the hair. Nicotine is not a stage; nicotine is an addiction. And kids who start early have the hardest time giving it up."

"Where'd you hear that?"

She had no idea. It sounded logical, but if anyone was the authority on addictions, it was Mack. On the other hand, all you had to do was watch him with Will to know he didn't have the same expertise with kids.

The third time she ran into Nell was at the beach again. This time it was high noon, and the place was mobbed with naked children digging in the sand and half-nude teenagers strutting their mahogany flesh; elderly women in dressmaker suits and barrel-chested men in postage-stamp trunks; people playing volleyball and Frisbee, eating and sleeping, reading and swimming, flirting and necking, diapering infants and swinging giggling babies above the waves and dragging screaming children from the surf. Bailey saw the riot of humanity as if from the wrong end of a telescope. The vast expanse of sea and sky still yawned dangerously. Even the solidity of Charlie sprawled on the blanket beside her was no anchor. When he went in for a swim and his elegant head disappeared beneath the foam of a breaking wave for an endless stretch of minutes, she dug her knuckles into the sand to keep from spinning out.

Charlie came back to the blanket and announced a gnawing hunger. They walked across the wide beach to the rickety shack that changed its name every summer, but continued to turn out the same greasy hot dogs and overly breaded fried clams and bizarrely colored Popsicles year after year. The line of women with eyes bleached from too many hours spent watching too many children in the too bright sun and salty kids clamoring for sugar was long and unruly, and they were almost at the counter before Bailey noticed who was working behind it. Nell's hair was brown again, though it was still short, and there was no cigarette dangling from her mouth. She was taking orders, and shouting them back into the hot shack that reeked of rancid grease and sweet suntan lotion, and making change without missing a beat.

The woman in front of them gave her order and herded the toddlers clinging to her naked legs to the bench to wait for it. Charlie and Bailey stepped up to the window. Nell's eyes widened. She looked as if she wanted to bolt. Instead she chanted the hi-can-I-help-you mantra of the fast-food outlet in a robotic voice. She might never have laid eyes on Bailey, let alone spent hours trading confidences.

Charlie said he wanted a clam roll. Bailey said she'd have one, too, and asked Nell how she was.

Nell shouted the order back into the pungent darkness. "Will that be all?" she chanted in the same flat singsong.

Behind Bailey big feet shuffled impatiently on the wooden deck. "I didn't know you were working here," she said.

Nell made a noncommittal sound.

"This is Charlie," Bailey said, then told Charlie this was Nell. "You met in the Talkhouse," she added.

"Hi, Nell," Charlie said.

Nell looked at Charlie; then away, then, as if she couldn't help herself, back at him. "Hi," she mumbled.

Behind them a voice urged them to get on with it.

"And a lemonade," Charlie said.

"And an iced tea," Bailey added.

Nell called the orders back and handed over their change.

"Why don't you stop by one of these days?" Bailey said as someone jostled her from behind.

Nell turned to the next customer.

Bailey stood her ground. "Edward's disconsolate without you."

Nell turned back to Bailey. She still looked as if she wanted to run, but she couldn't help herself. She smiled.

Twenty-Two

Bailey was surprised to see Howard Iselin come strolling into the store. She knew he wasn't there to browse. He said he was on his way back from the Prinzes and wondered if she had time for a cup of coffee. Maude said she did.

They went to the grill a few doors away. It was midafternoon of a hot, cloudless day, and the place was empty. Iselin maneuvered his bulk onto the spindly wooden chair and straddled it with his legs wide apart and his elbows on the table. He was big but agile, like a circus elephant trained to do dainty tricks.

He tore open four packets of sugar and dumped them into his glass of iced cappuccino in quick succession while he told her the judge still hadn't set a date, which was good news no matter how crazy Charlie and his loved ones were going with the wait. Then he leaned back in the rickety chair and looked at her. "Caroline tells me he sees a lot of you."

She wondered if that was a complaint. She still hadn't got a fix on Caroline, and the enigma went beyond the abnormality of their own particular connection. Caroline's discontent was discreet, like a single strand of pearls, so understated they can be worn for any occasion. It also had the burnished glow of an heirloom she'd had for some time. Bailey suspected the disquiet had to do as much with her own life as Charlie's problems.

"He doesn't have much of a choice. He's confined to the county. Caroline has her practice in town. Eliot's got the world to cover."

"What about his friends? The way I hear it, he was Mr. Popularity before this happened."

"Exactly. Before this happened. He doesn't see many of his friends these days."

"What about sex?"

"What?"

"What does he do for sex? I mean, let's get real here. We've got this six-foot-three package of throbbing glands who, judging from what happened that night, isn't exactly a Boy Scout. He says he's gone cold turkey. Eliot believes him, but then, Eliot likes to think the best of his fellow man." Iselin shook his head. "Sometimes I wonder if he's beginning to believe his own public image or if he got the image because he's a true believer. But that's beside the point. Eliot's image isn't the one that worries me. Charlie swears he's given up sex for the duration. Just saying no. I'm not sure I believe him."

"And you're asking me what I know?"

He nodded.

"I told you he doesn't see many people. There's one girl. She was Juliet's best friend. But I get the feeling that's more solace than romance."

"You mean the Sophie kid? She doesn't worry me. Hell, she'd be a boon. Nice fresh-faced preppy who just happens to be the deceased's best buddy. A little zaftig so she's not going to threaten the women on the jury. I'd love to truck her into court and have her sit there looking up at Charlie with a shit-eating grin. You know, the way Nancy used to look at Ronnie. But apparently that's not going to happen. She doesn't have the inclination, and her folks put their collective feet down. Are you sure there isn't anyone else in the picture?"

"Of course I'm not sure, but, I told you, he doesn't see his old friends much."

"That's what worries me."

"What do you mean?"

"I mean the locals. I mean the class war between the summer haves and the local have-nots, who tend their gardens and clean their houses and service their pools. If I find that Charlie has some little townie servicing him, an arrangement which I don't have to tell you will delight our friends at the *National En-quirer* and other journals of intellectual discourse, I will drive out here and personally do a number on him that will make Lorena Bobbitt look fainthearted. I am not about to go down in flames on a case like this because Charlie is into sport fucking." He lifted his hand to catch the waitress's attention, outlined a check sign in the air with one thick finger, and turned back to Bailey. "No offense intended. I'm just doing my job and looking out for Charlie's interest."

"You don't think much of Charlie, do you?" she asked when they were outside the restaurant on the way back to the store.

"Because I think he might be boffing some townie? Hell, that ain't a crime, it's just bad PR. Under other circumstances, I'd say more power to him."

"More than that. The way you treat him. The way you talk about the case."

He stopped walking and turned to her. "Are we talking about me, or you?"

She started walking again. So did he.

"I'll tell you something I learned during my long and stellar career as a defense attorney. You think I'm going to say that I don't give a flying fuck whether someone's innocent or guilty, because according to the hallowed Constitution of this great land of ours, even the lowest scumbag, once accused, has a right to representation. Call me a frigging idealist, but I believe that. So when I started out as a defense attorney, I never asked myself whether my client had raped the old lady or murdered the kid or embezzled the cash. All I asked was how I could prove there was a reasonable doubt he hadn't. Well, the big surprise was the number of times I found or came to believe the accused scumbag was innocent. Maybe not an upstanding member of the community. Maybe not a nice guy. But innocent of the charges in question." He turned his sweat-stained face to her. "That make you feel any better?"

"Loads. Charlie's a scumbag, but according to your intuition and the laws of probability, there's an outside chance he's an innocent scumbag."

He shook his head. "Charlie's an okay kid. Not the sweetheart Eliot thinks he is, but not what you're afraid of either. At least that's one thing we got from the diary."

"I thought there wasn't anything in it."

"No evidence, if that's what you mean, but a telling picture of our boy. He wasn't the one who did the roughing up in that relationship."

"What do you mean?"

"I mean the late lamented Juliet could be a real pain in the ass."

She stopped walking and turned to him. She had no rights here. And she agreed with Eliot; it was emotional trespass. But once again the moral niceties were no match for this instinct she'd tempted back to life. "Will you let me see it?"

He tilted his big perspiring face to one side as if he was trying to put her in focus. "Sure. Why not?"

A photocopy of the diary was waiting for her when she got home two nights later. She tore open the envelope and stood, her bag still slung over her shoulder, flipping through the pages. The handwriting was bold, with self-consciously artistic flourishes. At least she wouldn't have trouble deciphering it.

There was almost an hour of light left to read by. She took the pages and a box of matches for the citronella candle out to the deck, stretched out on one of the chaises, brought her knees up to rest the papers on, and began to rifle through them again. Hearts and stars, flowers and sunbursts marched down the margin and into the text itself. Iselin had said the diary was full of doodles. She remembered her own childhood diary with the small brass lock and key, and a comment Nell had made when Nell was still speaking to her. The diary Bailey had given her for her birthday had fallen out of her backpack as she was getting out of the car one evening. Bailey had said she was surprised Nell carried it around with her. "Are you kidding?" Nell had answered. "It's the only way to keep my mom from getting her hands on it."

Bailey had a feeling these weren't aimless doodles. Juliet had worked out a code. From the looks of it, it wasn't exactly Enigma.

She turned back to the first page. Juliet had started

the diary almost two years earlier, but she'd been an erratic writer. For a week or two she'd make entries daily, then a month would go by without a word. There was no mention of Charlie in the beginning, though there was a Jeremy she was breaking up with, and a Josh who was really cool, and a B who was really good at something that was signified by a sunburst. There was also a shopping expedition with Sophie after which they went back to Sophie's house and spent a couple of hours trying on clothes and makeup. Sophie worried about her weight. Juliet confessed to reservations about her own thighs, and to feeling horribly sorry for poor Soph. They went out to some clubs. They picked up some cute guys, but dumped them after a while. The diary wasn't improving her opinion of Juliet.

Spring break ended. Juliet went back to school. New men appeared, others disappeared. Poor Soph remained eternal.

Juliet met Charlie. The next several entries were filled with reports of how cool he was, and cute and sexy. He excelled at something that was indicated by a star. He took her to the opening of a new club where the great unwashed public gawked in envy outside while they were ushered inside. Bailey knew she was reading from the vantage point of middle age, but, my God, didn't the girl have any values at all? And if she didn't, what was Charlie doing with her?

Several months of silence followed, and by the time Juliet began confiding again, she'd decided to break up with Charlie. Sophie told her she was crazy. Charlie told her he loved her. Bailey told herself she shouldn't be reading this. Juliet told Charlie she loved him but wasn't in love with him. Bailey had forgotten how young these kids were.

Charlie's name disappeared from the diary for several pages. Someone named Noah appeared. This could be love. Juliet and Sophie went to a party. Charlie was there with another girl. Juliet realized she'd made a big mistake. Juliet went home with Charlie. They broke a record. Juliet didn't say what the record was, but Bailey had a feeling it wasn't the old-fashioned vinyl kind.

She went on reading. Juliet broke up with Charlie again and got back together with Charlie again. Bailey felt sorry for Juliet, who, if she wasn't seriously screwed up, was, as Charlie had said, a high maintenance woman. But she wanted to shake Charlie. She remembered staring at those pictures of him in the newspaper, before she knew who he was, deconstructing the lock-up-your-daughters smile, and coming up with a lady killer. She'd been way off the mark.

She went back to the diary. Despite the volatility of the relationship, when Charlie and his parents went to St. Barth's for a week, they took Juliet along. It was heaven and this was love. Again.

Back in New York, Charlie's parents gave a party. Caroline introduced Juliet to Mel Gibson. Mel said hi, and wasn't it a nice party, and something about the Knicks. Juliet had underlined the entire experience with a pink marker.

A few weekends later Charlie took Juliet to his parents' house at the beach for the weekend. When the weather turned cool, Caroline loaned Juliet an awesome sweater to wear out to dinner and told her to keep a pair of really cool earrings that Caroline insisted she must have been under the influence of something to buy at her age. Juliet compared Caroline with her own mom. Mrs. Mercer did not fare well.

Eliot remained a more distant and lofty figure. Juliet admitted to being a little afraid of him, but agreed with Charlie that he was pretty cool for a dad. Once when she and Charlie were just hanging out, Eliot came in and sat down and started asking them questions. Not the kind of questions parents usually ask, but questions like what did the word *feminism* mean to Juliet and her friends, and did she consider herself one, and what did she think about having a career and children and all that.

Juliet continued to torture Charlie when they were together and herself when she was alone. He was such a guy guy. He didn't know how to communicate. He wasn't in touch with his feelings. He didn't care about hers. He was too possessive. Except that time when she was really depressed and wanted him to come over and he went to some game with the guys. Nonetheless, she might as well go to the beach house with him for the weekend. She didn't have anything better to do, and if she went out alone Fri-

day morning, she could get a head start on her tan.
Besides, his folks were giving a party on Saturday
night with all kinds of totally cool people.

It turned out to be the best weekend of Juliet's life.
Now when Charlie appeared, he was simply *he* circled with a pink Magic Marker heart.

A few weeks passed, and when Juliet began writing again, she was beginning to worry about her period. It was way late. She and Sophie bought a home
pregnancy kit. They chanted a mantra to keep the
stick from turning pink. The mantra didn't work.

Sophie said Juliet had to tell Charlie. The he's,
sexed-up by the pink Magic Marker, were gone. Charlie was Charlie again.

There was one more entry. It was dated two days
before Juliet's death. She still hadn't told Charlie she
was pregnant. "Sophie is the only one who knows,"
she wrote. Nonetheless, things were looking up for
Charlie. He was once more a pronoun encased in a
throbbing pink circle.

Or was he? According to the diary, the party that
weekend had been filled with lots of celebrities
and totally cool guys. Setting Juliet loose in that
must have been like sending a hunter into an un-
posted wood overpopulated by deer. Mel Gibson
wasn't on the list, but there were several names
Bailey recognized vaguely and an entire paragraph
about a friend of Charlie's who'd just flown in
from Paris. Alain spent his life sailing on some-

one's yacht or climbing mountains on someone's expedition or staying at someone's ski house to perfect his snowboarding technique. He sounded like a freeloader to Bailey, but he was way beyond cool to Juliet.

Bailey sat staring at the hallowed *he* snuggled into the lovestruck pink circle. It could be anyone.

She put down the diary. Iselin had been wrong. It made Charlie appear more pathetic but not more innocent. He'd said the stories about other men had stopped bothering him once he'd realized that was what they were intended to do, but a man could stand only so much.

The more Bailey thought about the diary, the more logical the idea seemed. Sophie might not know what had gone on that night, but she did know what had gone on in Juliet's life. Bailey wasn't going to grill her. She just wanted to talk to her.

When Charlie had dropped by with Sophie one evening, the girl had mentioned she often took her twin half-sisters to the beach in the morning. She wasn't actually the au pair, but since she was staying with her father and stepmother for the summer, and since she hadn't got around to getting a job because she'd been so torn up about Juliet, her stepmother had said the least she could do was help out.

The beach was already crowded when Bailey got there, but it didn't take long for her to spot Sophie.

She was standing at the water's edge watching the twins splashing in the shallow waves.

Bailey said good morning. Sophie said hi and looked uneasy. Maybe she knew Bailey was after something. Or maybe she thought all adults were.

Bailey inched into place beside her, and they stood watching the children in the on-the-*qui-vive* attitude of two women who might pass the time of day but weren't about to forget their obligations. She started obliquely by asking about the twins, though she had to be careful about that. She had a feeling they weren't Sophie's favorite topic of conversation. They talked about the responsibility of caring for two little girls, and the scarcity of jobs, and the advantages of being able to spend the summer out here, or rather Bailey asked about all those things and Sophie answered, sullenly, grudgingly, but she answered. She might be miserable, but she was incapable of being rude. Clearly this was a girl who'd internalized every etiquette lesson she'd ever been taught.

"It can't be the easiest summer for you," Bailey said after a while.

They were still standing side by side, and Sophie glanced at her briefly.

"I mean because of Juliet. You must miss her a lot."

Sophie reached up and slid a finger under her dark glasses to wipe something away. "It's not fair."

This wasn't the time to let Sophie in on the secret that life seldom was. "Of course it's not. To Juliet.

To you. Or to Charlie. That's why we have to find out what really happened."

"I can't talk about it. My dad told me not to."

"Your dad's right. You shouldn't talk to the press or anyone like that. But this is different."

Sophie folded her arms across her chest and went on watching her half-sisters.

"I thought you were a friend of Charlie's," Bailey said.

"I am."

"According to him, you're just about his best friend." She watched that sink in and knew she was right about one thing: Charlie might think of Sophie as a buddy, but Sophie was intoxicated with Charlie as only a nineteen-year-old woman with a shaky self-image and a complicated situation on the home front can be. "So if you know anything, or even think anything about what happened that night between Charlie and Juliet, you shouldn't keep it to yourself."

Sophie took her eyes from her half-sisters long enough to turn to Bailey. "Even if it looks bad for Charlie?"

Bailey stood staring back at her. *Forget it. Forget everything I said. Your father's right. Don't talk to anyone. Not me. Not Charlie's lawyer. Not a soul.*

"What looks bad for Charlie?" Bailey waited. Sophie went on watching the twins, but she looked as if she was about to cry, not the single tear that had leaked out at the memory of Juliet's death, but a Niagara of misery at her own predicament.

"Nothing," Sophie said. "I don't know anything about what happened that night. I wasn't even out here. All I know is that Juliet's dead, and Charlie's in trouble, and I wish everyone would leave me alone." The waterfall started. It was, as Bailey had feared it would be, a Niagara. And though she barely knew Sophie, and had a feeling Sophie didn't particularly like her, she put her arms around the girl and let her sob her heart out. And Sophie did. She cried so long and so hard that even the heedless hedonistic twins noticed and came running out of the water to find out what was wrong. But whatever it was, Sophie wasn't saying.

Twenty-Three

At first Bailey thought it was another ghost-sighting of Nell. The situation was too unlikely to be the real thing.

She was crouched in the store window rearranging the display when she looked up and saw the red convertible stopped at the traffic light. Charlie was behind the wheel, and beside him in the passenger seat, which was closer to Bailey's line of vision because the car was heading east, sat a girl who looked like Nell. Bailey told herself it was her overheated imagination; either that or the blue-and-white-checked baseball cap that cast a shadow over the girl's features. Bailey blinked, then widened her eyes. The passenger seat was closer to her, but it was still the width of two traffic lanes and a sidewalk away. The profile looked like Nell's, but it couldn't be Nell's. The light changed. The car turned left. Charlie and the girl who might or might not be Nell cruised beyond her reach.

She told herself there was no reason for concern, even if the girl was Nell. But Iselin's speculations about Charlie's sex life had left a slimy residue.

She told herself Nell was only a child. But not so much of a child that Charlie hadn't gone up to her in the Talkhouse.

She told herself she wasn't going to ask Charlie about it. She didn't want him to think she didn't trust him. She brought it up the next time she saw him.

"Yeah," he said as if it were the most natural thing in the world, and of course it was. "I passed her walking home from the beach after work, so I gave her a lift."

"That was nice of you." She was trying to sound appreciative rather than suspicious.

"Rule of thumb. Always give a ride to a cute babe."

Bailey's head snapped up from the chicken livers she was slicing for Edward. He was the only one who didn't sense the change in temperature in the kitchen.

"Hey," Charlie said, "that was a joke. She's only a kid."

She dumped the livers in the bowl and put the bowl on the floor. Edward lit into it. She straightened.

"You're right," she said. "She's only a kid. Sixteen, to be exact. And there are men your father's age for whom that would be an inducement."

He sat on the stool in the corner staring at her, and she felt suddenly awkward and self-conscious, as if she had food on her face or lipstick on her teeth, but the real smudge, she knew, was the stain of distrust he could see on her soul.

"Yeah," he said. "The world's full of dirty old men. But I don't happen to be one of them."

Only later, after he left, when she was still kicking herself for the conversation, did she spot the hole in the story. If he'd given Nell a lift from the snack bar at the beach to her house, a fairly straight route from south to north that didn't go near the center of town, what were they doing stopped at a traffic light on Main Street? Bailey knew her suspicions were absurd. Either of them could have had an errand to take care of. Or maybe neither of them had anything to do except enjoy the summer afternoon tooling around town in his flashy car. Charlie was lonely. Nell was dazzled. And that was exactly what she was worried about. Goddamn Iselin and his slick, sick mind.

Twenty-Four

A few mornings later Eliot called the store about several books he said he needed for his work. Bailey told him she'd have to order most of them, but two were in stock. He said he'd pick them up around four. She told him she'd leave them behind the desk with his name because this was her early afternoon. That was when he came up with the suggestion. Why didn't she drive over with the books, spend the afternoon with them, and stay for dinner? "Caroline's in town," he said, "and Charlie and I are just rattling around the house." He lowered his voice. "What we're really doing is driving each other nuts. Iselin says we should have a trial date any day now, which hasn't exactly ratcheted down the level of tension around here."

Charlie was just getting out of his car when she pulled into the driveway. He stood scowling at her from behind his dark glasses. His long face looked sharp as an ax.

"I brought these for your dad." She hefted the books in one hand.

"Nice to know you're a full-service operation."

"With a smile," she said and pasted one on her face. If Eliot could turn the other cheek, so could she.

"He's probably in his study."

She started to say she didn't want to bother Eliot and would rather stay with him, but he cut her off. "Wouldn't want to keep the great man waiting. To the left of the living room and through the sunporch. Just look for the shrine."

She made her way through the house according to Charlie's directions. He'd been sarcastic, but not inaccurate. Framed photographs of Eliot with world leaders and national politicians and other instantly recognizable figures covered every surface and all the wall space that wasn't devoted to bookshelves. Most of them were signed. Under normal circumstances all those flash-frozen moments of success intended to rub the viewer's nose in her own comparative failure would have depressed Bailey. Now she found them encouraging. The room screamed of Eliot's power and connections. That had to mean something for Charlie.

Eliot was sitting behind a long refectory table

piled with papers and books and electronic equipment. Behind him she noticed another photograph. This one, unframed and unsigned, had been clipped from a newspaper and taped to the inside of a cabinet that housed more electronic equipment. She recognized the photo from the news coverage of the evacuation of Liberia. In the foreground a man was carrying a child toward an airplane. Behind them a woman in combat uniform stood sentry with a rifle. She looked from the news clip to the framed and signed photographs, and thought again that Charlie had been luckier than she'd deserved.

They came out of the house to find Charlie lying on his stomach on a chaise, his face buried nose down in the cushion. The sight stopped Eliot. "I know this is hard on him," he muttered under his breath, "but I can't help thinking it wouldn't be quite so hard if he'd get off his duff and do something."

"I heard that." Charlie pulled himself up and sat with his feet on the stone patio and his elbows on his knees. "He's been trying to find projects for me all summer," he said to Bailey. "A little community service to buff up my image."

"It might also get your mind off our troubles."

"Our? Hey, I didn't know the grand jury indicted you, too."

Eliot didn't answer.

"Anyway," Charlie went on to Bailey, "he thinks

I ought to rack up some good works. Public good works, of course. Won't do *us* any good if nobody knows about them. So I was just lying here wondering what I could do. You know, one small step for mankind, one giant leap for Charlie Prinze. And suddenly it came to me. I've decided to volunteer at the battered women's shelter."

"That's not funny," Bailey said.

Charlie shook his head. "Some people have no sense of humor." He stretched out on his back with his hands behind his head. "Okay, we'll deep six volunteerism. How about self-improvement? I'll take a course. Something practical I can use in the future. That's another of his ideas." He turned his head and smirked at Eliot. "Let's see, there's Introduction to License Plate Making. Or How to Run a Prison Laundry. Wait, I've got it!" He sat up again. "The basic essential for life behind bars, Rape Prevention 101, aka Watch Your Ass, Motherfucker."

"Stop it," Eliot snapped.

Charlie shrugged again, a small movement of his shoulders that carried cosmic implications. It devalued everything. "You said you wanted me to do something."

"Right," Eliot said. "Why don't you haul some of that hostility over to the court and take it out on me. Could be your day to finally whip my ass."

Eliot wasn't just turning the other cheek. He was begging Charlie to slap it.

"What about Bailey?" Charlie was looking at Eliot rather than her.

"I'll watch," Bailey said.

They walked across grass that was springy as a crew cut. Tall oaks made a canopy over the court, and as they began to volley, the ball flashed back and forth through a paisley pattern of shadow and sunlight. The thwack, bounce, thwack, bounce rhythm beat steady in the quiet afternoon. She settled in one of the Adirondack chairs arranged along the side. It was hard to believe the world could still put on such a benign face.

After a while Eliot asked if Charlie was ready, and Charlie said he was.

"You serve," Eliot said.

"No way. We'll spin the racket. We're going to do this by the books." He flashed Bailey a mean smile.

They spun the racket. Charlie got the serve. He turned and started back to the baseline. His big sneakers sprang over the surface of the court. His body bounced like the ball he kept in motion with his racket as he trotted. She couldn't tell if he was limbering up or putting on an act.

He reached the baseline and turned. His face was set in concentration. He tossed a ball in the air with his left hand, then let it fall without swinging. He tossed again, and this time his right arm came back at the same time. She heard the smack of racket connecting with ball, saw the blur of movement through the air, heard the dull thud as it hit the white tape of the net. It spilled over and dribbled to Eliot's feet.

She looked across the rippling mosaic of sun and shadow. Charlie was rotating his head as if to loosen his neck. She'd always resisted the idea of sports as a metaphor for anything, but she prayed he wouldn't double fault.

He served again. The ball sailed over the net. Eliot ran for it. Another solid crack. Eliot's return was a little high. It gave Charlie time. He returned it with a tremendous overhead smash. The ball whizzed past Eliot and bounced beyond the baseline.

"Don't muscle it," Eliot called. "Use your body, not your arm."

Charlie moved to the other side without answering and served again. The ball landed squarely within the service box. Eliot's return was wide.

Charlie took the first game, Eliot the second. Charlie served again. He was hitting his stride now. She watched him set himself up for a backhand. He'd moved in too close to the ball. It hit the net.

"You're crowding the ball," Eliot called.

Charlie still didn't answer. He bounced a ball up from the court with his racket, caught it, and shoved it in his pocket. He struck a second ball with the racket. It skidded away. He tried again. And again. Finally he bent and picked up the ball. She could see his mouth moving. She didn't have to be a lip reader to get the message. She wanted to tell Eliot to back off, but no one had asked her to referee.

Charlie recovered and took the third game with a deep, slamming backhand.

"Way to go, Ace," Eliot called.

Again Charlie didn't answer, but his moving lips were eloquent.

Eliot served. His face was flushed, but his game remained consistent. Charlie's was growing more erratic again. Some shots were acts of beauty, others were awkward blunders. At least Eliot stopped pointing them out.

Eliot took the fourth game. Charlie served again. The ball went wide. He stood at the baseline, head down, knees slightly bent, trying, Bailey knew, to will himself into a state of physical and mental beatitude. Her own muscles prickled with tension.

The sun lurched down the sky an inch, broke through a hole in the branches of one of the oaks across the court, and seared her eyes. She raised her hand to her forehead to make a canopy of shade and squinted at Charlie. He took a ball from his pocket, rotated his head on his neck, then his shoulders in their sockets. In a single smooth motion he tossed the ball and brought his racket back. She heard the crisp sound of contact and lifted her face to follow the pale blur of motion against the shadowy oaks. The ball described a long, graceful arc over the court and bounced to the ground just inches beyond the service box.

Charlie muttered. This time she could hear the expletive.

"In," Eliot called.

"Yeah," Charlie said, "and I'm Pete Sampras."

"It was," Eliot insisted.

Charlie walked to the net. "The ball was out."

Eliot turned to Bailey. "You saw it. Tell him it was in."

They stood facing her in identical poses, hands on hips, heads cocked to one side, waiting for her call.

"For Christ sake," Charlie said, "tell him it was out."

"It was in," Eliot said again.

She squinted into the dizzying pattern of sun-dappled light. A small, smooth smile creased Eliot's face as he watched her. *Trust me, I know what I'm doing.* Charlie's shoulder twitched.

"It looked out to me," she said.

"Right!" Charlie crowed.

Eliot shook his head. "Myopia. It must be hereditary."

Charlie jogged back to the baseline, turned, and served. He hadn't scored the point, but he had won something, and the victory had loosened him up. The ball cleared the net by an inch and sailed beautifully into the service box. Eliot bobbled the return into the net.

Charlie moved to the other side and served again. This time Eliot returned the ball. Charlie drove it back and made the point. A while later he took the game, and a little after that, the set.

Eliot trotted around the net to Charlie's side. His pink polo shirt had turned blood red under the arms and down the small of his back. He grabbed Charlie's shoulder and shook it. "You did it! You finally did it."

Charlie shook off his hand. "Not so fast. That was only one set."

Eliot stood for a moment, his chest under the dark-stained shirt rising and falling slowly. Then he shrugged and grinned. "Whatever you say, Ace."

Charlie moved to the other side of the net. He was on a roll now. He loped around the court, setting himself up for every shot, swinging his racket with long, easy movements, putting the ball exactly where he wanted.

"Don't muscle it," he called when Eliot smashed a ball into the fence behind Charlie's head.

"Use your body, not your arm.

"You're not bending your knees.

"Way to go, Ace," he crowed when Eliot made a good serve. His game had improved, but not his disposition.

He took the second set in less time than the first.

"Uncle," Eliot called and wiped his soaking face with a towel. His complexion was deep mauve, breathtaking in a sunset, but alarming in a man.

"Are you all right?" Bailey asked, and knew from his tone of voice when he answered he was fine that she shouldn't have. For a moment she thought he was going to drop to the grass and toss off a few push-ups to prove it.

They walked back to the patio. Charlie slapped his father on the back. The smack of his palm on the wet shirt echoed through the dusk like a gunshot. "You've got the game, Ace, but I've got the psychological edge."

Eliot didn't say anything. Bailey didn't dare.

Charlie went into the house to shower. When he came out, he was carrying a tall glass half full of clear liquid. A lime floated on the surface. Something about the way he swaggered across the patio with the glass held ostentatiously in front of him told her he'd made up his mind to get drunk. She had an uneasy feeling it wasn't in celebration.

Eliot went in to shower and came out with that cat-licked-clean look peculiar to small children and sun-tanned men after a day of outdoor play followed by a good scrub. His dark hair was slicked close to his head. He smelled aggressively of soap. He seemed to have recovered from his defeat.

They settled around the wrought-iron-and-glass table with drinks. Charlie was on his third, though Bailey was trying not to count. Eliot was less fastidious, but then, Eliot had rights. "You're going to be on your ass," he said when Charlie stood, walked to the tea trolley that served as a bar, and topped off his glass again.

"You're the one who said this calls for a celebration." He turned and grinned at Eliot. "Ace." He came back to the table and sat. "And I owe it all to Bailey." He turned to her. "Couldn't have beaten the old man if it weren't for you."

"Please," Bailey said, "leave me out of this."

Charlie stared into his drink and shook his head. "Nope, it's the truth. Couldn't have whomped his ass if you weren't here. Not just 'cause you stopped him from throwing the point." He swung his head to Eliot. "If you're going to patronize me, Ace, you gotta be subtle." He turned back to Bailey. "But I couldn't have rattled him that much if he hadn't had an audience. A feminine audience." He lifted his head to Eliot. "Right, Ace?"

Eliot's smile was unruffled. "Return with us now to those golden days of yesteryear when Charlie Prinze was a mere slip of an adolescent, raging with rebellion and doing his damnedest to drive us all crazy."

Charlie shrugged and smirked. "Hey, I can't afford to grow up. I've got a dad who's eternally young."

"It's not nice to make fun of those of us who are youth-challenged," Eliot said.

"Look at him, Bailey. Nothing rattles the guy. It's called sangfroid." Charlie made a popping sound with his mouth as he pronounced the words. "Didn't flinch in the face of Desert Storm. Didn't flee when the Taliban marched into Tashkent. Even kept his cool when I dragged him into this mess with Juliet."

Eliot's smile was growing tighter. "That's enough, Charlie."

"Well, maybe this business with Juliet has rattled him a little. After all, this one tarnished the old image. Shaved his TVQ rating. Put a dent in his demand."

"That's not your fault," Bailey said, though they all knew it was.

Now Charlie turned the smirk on her. "I know. He told you. He doesn't hold me responsible. *I* haven't let *him* down."

"I said, that's enough," Eliot repeated.

"Right." Charlie bowed his head to Eliot. "Ace." He swiveled back to Bailey. "But what if we turn the question around? Ask not whether I let him down, but whether he let me down."

"Stop it, Charlie," Eliot said.

"And the answer," Charlie went on without looking at his father, "is no way. We have jury experts. We have market researchers. We have PR firms. Not to mention the best damn defense lawyer money can buy. If you don't believe me, ask Iselin. My dad, Eliot Prinze, has spared no expense."

"Perhaps we could save this until after Bailey has left," Eliot said through lips narrow as a pencil line.

"Why?" Charlie's eyebrows rose in twin arches of innocence. "Bailey's family. Isn't that what you said to her the first time you met?" He leaned across the table and held out a hand to her. "Welcome to the family," he crooned in a mean imitation of Eliot. "Jesus," he muttered in his own voice, "isn't anyone off limits?"

"You're embarrassing Bailey."

"Embarrassing her, hell. I'm not the one who's hitting on her."

She wanted to say Eliot wasn't hitting on her, because he really wasn't, but she kept her mouth shut. This had nothing to do with her.

"Christ!" Charlie said. "First my girlfriend, now my birth mother. I'm beginning to feel like a fucking pimp."

Bailey couldn't tell whether the world had really gone silent or if her consciousness had merely slammed closed, as if she'd put her hands over her ears to shut out the words she didn't want to hear. Maybe she hadn't heard. Or maybe she'd misunderstood. Charlie couldn't have meant what she'd thought. Only, she looked from one to the other of them, from the rash-red rage that made Charlie look like a child on the verge of a tantrum to Eliot's alert air of a man with his eye on the exits, and knew she'd heard correctly and understood perfectly.

Eliot turned to her. His face was smooth, his smile self-deprecating. Damage control was already under way. "So now you know. Another of our little family secrets."

"Little?" Bailey repeated.

"It only happened once." Charlie let out a nasty laugh. "Or so he says. Juliet's story was a little different. She was in lu-uv. Hey, for all we know she was going to"—he pretended to strum a guitar—

"have his baby," he sang to the tune of "If I Were a Carpenter." "Not mine."

"I don't believe it," Bailey muttered, though of course she did. Part of her wasn't even surprised. She'd covered too many scandals that made this look like penny ante stuff. So Juliet had been half his age. Did anyone even notice anymore? So she'd been his son's girlfriend. Bailey could cite half a dozen similar stories about the patriarch of America's favorite political dynasty. Only this wasn't someone else's story. This had happened to Charlie. Her son. Perpetrated not by a greedy dead patriarch she'd only read about but by the man to whom she'd entrusted her child.

"You and Juliet?" She was still trying to wrestle the information into some form that made sense.

"It was, as Charlie pointed out, even if he was being sarcastic, a single indiscretion—mistake—on my part."

"But memorable for Juliet." Charlie turned to Bailey. "The old earth moved. The old colored lights went off. Hell of a guy, my dad."

"Stop it!" Eliot's voice rang with authority. He was the one who'd screwed his son's sweetheart, but his son was the one who was behaving badly.

Charlie raised his arms, palms toward them. "Hey, I'm just telling you what Juliet said."

"You were supposed to take care of him!" The cry exploded from her.

Eliot turned slowly from Charlie to her. "The way you did?" he asked quietly.

The words were a fist in her face. Her ears rang, her vision blurred.

"Why didn't you tell me?" she asked Charlie. "Or Iselin or someone?"

Charlie gave her another of those cosmos-destroying shrugs. "Hey, he's the guy who's footing the bills. Not to mention the fact that it does give me a pretty nifty motive. Son kills girlfriend in jealous rage over devastating dad."

"You didn't!" It was half question, half prayer.

He stood and shook his head. "You see what I mean," he said quietly. "A terrific motive." Then without weaving, without missing a step, he walked a straight, sober line into the house.

She sat staring after him, sickened by Eliot, sick of herself. She was the one who'd turned Charlie over to him. She saw herself walking across a room and placing a blue-blanket-wrapped Charlie in Eliot's arms, though the event had never occurred. She saw herself stupid with trust, blind with self-indulgence, reckless with youth. She shook her head to drive the image away. The consequences pressed closer in the soft evening air.

"This doesn't change anything," Eliot said quietly. "I still believe in Charlie. I still love him."

"You have a damn funny way of showing it."

He closed his eyes and rubbed his forehead with his thumb and forefingers. "I made a mistake. One night. Not that the lack of repetition makes it any less reprehensible. I know that. Still, you have to understand—"

She stood. "I don't want to hear about it."

He sat looking up at her. "You do, because it concerns Charlie. It explains why he's been acting the way he has, the way we definitely do not want him acting at the trial or in front of other people."

He went on staring up at her and waiting. She sat. He began to talk. He walked her through the whole night, how Juliet had come out by herself one Friday morning because the weather was nice and she wanted to get a tan, and how Charlie had planned to drive out that evening but had got tied up at work; how Eliot and Caroline had planned to arrive the next morning, but Eliot had got off a plane at JFK and decided it was silly to drive back to town just to turn around the next morning and face the traffic out to the East End, especially since he'd left the Jaguar in the long-term parking lot, because he'd found years ago that getting behind the wheel of his own car was better for getting out the kinks of a long plane ride than sitting in the backseat of a limo. "The Mario Andretti of middle-aged philanderers," she muttered, but he just kept going, explaining how he'd called Caroline from the car to tell her his change in plans, and she'd warned him that Charlie and Juliet would be at the house, and how he'd been annoyed when he'd first got there and found Charlie hadn't made it, because he was tired and jet-lagged and just wanted to have a drink and go straight to bed.

"And so you did." She stood again. She'd had enough. His voice, as he'd told the story, had been hushed with contrition, but she'd heard the barnyard crow beneath the mea culpas. He might as well have stood up, flapped his arms, and shouted cock-a-doodle-doo. This was the man who'd raised her son.

He looked up at her. "You're right. I have no defense. About the only thing I can claim is that I never let it happen again. Despite Juliet's fantasies of a great love affair. And I never told Charlie. Not that I wasn't dying to. But that would have been for me, not him."

"No, you left that to Juliet. And now she's dead, and he's on trial for manslaughter."

"Charlie's innocent. I'm still convinced of that."

Night had moved across the yard, and she could barely make out his face in the darkness, but she could see the solid bulk of shadow.

"Look, I admit it. I screwed up. Badly. No excuses, no extenuating circumstances. But that doesn't mean I don't love Charlie. It certainly doesn't mean I'm not determined to get him through this thing. If anything, I'm more determined. It's the only way I can begin to make things up to him."

Twenty-Five

Charlie didn't mention what had happened between his father and Juliet again, and Bailey didn't bring it up. Life went back to normal, or what passed for normal with a trial for manslaughter hanging over their heads. Charlie went on trying to fill the minutes and hours that slowed his days to a crawl. It wasn't easy. One afternoon he even went fishing with Mack.

Bailey wasn't sure how that happened. Maybe Charlie was in the market for a new role model, though Mack wasn't exactly a likely candidate. Maybe Mack knew she was worried about Charlie. But there was probably less to it than that. Mack and Charlie were men. They didn't have to have a reason or even particularly like each other to spend long hours cheek by jowl in eighteen feet of fiberglass.

They had a run of luck. A little after sundown they came walking across her yard carrying a big plastic cooler between them. Will was a few steps behind. They put the cooler down on the deck and opened it. Seven massive bluefish lay bloody and lifeless inside.

A little later after they'd taken the cooler into the kitchen to clean the fish, she went back out to the deck to start the grill. The patch of sky overhead was still blue, but night had closed in on the yard. She stood in the gathering darkness looking into her brilliantly lit kitchen.

Mack was teaching Charlie to fillet a bluefish. They stood shoulder to shoulder, the classic stance of male heterosexual coupling, their heads bent in concentration and consecration over the scaly, smelly, sacred fish that bound them. The picture was corny. Norman Rockwell or an ad designed to make you believe in things you'd long ago learned weren't true. But it was seductive.

She heard a noise at the other end of the deck and turned to see Will, his hands jammed into his pockets, his body shriveled into a parenthesis of loss, his nose practically touching the sliding glass door that separated him from Mack and Charlie. This was no sugar-coated illustration or seductive ad. This was the naked face of love with all its scars.

* * *

A few days later Mack came into the store just as she was about to leave and asked if she felt like going out on the water for an hour or so. He had to check his lobster traps.

They motored out of the harbor under an overcast sky that pressed down on them like a sheet of tin. The only breath of air was the faint breeze made by the movement of the boat. The sea was flat as a sheet of Plexiglas.

It took close to two hours to cover all the territory. She sat watching him haul in the unwieldy wooden boxes and empty the catch and reset the traps. It looked simple and mindless, but she knew it wasn't. She also knew from the economy of his movements that he took pride in his competence. It was one of the few things he did take pride in. *I am hunter-gatherer, hear me roar.*

By the time they turned back into the channel leading to the harbor, a greasy black stain of night had begun to spread over the eastern horizon. She could almost see the humidity in the air.

Just inside the breakwater, he cut back the engine, and when he spoke he didn't look at her. "Money has started disappearing from my wallet."

"Are you sure?" Mack wasn't the kind of man who kept his bills neatly arranged by denomination and knew exactly how many he had of each. She was surprised he even had a wallet. Whenever she saw him, he was pulling handfuls of crushed bills from various pockets.

"No, I'm not sure. But a couple of times I've had the feeling there was less there than I remembered."

"You think it's Will?"

"Who else?"

"Have you asked him about it?"

"What's he going to say? 'Gee, Dad, yeah, forgot to mention I filched a couple of twenties from you'?" He cut the engine back a little more and eased the boat around a channel marker. "I hate to accuse him. There isn't a hell of a lot of room for more misunderstanding between us."

"What are you going to do?"

"Hope it doesn't happen again."

"The MacKinley Reese school of child rearing."

He lowered his head and looked over the top of his dark glasses at her. "You have a better suggestion?"

"Me? The authority on parental trust? I mean, all you have to worry about is petty larceny. I—" She stopped. There it was again. Her dirty little secret. "I just meant—" she started to explain.

"I know what you meant. It's okay."

She sat watching the foamy ribbons of wake unfurl behind them. It wasn't okay, no matter what he said. "It's just that I don't know him. I love him. I'm worried sick about him. But I don't know who he is. There's too big a space where our history should be."

He leaned over and put his big, competent hand,

fingers splayed, on her knee, complicitous rather than seductive. "I've got a news flash for you. You could have spent the past twenty years with him, driving him to Little League games and washing his underwear and taking his temperature when he got sick, and you still wouldn't know him. They're alien little buggers. From another planet. You can love their asses off, but that doesn't mean you know what's going on in their heads. And maybe it's better that way. Think of what it would be like if we really knew what they were up to. Not to mention what they were thinking. Living hell."

Twenty-Six

He'd have to take a bus for the first part of the trip. He couldn't take the chance that someone would see him hitchhiking. That was okay. That was no big deal. He could take the money from the asshole's wallet. He'd never even know it was gone. Not like his mom. She missed fucking dollar bills. But He never noticed anything. Once he'd taken a twenty and two tens, and He was just like "Hey, Will, you didn't see any money around here, did you?" The asshole. It was the same with the story he'd told Him this morning. All he'd had to say was I'm going camping with Reid and his dad. His mom would have wanted to know every fucking detail. His mom would have wanted a fucking map of where they were going. But He was just like, great, have a good time. Then He'd got the brilliant idea about the sleeping bag. Like anybody in his right mind would sleep in that stinking old pissbag. But it had given him the idea. Before that he hadn't known where he was going. He'd thought maybe Las Vegas, which would be cool for a while, but then he'd just end up with his mom and Ari, which would be the same thing all over. But the minute he saw that totally gross sleeping bag he knew what he was going to do. It would kill the asshole. He raised his hand, cocked his fingers like a gun, and took aim at his imaginary target. *Pow! Pow! Pow!* It would blow him away.

Mack felt disoriented. It had been months since he'd walked into an empty house. Even when Will, sprawled in front of the television, wasn't the first thing he saw as he came through the door, he knew Will was there or on the way. But not tonight. Or tomorrow. He had a twenty-four-hour pass. He felt suddenly light, more insubstantial than carefree. The habit of worrying about Will—not the cosmic worries, like was he going to get smashed up in a car accident or hung up on drugs, but the mundane worries, like had he eaten or was he staying up all night watching television—was hard to shake. Willworry permeated the place. Like the stain sweated into the bedroll he'd hauled out that morning.

How in hell had he forgotten that stain? He could still see the disgust on Will's face. He'd stood there staring at it for a moment, and Mack had seen his eyes grow wider as he'd made out the shape. It was the putrid yellow shadow of a man. His father.

The funny thing was that Will had been nice about it. He hadn't screamed *Gross!* or made any of his exaggerated comic-book sounds of revulsion. He'd just said that was okay, Reid's dad had an extra sleeping bag he could use. Maybe Will was growing up. Maybe they were reaching a new plateau of mutual understanding and respect. And maybe pigs could fly.

He put the two lobsters he'd kept from his haul in the refrigerator and went into the bathroom to shower. He hadn't reached a new plateau, merely got some time off for R & R, and he figured he might as well drop in on Bailey.

He arrived bringing two lobsters from his traps. She told him she still had enough bluefish in her fridge and freezer to feed the starving hordes of North Korea. He said he thought she didn't like bluefish, and besides, they were celebrating because he had time off for good behavior. Furthermore, he didn't want any of her bunny-hugging crap about boiling the lobsters because it was more humane. "We're going to steam these babies in a little water and one can of beer."

"Real beer?"

"Real beer. I'm living dangerously tonight."

After dinner they sat on the deck, side by side, their feet propped up on the railing, boating moccasin, torn boating moccasin, new espadrille, new espadrille, their faces turned to the trees, which hung heavy and still in the thick night.

"Where is Will, anyway?"

"Camping with a buddy and his dad."

"Sounds suspiciously all-American." Maybe she'd been wrong the other night when she'd stood on the deck watching Will watching his father and Charlie like a starving man watching a banquet. Maybe things were going better than that single moment made them appear. "I guess you really are doing something right."

"Hell, I'm not the one who's taking him camping," he said, but the pleasure hummed in his voice like the outboard of his boat when he'd just had it overhauled.

That was when the phone rang. She looked at her watch. The hands glowed eerily in the darkness. It was close to midnight. The only people who called at that hour were ill-wishers who wanted to harass or bearers of bad news. As she slid open the screen door and went inside, her imagination raced from who wanted to threaten her to what misfortune might have befallen Gilda or Charlie. She picked up the receiver. A man's voice asked for MacKinley Reese. The wave of relief shamed her.

She put her hand over the mouthpiece and called to Mack. He was out of his chair and into the house in seconds. He knew trouble when he heard it.

She stood in the doorway between the kitchen and dining room, leaning against the wall with her arms crossed in front of her chest, trying to make out what was happening. Mack wasn't saying much. Yes, he was MacKinley Reese, the father of William Reese. No, he hadn't known. Yes, he understood. But his tone was eloquent, half rage, half relief, the primal scream of parenthood. Then he said, yes, he'd like to speak to him, and she could tell by the way Mack notched up his voice that Will was on the other end of the line.

He asked Will what the hell he'd been thinking. He wondered if Will were out of his mind. He said didn't he know he could get in big trouble that way? Then Will must have given the phone back to whoever had called, because Mack got the panic-driven anger under control again. He said yes, and certainly, he'd leave right away. He added that he figured it would take him five or six hours to get there.

He hung up the phone. She asked if Will was okay. It was a stupid question. What she meant was, was he hurt.

"The cops picked him up. The Washington cops."

"D.C.?"

He'd been standing with his palms flat on the counter, his head bent, staring at the floor. Now he looked up at her. "It would have taken him longer than a day to hitchhike to Washington state."

"What did they pick him up for?" She expected drugs. He'd be lucky if it was merely alcohol.

"Vagrancy."

"Vagrancy? What does that mean?"

"It means they found him asleep in a public park. In the rain. Apparently, it's been thundering and lightning all the hell over the D.C. area."

She didn't get it. New York would have made sense. She wouldn't have been surprised at Las Vegas. But the Beltway wasn't exactly a mecca for disgruntled kids. "He ran away to some park in D.C.?"

"Not just any park. The cops picked him up at the Vietnam Memorial."

"Oh."

"Yeah. He was asleep among all the junk. You know, the stuff people leave there. Old dog tags and roach clips and beer cans. Medals nobody wants anymore and women's underwear and God knows what kind of crap. It's supposed to be social history." He slammed his fist on the counter. "Social history, fuck. Detritus is more like it. He was throwing himself away."

She told him he'd better take her car. The truck wouldn't make it.

He stood looking at her for a moment. "I don't suppose you'd like to come along for the ride. See your nation's capital."

She could think of half a dozen reasons right off the top of her head why she wouldn't. She told him sure.

They traveled the Long Island Expressway in darkness. He was going too fast, but she didn't say anything. The New Jersey Turnpike was a grim ghostly white in the glare of the refinery lights. They stopped

for coffee outside of Philadelphia. As they came back
to the car, she asked if he wanted her to drive. He said
he didn't. It began to drizzle around Wilmington,
more mist than rain. He kept turning the windshield
wipers on and off. He cursed quietly each time he did.

By the time they hit Washington, the sky was beginning to fade to a polluted gray. They got lost trying to find the police station, and it was after six
when they finally located it.

She hadn't been in a stationhouse since she'd left
her old life. Nothing had changed. The waiting area
was crowded with women and children and victims
and enablers. The perps, the real stars of this drama,
were off in another area, presumably under lock and
key. Bailey tried not to think of Will shut up in a holding pen with a bunch of pimps and muggers and murderers. She refused to think of the possibility of Charlie's being locked up there for God knew how long.
She concentrated on the people around her. They
wore a look of early-morning exhaustion. The place
had a morning aroma too. The odor of urine was
stale, but the disinfectant and coffee smelled fresh.

Mack went straight to the desk. Bailey hung back
and watched. He showed identification and signed
papers. The desk sergeant picked up a phone. Mack
turned toward a door at the other end of the room and
stood waiting. She'd never seen him so awkward. He
looked as if he were about to spring, or run.

The door opened. Will shuffled out, his eyes on

the floor. He dragged them up to Mack's face for a moment, just long enough for Bailey to see the fear, then dropped them again. He stopped walking and stood a few feet from Mack. Mack went on standing there. She remembered a time she'd watched the two of them walk across a parking area toward the pickup. They'd started out side by side, but moved as if they were on divergent paths from some accidental vortex. By the time they'd reached the truck, they'd put a good ten feet of space between them.

Mack's hands closed into fists, then relaxed again. He took two steps, opened his arms, and crushed Will against him. She couldn't tell if he was trying to hold him or break every bone in his body.

They stopped at the same fast food outlet on the New Jersey Turnpike. Will was asleep on the backseat, curled on his side with his fist in front of his mouth. He might have been sucking his thumb, or stifling a scream. Bailey whispered that she'd stay while Mack went in for the coffee and whatever else looked as if it hadn't been deep fried in a vat of year-old grease. Mack got out and slammed the door. Will turned over and opened his eyes. When he saw Bailey, he sat up, but didn't say anything.

"How're you feeling?"

He shrugged.

"Your dad went in to get lunch. If you want anything in particular, you'd better go after him."

He mumbled that he didn't.

She leaned against the window on the passenger side, not facing him, but not turned away either. He huddled in a corner of the backseat.

"So, what'd you think of the memorial?" she asked after a while.

He shrugged again.

"I've never seen it."

His superior experience seemed to encourage him. "It's okay."

"I read that people leave all kinds of stuff there. It's supposed to be a social statement."

"He ought to leave that dumb sleeping bag."

"What sleeping bag?"

The grate slammed down. She'd displayed too much interest.

"Your dad's sleeping bag?"

He pulled his knees up, hugged them to him, and stared at her for a moment. "He's got this really gross sleeping bag. From when he was there. He brought it out yesterday morning. Like I was supposed to use it." He made a sound as if he were about to throw up.

"That bad?"

"It's got this big stain. But the really gross part is the stain's in the shape of a dude. I mean, beyond gross. It—"

Mack's body appeared outside the window on the driver's side. He opened the door. Will closed his mouth.

* * *

It was late afternoon by the time they pulled into the clearing in Bailey's yard. Mack's pickup was still parked there, and the outdoor lights she'd turned on to help them find their way in the darkness were still on.

Will jumped out of the backseat. He was the only one with any energy. He was also the only one who'd had any sleep in the past thirty-six hours. Bailey had dozed for a few minutes in the front seat. Mack hadn't even done that. When she'd offered to spell him behind the wheel, he'd said there was no point. He wouldn't be able to sleep anyway. She glanced over at him now. His skin, beneath the deep tan, looked ashen. He had the drawn and shaky air of a man with a hangover, only this binge had been emotional.

Will started down the driveway.

"Will!" Mack called after him. The boy kept going. "Will-yum!" Mack shouted.

Will turned around, but didn't take off his earphones or even make a move to turn down the sound. He wasn't defiant, but he wasn't giving much either.

"Where're you going?"

"Reid's."

"I thought Reid went camping with his dad."

Will glanced at Bailey and rolled his eyes. *Can you believe how dense this dude is?* He turned back to Mack. "I'm just going over there." He hesitated. "I'll be home for supper."

Mack stood looking at him. Will didn't drop his eyes.

"Scout's honor?"

"I'm not a Scout."

She was surprised and knew by the expression on Mack's face that he was too. It was a verbal exchange. It was almost an attempt at humor.

"I'll be home for supper," Will repeated, then turned and started down the driveway.

They stood in the clearing watching him.

"You think he means it?" Mack asked.

"I won't swear his hitchhiking days are over, but I don't think he's going anywhere in the immediate future."

They went into the house. He took a fake beer from the refrigerator. She poured herself a glass of iced tea. They went out on the deck.

She hadn't planned to bring it up. It was none of her business. And he'd had enough for one day. They all had. But somehow the longer they sat there, the more important it seemed.

"Will and I had a talk when you went in to get lunch."

"A talk. You must be kidding."

"Nope. Several sentences. We discussed the Vietnam Memorial. And the artifacts people leave around it." She hesitated. "He also mentioned a sleeping bag."

He didn't answer, didn't even turn to look at her, but she could sense the change in him, like Edward tensed with watchfulness when he scented danger.

"The one you thought he might want to borrow."

He still didn't say anything.

"He seemed to think it belonged with the mementos people leave at the monument. The detritus."

"Why don't I just burn it instead?"

"Why didn't you?"

She knew from the trapped look on his face it was the question he'd been asking himself. His mouth opened, then closed. He heaved himself out of the chair with the wild, lumbering movement of an animal trying to crash out of a trap and told her he'd better get going.

Twenty-Seven

The judge finally set a date. They'd begin jury selection in three weeks. Eliot came into the store one
morning to give Bailey the news. She had to hand it
to him. He acted as if that evening at the house had
never happened. He acted as if he were still Dad of
the Year. And in a funny way he was. Charlie might
have lost faith in him, but he still had faith in Charlie. He told her the trial date was good news. "The
sooner Charlie puts this behind him, the better."

She didn't think Charlie was going to slough
things off as easily as Eliot seemed to, but there were
more important issues at hand.

"You're that confident he's going to be acquitted?"

"Absolutely. I keep telling you, we don't have to

prove Charlie's innocence, only a reasonable doubt of his guilt."

The conversation kept roiling around in her head. Every time she looked at the calendar hanging on her refrigerator door and saw the date jury selection was to begin—she hadn't marked it with a cross or circled it in red, but it stood out as if she had—she came face to face with her own damnable doubt. And gradually she began to realize that she wasn't thinking only of Charlie.

When she'd first read about Charlie, before she'd known who he was, she'd wondered how it would feel to have raised a son like that. Now, at three in the morning, when fear sat on her chest heavy as Edward, she cringed to think what she'd done by not raising him. In the bright rationality of day, she, like Eliot, would settle for Charlie's acquittal. In the blackest hours of her own personal night, when the ghosts of Juliet and Juliet's parents and Nell lurked in the corners of the bedroom, she needed him innocent. If Charlie were guilty, she was culpable. It was the quintessential maternal fear. Maybe that was why Gilda spotted it.

Bailey had sworn she was going to keep her mother out of the loop this time around. Gilda had other plans. For weeks she'd been begging to meet Charlie, and for weeks Bailey had been saying she didn't want to hit him with too much at once, and didn't add that she found Gilda's impatience peculiar after years spent denying his existence and months warning of his danger. There was no point. To Gilda consistency was merely the crutch of the cowardly. Finally Bailey ran the suggestion past Charlie, and he said sure, he'd like to meet her.

Bailey warned him about the Towers on the drive out. She wanted to warn him about Gilda, but her loyalties were divided. As it turned out, she'd had nothing to worry about. Within minutes Charlie and Gilda discovered the instinctive bond that skips a generation, or perhaps only unites against it. They didn't exactly gang up on Bailey, but they did have a little fun at her expense. They had other things in common as well. By the end of the visit they were comparing notes on driving Route 66.

"She has a lot of snarl," Charlie said in the car on the way home. He meant it as a compliment.

Gilda was simply besotted. She was also convinced he couldn't possibly have done the things the state was saying he had.

"Why?" Bailey shouted at her on the phone that night. "Why is he incapable of having done those things? Because he's your grandson? Because he's my son? Because he has our genes and blood and infinite goodness of heart?"

Gilda's rings clattered against the plastic receiver like castanets. "Is that any worse than having him guilty because he has your genes and blood and infinite blackness of heart?"

Bailey shriveled. "I thought it was supposed to be different. More selfless."

"Whoever told you love wasn't ambivalent."

"Even maternal love?"

At the other end of the line the rings danced faster. "Maybe especially maternal love."

Bailey thought about that for a moment. "Not you, that's for sure."

The realization came to Bailey in the empty black hours of the next morning. She'd always been disdainful of her mother's optimism: Smile and the world smiles with you; every cloud has a silver lining; keep your sunny side up. She'd always been scornful of a woman of such infinite hopefulness that she'd driven halfway across the country on a whim before she'd had to face reality and, tail between her legs, turn around and head home. Bailey lay in bed picturing Gilda's return so many years earlier. At the end of each day, the sun would have been sinking behind her, a bloody disappointment in the rearview mirror. But that wasn't the way Gilda saw it. Even all these years later she'd sworn to Charlie that the trip out had been worth it. Bailey had been wrong about her mother. She wasn't merely optimistic. She was resilient.

Twenty-Eight

The first thing Mack saw when he came through the door was the big television screen, black and silent as a granite slab. The house was so quiet he could hear the drip of the kitchen faucet he kept meaning to fix. He eased his body into the big club chair where Will lived, put the pile of textbooks and lesson plans and forms for the coming year on the floor, and rested his head against the back of the chair. This time he knew where Will was. He'd called Reid's mother to make sure. Will had screamed bloody murder. "Everybody will think I'm a complete wuss."

"The consequences of earlier actions," Mack had told him. "Get used to the concept. You're going to have to live with it for the rest of your natural life."

They hadn't talked about Will's flight. Mack had tried to, but Will had clammed up, so he'd decided to let it go. Let it go, hell. He'd practically hugged the kid for letting him off the hook. But Bailey hadn't let him off. He still couldn't figure out how he'd forgotten the stain on the bedroll.

When he'd first got back, he'd lived in a room that made this place look like a palace. There'd been a bed, but that had been about it. One old packing crate. No other furniture. Certainly no sheets and blankets. That had been okay with him. The room had felt strange, but the bedroll on top of the bed had been familiar. As familiar as the night sweats. His old companion. His old bedmate. As much a part of him as the sweet, shameful wet dreams of youth, or the self-sufficient pleasures of masturbation, or certainly any woman he'd ever slept with. In the mornings the whole damn room had reeked of them. It had been the first thing he'd smell as he'd struggled up to consciousness. When he'd finally dragged himself out of bed, he'd see the stain in the shape of himself on the bedroll. The same putrid yellow shadow of a human being Will had recognized that morning.

He could still see Will standing there as he'd dragged the damn thing out of the shed, carried it across the yard, and started to unroll it. *Here you go, Will. A little memento from the old man. Your patrimony.* And then, before it was all the way open, but still too late to stop, he'd remembered the stain.

Or maybe he'd never forgotten it. Maybe he'd done it on purpose. Maybe he'd been grandstanding. Rubbing the kid's nose in it. Getting himself off the hook. He talked a good game. He was always the first to say

you couldn't blame it on that. And he didn't. Look at
all the guys who hadn't come back messed up. Senators and brain surgeons and fucking Oliver Stone. He
bet they didn't keep their stinking, stained bedrolls
stashed away, just waiting for an occasion to whip
them out and show them off. His eyes snapped closed
at the memory. He leaned over with his elbows on his
knees and his face in his hands, but the image didn't
go away. He saw Will staring down at the stain, and
he saw something else, himself, sitting here in the big
club chair, alone in the empty house, hunched over,
curled in on himself, nursing his pain like a wound.

He sat up and dragged his hands down his face so
hard his beard scratched like sandpaper against his
palms. That must mean something, a vital sign of
sorts. His beard went on growing, his hair was turning gray, he was getting shorter while his son got taller.

He stood, left the house, and crossed the patchy
grass to the shed. The combination lock was set to
Will's birthday. He spun it and yanked open the door.
The darkness smelled of mice and mold and the damn
bedroll. He carried the thin, loosely tied mattress out
of the shadows, into the daylight, and flung it on the
ground. Particles of dust rose from it and danced in
the slanting rays of the late afternoon sun, the miasma
of his own stinking fear and failure. He unrolled it. The
sick yellow stain lay on the ground like a dying man.

He picked up the roll, carried it to the metal trash
can, and shoved it in. It didn't take much space. There

were no matches in his pockets. One more vice he'd sworn off. He went into the house for a box. On his way back to the trash can, he took the plastic container of charcoal starter from the grill, just for good measure.

The thing caught in a flash. It burned for fewer than ten minutes. When there were only ashes left in the bottom of the barrel, he dragged the hose over and doused them. A small cloud of steam rose, nothing more.

He arrived bringing two lobsters from his traps again, but this time there was no talk of celebrating. She asked how Will was. He said he was staying at the legendary Reid's, and this time he really was. He asked how Charlie was. Her eyes moved to the calendar on the front of her refrigerator. She said he was okay, considering.

They didn't mention Will or Charlie again while he steamed the lobsters, and she melted the butter, and they carried everything out to the deck, but she might as well have set two extra places at the table.

"Do you want to talk about it?" he asked when they were sitting on the side deck again after she'd put the dishes in the dishwasher and he'd scrubbed the lobster pot.

She shook her head no.

A breeze rattled the leaves like rain and walked across their shoulders. He reached over and put a hand on her thigh. She felt him watching her and turned to him. His face was tanned as dark as the night. All she could make out was the faded light of his eyes. There was no humor in them. This wasn't a joke. He hadn't even left himself that narrow corridor for retreat.

He moved his hand, a feint north. The callus at the base of his thumb scraped her flesh, an itch begging to be scratched. She remembered the last time he'd done that, the night he'd hit Will, the weekend she'd dumped the newspaper stories about Charlie. Mack had been asking for, and offering, solace that night too. It should have been so easy. She couldn't figure out why it wasn't.

She'd come of sexual age, they both had, in an era of instant and constant gratification, of easy tumbling into bed with near strangers, of the raucous celebration of self on the ground zero of someone else's body. But she was no longer a kid, and they weren't strangers. They were a couple of war-weary veterans with wounds that, if there were any justice in the world, would qualify them for disability payments. Instead, they were merely wary.

She remembered the old fears. In her youth, people had whispered about pregnancy, and, as it turned out, they hadn't been crying wolf. In her young womanhood, doctors had warned about STD's. Women's magazines still alerted her to the perils of commitment and the greater risks of fear of commitment. But sitting with Mack, separated from him by a few inches of night, she knew those fears were child's play. You could call it love or sex, commitment or entanglement, but naming it didn't tame it. That was the point. It couldn't be tamed. It was a disruptive force. It tore apart society, and unhinged individuals, and made people do things they thought they never would. It made them shoot other people and drown themselves; write sonnets and cry at operas; lift their faces, tuck their tummies, and lie about their ages; squander money, steal time, and cheat on their nearest and dearest. It transformed them into other selves. She'd spent a good part of her life and more than a little effort keeping it at bay. Having Charlie back had made her see that. Now as she sat watching Mack's face getting bigger as it leaned into hers, she felt the fight go out of her.

And later, in her bed in her house in the middle of the woods in the middle of the night, that was something to howl about.

She heard the screen door slide open and closed behind her but didn't turn around.

"Getting up in the middle of the night to commune with nature is one thing," he said. "Taking the covers with you is something else."

She hugged the quilt around her. "I left you a blanket."

He sat in the deck chair beside hers. He was wearing only boxer shorts, and the long jagged scar glowed white against the dark flesh of his thigh. "That was supposed to be a joke. Do you want another blanket?"

She shook her head no.

"Do you want talk now?"

She realized suddenly that she did. The subversive force was already at work. It had made a crack in the glassy surface of her isolation.

Once she started she couldn't stop. She told him about her fear that Charlie wouldn't be acquitted and her terror that he might not be innocent; her lust to believe in him and her shameful need to absolve herself. She spun the words out into the darkness, whirled them around him, pulled them back in a lasso of need. She cataloged her doubts and contradicted them with her convictions. She cursed the world and blamed herself and berated Eliot. And she kept coming back to his unswerving faith and her own inability to cling to it.

"Come on, Bailey, the man's a public figure. He's accustomed to the big lie. Not that Charlie's innocent," he went on quickly, "but that he has no doubts."

"No, it's more than that. He really believes in Charlie. He says he knows him."

He reached over and put his hand on the back of her neck. The heat of it burned through the quilt. "No one knows another human being that well. Hell, people don't know themselves that well." He thought of the stain he'd managed to forget and the sleeping bag he'd neglected to burn, but he didn't want to talk about that now. "They think they're incorruptible, until the bribe reaches seven figures. They believe they're happily married, until love walks in the door. Look at your mother. She went out for a quart of milk and ended up halfway across the country. And it's not just the big things. The world's full of people who decide to play hookey from work on a whim, or go shopping for a family van and come home with a slick, I'm-not-over-the-hill-yet sports car, or—"

The words spiraled off into the night, dragging her after them. Or get off a plane and into a car and go east rather than west, young—or in this case, middle-aged—man. Eliot had told her so himself. There was nothing he liked better after a long flight, especially when his body clock was running three hours early on Pacific Time, than to get behind the wheel of his racing-green tribute to automotive engineering and his own consumer power and open her up on the open road. He'd done it once and surprised Juliet there alone. Who was to say he hadn't done it again? He said he hadn't, but his word wasn't exactly the coin of the realm.

She knew it was a long shot, but then, much of her life had been the result of long shots. Finding Charlie was one. Getting pregnant with Charlie had been another.

There was one more reason she was willing to bet

on this particular long shot. It would explain why Eliot was such a trusting father, and she was such a suspicious bitch of a mother.

Twenty-Nine

She left Mack asleep in her bed. He was still on a twenty-four-hour pass, but she had things to do today.

She made good time into town and went straight to the garage where, according to Eliot's enthusiastic secretary, who was happy to pass the information on to Charlie's birth mom, Eliot kept his car. Her only surprise was that no one else had bothered to go there. Then again, Eliot's whereabouts weren't the whereabouts in question that night.

The garage attendant didn't recognize her. She might be a celebrity on the East End, but in the greater world her fifteen minutes of notoriety were over.

She still had an old press pass in her wallet. She also had several twenties that fell out on the attendant's desk. She had a moment's misgiving about that, then remembered: This wasn't someone else's news story. She was allowed to pay for it. She already had.

The attendant remembered that Mr. Prinze had brought the car back just before five-thirty that morning. He recalled the night because the next day the news had broken about that girl falling from the deck or the boy pushing her, and he'd figured Mr. Prinze had been up all night taking care of business with his son and the police and lawyers.

She asked if he was sure of the time.

He said he'd put money on it. He and Mr. Prinze were both classical music fans. The radio in the Jag was usually tuned to WQXR. As Mr. Prinze got out of the car that morning and he got in, Nimet, the night announcer, was just signing off. He knew, because Mr. Prinze had made a crack about how not only did she have the sexiest voice in the business, but she certainly knew the score musically. They'd both laughed at that.

She didn't break Eliot's record on the drive back, or even Charlie's, but she scored her own personal best; a cool eighty on the expressway, and only a little less on 27, despite the traffic, but thanks to turning lanes and shoulders. She was only fifteen minutes away when she heard the siren. The police car came abreast of her and motioned her over.

She pulled out of the traffic lane and stopped. The police car cruised to a halt behind her. She glanced

into the rearview mirror. The cop was taking his
sweet time getting out of the car. Her hands clenched
the wheel. Her foot itched to floor the gas pedal. She
was so close. Charlie was so close.

In the rearview mirror the cop sauntered toward
the car. John Wayne was alive and well on the East
End of Long Island. He came around to the driver's
side and stood with his hands on his slim hips staring down at her. She tried to look innocent. The itch
in her right foot didn't make it easy.

He asked for her license and registration. She
handed them over. He stood studying them as if they
were written in some code he was trying to break.
Out of the corner of her eye she noticed the digital
clock on the car radio swallow another minute.

He asked if she'd seen the sign with the flashing light
that indicated she was passing a school. Some crazed
demon inside her head, rowdy with tension, said that
was like asking if she'd stopped beating her husband.
She was damned if she'd seen it, damned if she hadn't.
She made a noncommittal sound. He launched into a
short lecture on children. They didn't always look both
ways before crossing. They darted out into the road
after a ball or a friend. They were, in short, unpre-
dictable little critters. Didn't she know it. It was up to
her to take care. Damn it, she was trying to. She held
human life in her hands. Her fists clenched the wheel.

The cop asked her how fast she'd been going.

She said she wasn't sure and thought of Eliot's

record-breaking trips to and from town. The garage attendant might remember where his loyalties lay and call Eliot. He could be on the way to the airport now. It was unlikely but not impossible.

She said she hadn't meant to exceed the speed limit, but there was something urgent. Even she could hear the hysteria simmering in her voice. This was a woman about to boil over.

The cop put his hands on his hips again and stood staring down at her. "You been drinking?"

She saw herself disappearing into a Kafkaesque labyrinth of Breathalyzer tests and red tape. She'd never get to Charlie. She swore she was sober as a judge. She said she seldom drank anything stronger than wine anyway. She warned herself to shut up.

He went on staring down at her. Smooth and showy as a gun draw, one hand moved to his pocket and withdrew a book of tickets. She thanked him profusely.

She reached the house by midafternoon. Sprinklers whispered in the silent, sun-baked air. The grass lay wet and green and glistening. The house was so white it looked scrubbed. Bright red geraniums glowed in the clear East End light.

As she pulled into the driveway, she noticed Iselin's white Rolls among the various Prinze automobiles. He might want people to underestimate him, but not his buying power.

She parked her car, climbed out, and followed the

sound of voices around the house to the yard. Charlie and Eliot stood face to face on opposite sides of the tennis net. Even from this distance she could make out the grim concentration on Charlie's face, as if he could see nothing beyond the fence surrounding that court, as if he were condemned to spend the rest of his life playing out this game. Caroline and Iselin sat side by side in Adirondack chairs watching them.

Eliot waved hello. Charlie didn't even glance her way. Maybe he was afraid that if he took his eye off Eliot for even a minute, he'd be blindsided.

Caroline said it was nice to see her and started to ask if she'd like a cold drink. Iselin lifted a big, meaty hand in greeting. Bailey made her way past them and onto the clay surface. A ball whizzed by her. She kept going until she was standing center court. Maybe it was the look on her face. Maybe it was simply that she'd intruded onto the court. They stood, rackets hanging loosely at their sides, waiting. She'd finally stopped the game.

Eliot asked if something was wrong. She could tell by the alert look on his face that he had a pretty good idea of what it was.

She said she'd just come from town. "From your garage," she added. She told him about the attendant and his taste in music, and his recollection of what was on the radio that night when Eliot got out of the car and he got in it. She said she'd also checked with the airline. Eliot's plane had landed around midnight. She could sense Charlie on the other side of the net piecing together the information, but she couldn't gauge his response. Even when she turned to glance at him, she couldn't see behind the mask of disbelief melting slowly in the heat of the accumulated evidence.

She turned back to Eliot. He took off his dark glasses, rubbed his eyes with his thumb and forefinger, and shook his head. "I'm glad," he said. "I'm glad it's finally over."

It was his finest act, and she wanted to slap him for it, but as he walked off the court, and slumped into one of the chairs beside Caroline and Iselin, she began to think maybe it wasn't an act after all. In the unforgiving afternoon glare, the chiseled Mount Rushmore features had gone slack and weak and ugly, like the face of a man sleeping off a binge. He had the unconscious calm of a sleeping drunk too. Something in him—the father, the self-styled man of honor, or merely the exhausted actor—really was glad it was over.

He told them about the night. It was almost a replay of the first night, which hadn't been the only night after all. This time there was no rooster's crow echoing beneath the confession. He told them how once again he'd got off a plane, changed his mind on the spur of the moment, and decided to drive out here rather than back to town. And once again he'd found Juliet alone in the house. He admitted all that, but he was adamant on one point: Juliet had fallen by accident. He hadn't touched her, except to try to pull her down from the railing where she'd climbed in a melo-dramatic, alcohol-fueled threat of proof of love by suicide. After she'd fallen, his first instinct had been to call the police, but then he'd thought better of it. No one knew he'd driven out. Charlie had been gone for hours. Juliet had told him about the argument. There was no reason to complicate what was clearly a suicide.

No one spoke. Iselin sat behind his dark glasses like a slick poker player behind a full house. Caroline opened her mouth. Her breath came out light and whispery as the afternoon breeze, a wordless whimper of protest. Eliot caught her gaze and reeled it in. There was no threat in his look, only intimacy. She closed her mouth and averted her eyes. She'd been doing that all her life. It was too late to change.

Bailey looked from Caroline to Charlie. His face had broken up into a Cubist portrait. Her hand reached toward him. He shrank away.

She turned back to Eliot. Now she hated his relief. He wasn't entitled to it.

"And what about Charlie? When the police decided it wasn't a suicide, when they arrested Charlie, how could you go on pretending you hadn't been there?"

"Because I wasn't any more guilty than Charlie was."

"But you owed it to him—"

"What?" He cut her off. "What did I owe Charlie? What does a parent owe a child? Do you want to talk about that, Bailey?" The slack-faced weakness of the sleeping drunk was gone. A cruel tic of a smile tugged at his mouth. He was in control again. "No, I didn't think so. Well, let me tell you about it. They come crawling into this world, helpless, mewling, greedy. You probably remember that much. And full of wiles. You missed that part. The toothless grin you know is gas but can't help believing is love. The tiny fist that grabs your finger and holds on for dear life. The need that masquerades as adoration. They look up at you with wide-eyed hunger, and you look down at them and feel ten feet tall, and wham, the deal is signed, on their terms. So you agree to protect and provide; to fill their stomachs and open their minds and smack their bottoms; to curb their greed without crushing them, and to know when to shelter and when to shove them out into the world naked and afraid. You teach them how to tie their shoes and tell time and respect their fellowmen. And you give them things. A bike and hockey camp, a car and college, the tools for survival in a careless, uncaring world. That's the deal. That's what you owe. But what you do not owe, at least what I never felt I did, is sacrifice of self. And don't tell me that's because Charlie isn't my biological son. That's your conceit, not mine. This has nothing to do with genes or blood. I love Charlie as much as I could love any child."

She could feel the rage hammering in her chest. "Which unfortunately isn't quite enough."

"I suspect," Eliot said evenly, "that's true of both of us."

"Stop!" The howl ripped through the air. They turned to Charlie. He stood, his head down, his arms hanging like dead weights at his side, his chest heaving up and down with each breath, like a fighter who knows he's whipped but is steeling himself to go one more round. "Stop all this crap about parents and children and love." He lifted his head to the sky. "What about me?" He lowered it to face Eliot. "What about leaving me to twist in the fucking wind?"

"No one was leaving you to twist in the wind," Eliot said. "I always knew we could get you off. If I hadn't been sure of that, I'd never have let things play out this way. Never," he repeated quietly.

Bailey stood staring at the granite features chiseled with probity and suddenly she knew. He was going to get away with it—not unscathed, perhaps, but unpunished. Iselin would contact the district attorney. They'd cut a deal. The case against Charlie had been circumstantial and full of holes. Bringing it against Eliot would make it look as if the state were playing a game of pin the tail on the donkey. She was queasy with disgust.

She asked Charlie if he wanted to come with her. He stood holding on to the flimsy net as if it afforded some support and shook his head no. Her heart swooned to him, but she kept her distance. She'd been dreaming to think she could close it.

Thirty

Later she could have sworn that the sirens had wakened her in the middle of the night, but she knew that was impossible. The car crashed miles away. The only sirens she'd heard had gone off in her own head.

Mack brought the news the next morning. He'd heard it from one of the local cops when he'd stopped at the bait store. Instead of driving to his boat, he'd got back in the truck and driven to her house.

The car, he told her when he got there, had careened out of the lane, hit the steel guard, and folded like an accordion. The top had been down and the driver, who needless to say hadn't been wearing a seat belt, had kept going, over the guardrail, through the early morning darkness, and into the Shinnecock Canal. The police figured he must have been doing at least ninety.

They didn't have to dredge for the body or even search far. One tennis-sneakered foot had got caught on the rudder of a Bermuda 40 tied up in the marina. No one was aboard at the time, so no one heard the rhythmic thumps of human bone and muscle and flesh against fiberglass hull. Fortunately, the speed limit in the canal slowed marine traffic. Wakes were gentle. The body was still identifiable. Even the police and a handful of curiosity seekers, who roused themselves from bunks on other boats in the marina or swung off the road to see what was happening, recognized it on sight, though that didn't count as official identification.

The police were efficient. They had what was left of the car towed and the body on the way to the ME by the time the dawn of a perfect East End day was seeping over the horizon like a bloody stain.

Mack reported the facts, but he didn't pass on the speculation. There were rumors it hadn't been an accident. The stretch of road where the crash occurred was straight, no hairpin turns or even gentle curves to send a car out of control. Driving conditions had been good—a dry surface, a full moon. There hadn't even been traffic on the road to crowd the car into the guardrail or blind the driver with oncoming brights. At least, no one had come forward. The driver had simply lost control. Or relinquished it. With that kind of thing you never knew and would probably never find out. To illustrate the point, the cop told Mack about an accident he remembered from the days when he'd worked on a force upstate. A guy in a Ford Galaxy had driven head-on into an eight-wheeler, killing himself as well as a woman and child in a station wagon in the next lane. It looked like a case of failed brakes or mechanical malfunction or a heart attack, until the workers pried apart the wreckage and found a suicide note on the front seat of the Galaxy. At least in this case, the cop remarked to Mack, the driver hadn't taken anyone else with him.

There was no reason, however, to assume it had been a suicide. No note turned up in the convertible or on the body. There wasn't even a license or other identification. The official report listed an adult male, Caucasian. Height, five feet eleven and three quarters inches. Weight, one hundred and sixty-nine pounds. Hair, brown. Eyes, brown. Age, forty-five to fifty. Eliot would have loved that.

Charlie made the official identification. According to the cop, the minute the kid saw his father laid out on the slab like a piece of waterlogged bait, he lost it completely. They'd practically had to carry him out of the place. Mack didn't tell Bailey that either.

Eliot Prinze was buried on a sunny September day that glowed like a gold-backed promissory note for a brilliant autumn to come. Fifth Avenue, closed to traffic for a six-block area north and south of Temple Emanuel, teemed with mourners and fans and long black limos that glittered like jet in the hard light. Among those who came to pay their respects were a representative of the president of the United States, two governors, five senators, scores of lesser pols and dignitaries, and an army of celebrities with less specific titles but more recognizable faces. At the service, many of them got up to pay tribute or reminisce or, in one case, sing a spiritual Eliot was said to have found sustaining during his days on the civil rights front. From where Bailey stood in the back of the sanctuary, she saw Caroline's shoulders begin to shake. Beside her in the first pew, Charlie reached an arm around his mother.

A phalanx of police cars and spiffily uniformed officers on motorcycles, who looked a little too much like SS for Bailey's comfort, escorted the hearse and long line of mourner-carrying limos and cars up the FDR Drive, across the Triborough Bridge, and out the LIE to the cemetery. The crowd there was smaller than in town. Bailey stood nearer Charlie, though she was careful not to push too close. He didn't look at her. He didn't look at anyone. His eyes, behind dark glasses, were riveted on the black hole that yawned up from the loamy earth. Once she saw his long body sway toward it, then pull back.

The ceremony was brief, lip service to a God Eliot had never worshiped, a last-minute covering of bets he'd hedged. The sorrowing prayer wailed by generations of mourners died. A small mechanical engine coughed to life. The long pine box, suspended in two thick canvas slings, began to move. The coffin lurched unsteadily downward. Bailey watched Charlie watching the descent. On the smooth, shiny lenses of his dark glasses, twin coffins disappeared into the ground.

She didn't go back to the Prinze house after the funeral. She asked Charlie if he wanted her to. He said it was up to her. His eyes, still hidden behind the dark glasses, focused somewhere over her head; his face was blank as the moon. He added that there was bound to be a crush, and he hated those things anyway. It made him sick the way people stood around drinking and talking and pretending at grief, and then before you knew it, the whole deal had turned into a party.

She said she guessed she wouldn't go. He said whatever. She said she'd give him a call tomorrow. He said he was thinking he'd go back to town for a while. She said she understood.

Mack was waiting on the deck when she got home. He told her he was surprised to see her so early. She said in that case what was he doing there. But neither of them had the heart to keep it up.

She took the chaise beside his. Edward sat up on Mack's stomach, arched his back, padded around to a new position, and returned to his nap.

"I thought you'd go back to the house to be with Charlie."

She didn't answer, and he let it go. They sat that

way for some time. The silence wasn't consoling, but it wasn't uneasy. After a while Edward sat up again, stretched, and moved from Mack to Bailey. He settled onto her lap and rubbed his head against her thigh, begging for a scratching.

"It was too late," she said. "It was always too late."

Thirty-One

Nell heard the sound of the engine behind her and without turning around veered onto the grass beside the road. As the engine grew louder, so did the blare of music. Jazz, not rock. It drowned out the birds and the sound of her own breathing and, finally, even the engine.

She turned as the car came abreast of her and was surprised. He wasn't supposed to be tooling along in his cool red convertible blaring jazz so the whole neighborhood could hear the day after his dad's funeral. She knew the funeral had been yesterday, because her dad had seen it on the news the night before.

He was almost past her, when he slammed on the brakes. Then he sat, half turned around with his arm draped along the top of the front seat, waiting for her to catch up with him.

He asked if she wanted a lift. She said sure. He leaned over and pushed open the door. She'd been in the car once before, but it still felt funny. You didn't so much climb as crawl into it.

As they started moving, he asked if she liked Diane Schuur. She shrugged her shoulders because she didn't know what he meant.

"That." He gestured to the CD player.

"Oh," she said, "sure." But he reached over and turned it off anyway.

She wasn't sure what to say after that. She thought she ought to mention something about his dad, but she didn't know what. Her mom was always talking about finding peace and happiness with Jesus, but she wasn't going to say that. God, she especially couldn't say that. Charlie was Jewish. Then she remembered the time Maude's brother had died, and she and Bailey had taken care of the store. When Maude had come back, Nell hadn't known how to behave, but Bailey had just told Maude she was really sorry about her brother, and Maude had said thank you, and added something about its being a godsend after all this time, which Nell had taken to mean that he'd been really sick for a while, and then they'd all got back to normal.

"I'm sorry about your dad," she said to Charlie now.

His profile turned edgy as a hatchet. She could have kicked herself. Then he looked over at her and said thanks in a quick, flat way that sounded as if he were slamming a door.

She decided to keep her mouth shut for the rest of the ride. She was sorry she'd accepted it in the first place. But after a couple of minutes, he asked her in a perfectly normal way how was life at the snack stand. She said she was glad to be out of there now that school had started again.

"Bailey said you used to work at the bookstore."

"That was before." Ohmygod! *Before* meant before she'd found out about Bailey's being his mom and stuff. She never should have accepted the ride.

"Why the career change?"

"What?"

"From books to burgers. How come?" he asked as he pulled up in front of her house. He must have remembered it from last time he'd given her a ride home because he hadn't even needed directions.

"It's a long story."

He put the car in neutral, but didn't kill the engine. "I bet it's not. I bet I can sum it up in one word."

He smiled at her. She still thought he was nice, but she was beginning to think he was a little weird. How could he sum it up in one word, when she hadn't been able to make sense of it all summer? Bailey had lied to her, and let her down, and turned out to be different from what Nell had thought. That had scared her. She wasn't a scaredy cat. Even when she was a little kid, she hadn't been afraid of dogs or thunderstorms or anything. But after she'd found out about Bailey, she'd been afraid. It was as if all the dangers her mom had warned about really existed, and the only way you could keep from having horrible things happen to you was to stay away from people who were different and never do anything that hadn't been time-tested by her mom and her mom's sisters and her mom's friends and about a thousand generations of people just like them. And for a while Nell had. Only now she was getting as scared of that as she was of the other.

"Bailey," he said. "That's why you left the bookstore."

She didn't answer. She definitely shouldn't have taken the ride. She should get out of the car now. *Thanks for everything. See you around.*

"You were pissed at her. When you found out about me."

She swung around to face him. "It isn't your fault!"

He smiled and shook his head. "I mean, when you found out she'd lied to you, or at least hadn't told you everything. When you found out that just because you thought she was cool didn't mean she was perfect. When you found out she was human. They are, you know."

"What do you mean?"

"Adults. All they are is us grown up." He shook his head again. "Sometimes all they are is us grown older."

She didn't know what to say to that. The idea of her mom and dad as just older versions of her was almost as scary as the idea of her growing up to be just like them.

"Yeah," she said, "I guess so," though she wasn't sure she did. She had to think about it for a while. She thanked him for the ride and climbed out of the car. He said he was going back to town for a while, but he'd see her around, and to keep her nose clean in the meantime.

He put the car in gear, but didn't release the clutch. "Hey." He sat behind the wheel looking up at her. "Do me a favor?"

"Sure," she said, though she couldn't imagine what kind of favor she could do for him.

"Go see Bailey. You don't have to hang out there or anything. Just stop by and check her out. Her and Edward."

Before she could tell him whether she would or wouldn't, he released the clutch and pulled away.

Thirty-Two

Maude had already left when Bailey heard the bell above the door, looked up from the customer she was helping choose a cookbook, and saw Nell come into the store. She hadn't set foot in the place since she'd quit, or since her mother had quit for her. Bailey hadn't seen her on the street for a while either, though a couple of weeks ago, just after the funeral and before Charlie had gone back to town, he'd said he'd given her a lift home. She mumbled hi and kept going past Bailey to the paperback fiction. Beyond the customer's shoulder, Bailey watched the progress of Nell's head, which was all she could see over the tall displays. Her hair was getting longer again.

The customer left, but two more came in. Nell

kept browsing, while Bailey kept an eye on her and tried not to rush the customers. Nell was still there when they finally left. Bailey went straight to the table where she was standing paging through a book.

"Looking for some light reading, madam?"

Nell looked up but didn't meet Bailey's eye. "My dad sent me," she mumbled.

"Some light reading for him?"

"He says I need some stuff for, you know, taxes."

"You mean a ten-ninety-nine?"

Nell put her hands in the back pockets of her jeans. "Yeah."

Bailey thought about it for a moment. Don Harris might not be a financial wizard, but he was a functioning civil servant in the local post office. He knew nobody mailed 1099's in September. "Maude's accountant won't mail that until early next year."

Nell looked at the floor and shrugged. "I guess he made a mistake."

Bailey stared at the top of her head. She wanted to stroke the mink-soft hair.

"No problem," Bailey said, and then because Nell went on standing there, she asked how things were going.

"Okay." She looked past Bailey, but Bailey went on staring at her. Nell wasn't volunteering any information, but she wasn't leaving either.

"How's Kevin?"

"Okay, I guess."

She wondered if Nell guessed because she couldn't fathom the complexities of Kevin Lonergan or because she was no longer spending her life hanging out with Kevin Lonergan, but decided not to ask.

"If you hang around until I finish closing up, I'll drive you home."

There was a silence. Nell looked around the store again. She still wasn't meeting Bailey's eye. "Okay," she said finally.

She spent most of the ride home hunched down in the front seat with her shoes on the dashboard answering Bailey's questions about what courses she had this year and which teachers and—Bailey held her breath—whether she'd started her college applications yet. Nell's answers weren't exactly monosyllabic, but she wasn't giving away a lot of information. Finally Bailey gave up and drove in silence.

"It's funny," Nell said as they turned into her driveway. "Your being Charlie Prinze's mom, I mean."

"Birth mom," Bailey corrected her, "and I didn't know I was when we talked about him."

"Yeah, I figured that out."

"I didn't lie to you about anything."

Nell didn't answer.

Bailey waited for her to pick her backpack up off the floor, but she went on sitting there. "It must have been pretty bad for you," Nell said without looking at her.

"Pretty bad," Bailey admitted.

Nell continued to sit staring straight ahead at her parents' house. "At first I thought, what a slut. Not that you got pregnant, but because you gave the baby up. I thought you were really disgusting."

"I thought I was pretty disgusting, too."

Nell turned to look at her. "I'm sorry."

"Thanks."

"No, I mean I'm sorry I was so mean to you."

Bailey reached over and ruffled her hair. "Mean means you really care."

Nell picked up her backpack and opened the door. "Later," she said as she got out of the car and started toward the house.

"Later," Bailey echoed and gave Loraine, whose shadow had appeared in the front doorway, a faithless wave. Then she put the car in reverse and backed out of the driveway.

She drove with the windows open, though the rush of evening air bit at her skin. It carried the faint aroma of something burning, not charcoal barbecues but hearths. Other people's home fires always made her nostalgic, though she wasn't sure for what.

Like most year-rounders, Bailey was ambivalent about the passing of summer. She looked forward to deserted beaches, and less-traveled roads, and a small-town way of life, though the municipality in question bore about as much similarity to an actual small town as those backlot burgs the old movie studios used to create for Jimmy Stewart and Judy Garland, but she

worried if she'd squirreled away enough financial
and emotional acorns for the long winter of short days
and isolated nights ahead. This year she was especially worried. Charlie had called from town a few
nights earlier. He'd got a job with an international
human rights organization and would be living in
Paris for at least a year, probably longer. He said he'd
come out to say good-bye if he could manage it. She
told him she'd like that and herself not to count on it.

It was almost dark by the time she turned onto her
own street. Through the thinning trees, she could see
lights in her house. She didn't remember leaving any
on this morning. And if she had, she would have left
on one or two. This was a bonfire. Every fixture in
the place must be on, as well as the spots and floods
in the yard. She was surprised but unworried. The
phone calls and letters had stopped since the charges
had been dropped and Charlie was no longer in the
news. She still locked her doors when she left for the
day, but Mack had a key.

She turned into the driveway, and as she came out
from under the canopy of trees into the clearing, she
saw Mack's pickup. She'd expected that, but not
Charlie's red convertible parked next to it.

She climbed out of her car and started toward the
house. She still wasn't sure what was going on. The
place blazed like a stage set, but there weren't any
actors.

She went up on the deck and peered through the

NEW YORK TIMES BESTSELLING AUTHOR

ELIZABETH LOWELL

Janna is a survivor, protecting herself and the wild stallion she adores from the harsh realities of the Utah badlands. Then Ty Mackenzie disrupts her solitude, tracking her horse...and capturing her heart. Now Janna must follow Ty on a perilous trek through the blazing land, battling danger, the elements and her own reckless heart with a fury that can only be tamed by love itself.

RECKLESS LOVE

"For smoldering sensuality and exceptional storytelling, Elizabeth Lowell is incomparable." —*Romantic Times*

Available the first week of January 2000, wherever paperbacks are sold!

Visit us at www.mirabooks.com

MEL525

If you enjoyed what you just read,
then we've got an offer you can't resist!

Take 2 bestselling love stories FREE!

Plus get a FREE surprise gift!

Clip this page and mail it to The Best of the Best™

IN U.S.A.
3010 Walden Ave.
P.O. Box 1867
Buffalo, N.Y. 14240-1867

IN CANADA
P.O. Box 609
Fort Erie, Ontario
L2A 5X3

YES! Please send me 2 free Best of the Best™ novels and my free surprise gift. Then send me 3 brand-new novels every month, which I will receive months before they're available in stores. In the U.S.A., bill me at the bargain price of $4.24 plus 25¢ delivery per book and applicable sales tax, if any*. In Canada, bill me at the bargain price of $4.74 plus 25¢ delivery per book and applicable taxes**. That's the complete price and a savings of over 10% off the cover prices—what a great deal! I understand that accepting the 2 free books and gift places me under no obligation ever to buy any books. I can always return a shipment and cancel at any time. Even if I never buy another book from The Best of the Best™, the 2 free books and gift are mine to keep forever. So why not take us up on our invitation. You'll be glad you did!

183 MEN CNFK
383 MEN CNFL

Name	(PLEASE PRINT)	
Address	Apt.#	
City	State/Prov.	Zip/Postal Code

* Terms and prices subject to change without notice. Sales tax applicable in N.Y.
** Canadian residents will be charged applicable provincial taxes and GST.
   All orders subject to approval. Offer limited to one per household.
   ® are registered trademarks of Harlequin Enterprises Limited.

BOB99   ©1998 Harlequin Enterprises Limited

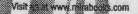